Praise for Kevin Crossley-Holland's

THE SEEING STONE

Arthur

BOOK ONE

✝ THE ✝

SEEING STONE

KEVIN CROSSLEY~HOLLAND

SCHOLASTIC INC.

New York   Toronto   London   Auckland   Sydney
Mexico City   New Delhi   Hong Kong   Buenos Aires

Arthur A. Levine Books hardcover edition, published by
Arthur A. Levine Books, an imprint of
Scholastic Press, October 2001

ISBN 0-439-43524-2

10 9 8 7 6 5 4 3 2 1   23 4 5 6 7/0

Printed in the U.S.A.   01
First Scholastic mass market paperback printing,
September 2002

FOR NICOLE

CROSSLEY-HOLLAND

WITH LOVE

the characters

AT CALDICOT

SIR JOHN DE CALDICOT

LADY HELEN DE CALDICOT

SERLE, their eldest son,
   aged 16

ARTHUR, aged 13,
   author of this book

SIAN (PRONOUNCED "SHAWN"),
   their daughter, aged 8

LUKE, their son who dies
   in infancy

NAIN (PRONOUNCED "NINE"),
   Lady Helen's mother

RUTH, the kitchen girl

SLIM, the cook

TANWEN, the chamber=
   servant

OLIVER, the priest

MERLIN, Sir John's friend and
   Arthur's guide

BRIAN, a day=worker

CLEG, the miller

DUSTY, Hum's son, aged 7

DUTTON, the pig=man

GATTY, Hum's daughter, aged 12

GILES, Dutton's assistant

HOWELL, a stableboy

HUM, the reeve

JANKIN, Lankin's son,
   a stableboy

JOAN, a village woman

JOHANNA, the wisewoman

LANKIN, the cowherd

MACSEN, a day=worker

MADOG, a village boy

MARTHA, Cleg's daughter

WAT HARELIP, the brewer

WILL, the bowyer

AT GORTANORE

SIR WILLIAM DE GORTANORE

LADY ALICE DE GORTANORE

TOM, Sir William's son,
   aged 14

GRACE, Sir William's daughter,
   aged 12

THOMAS, a freeman
   and messenger

AT HOLT

LORD STEPHEN DE HOLT

LADY JUDITH DE HOLT

MILES, a scribe

RIDER

OTHER

SIR JOSQUIN DES BOIS,
  Marcher knight

SIR WALTER DE VERDON,
  Marcher knight

FULK DE NEUILLY, friar

KING JOHN'S MESSENGER

KING RICHARD,
  COEUR = DE = LION

KING JOHN

ANIMALS

ANGUISH, Sir John's horse

BRICE, a bull

GREY, a mare

GWINAM, Serle's horse

HAROLD, an old bull

MATTY, Joan's sheep

PIP, Arthur's horse

SORRY, Merlin's horse

SPITFIRE, Sian's cat

STORM and TEMPEST, two
  running = hounds
  (or beagles)

IN THE STONE

KING VORTIGERN

THE HOODED MAN

KING UTHER

GORLOIS, DUKE OF CORNWALL

YGERNA, married first to
  Gorlois and then to Uther

SIR JORDANS

SIR ECTOR

KAY, Sir Ector's son and squire

SIR PELLINORE

SIR LAMORAK

SIR OWAIN

WALTER, a Saxon leader

ANNA, daughter of Uther and
  Ygerna

THE ARCHBISHOP OF
  CANTERBURY

THE COPPER = COLORED KNIGHT

THE SPADE = FACED KNIGHT

THE KNIGHT OF THE BLACK
  ANVIL

ARTHUR, boy and king

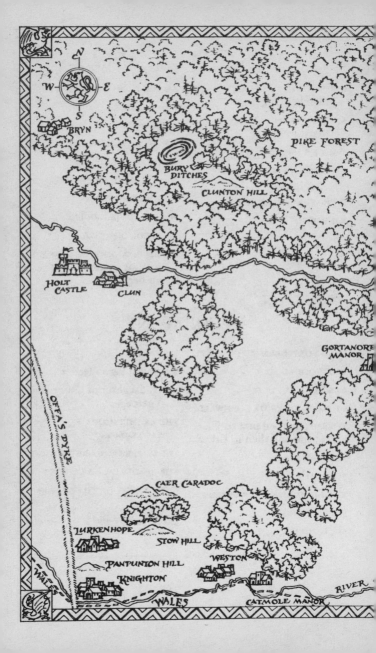

author's note and acknowledgments

It is fifteen years since I began to think about reworking Arthurian legends within a fictional framework, and I would like to thank Gillian Crossley-Holland, Deborah Rogers, Richard Barber, and my father, Peter Crossley-Holland, for giving me great encouragement on the first steps of my journey.

To write a book set in time past calls for a good deal of research, and I am extraordinarily fortunate in having for stepmother a distinguished medievalist who has not only helped direct my footsteps but given my first draft a meticulous and perceptive reading. To her the first part of this trilogy is dedicated.

I am so grateful to all four of my children, Kieran and Dominic, Oenone and Eleanor, for their enthusiasm, sharp comments, and contributions to this book-in-the-making. In addition, a number of people have kindly offered advice on specific matters: Ian Chance on the medieval fishpond or stew; Jeremy Flynn on armor and weaponry; Kathy Ireson on pregnancy; Colin Janes on archery; Carol Salmon on black pudding. I am indebted to them, and to Cecile Dorr for involving me in an Arthurian "occasion," Abner Jones for the loan of books, Janet Poynton for her great generosity in lending me a "safe" house last summer in which to live and write, Maureen West for rapid typing, and the Afton-Lakeland school library in Minnesota.

Hemesh Alles has drawn the splendid endpaper maps. Readers will discover that my imaginary Caldicot appears to be a predecessor of Stokesay Castle: it combines elements of that castle with Wingfield College in Suffolk, the home of Ian and Hilary Chance.

In Judith Elliott I have a superb editor/publisher and friend. She commissioned this book, commented in detail on every aspect of it, and has excited some interest in it. I thank you so much, Judith, and, finally, I thank my wife, Linda. You helped me to dream this book, put up with me while I was writing it, read the drafts with a keen American eye and a blue pencil, and helped to name the chapters. My name alone appears on the title page but many other people have given me thoughtful advice and imaginative support.

CONTENTS

I.	ARTHUR AND MERLIN	I
2.	A TERRIBLE SECRET	3
3.	INTO THE BULLRING	5
4.	MY BLACK KING=FINGER	13
5.	DUTY	14
6.	COEUR=DE=LION	18
7.	MY TAILBONE	21
8.	LITTLE LUKE AND PIGEON PIE	23
9.	TUMBER HILL	25
10.	THE SLEEPING KING	30
11.	JACK=WORDS	35
12.	FEVER	36
13.	KNOWING AND UNDERSTANDING	38
14.	JUMPERS AND MY WRITING=ROOM	44
15.	NINE	48
16.	THREE SORROWS, THREE FEARS, THREE JOYS	50
17.	TEMPEST'S TEETH	51
18.	JUST JACK	52
19.	NAIN IN ARMOR	53
20.	OBSIDIAN	54
21.	LANCE AND LONGBOW	57
22.	LONG LIVE THE KING!	62
23.	THE MESSENGER'S COMPLAINT	65
24.	ROYAL BROTHERS	67
25.	ICE AND FIRE	72

26.	MERLIN	73
27.	MUFFLED	76
28.	THE PEDDLER	77
29.	LUKE	80
30.	POOR STUPID	81
31.	THE SEEING STONE	88
32.	ON MY OWN	91
33.	NUTSHELLS AND GOOD EARTH	92
34.	DESIRE	99
35.	A FLYTING	104
36.	HALLOWE'EN	107
37.	PASSION	119
38.	STRANGE SAINTS	124
39.	UTHER EXPLAINS	126
40.	SCHOOLMEN, SCRIBES, AND ARTISTS	128
41.	MOUTHFULS OF AIR	132
42.	FOSTER CHILD	134
43.	CROSSING-PLACES	136
44.	LUKE'S ILLNESS	137
45.	PAINS	140
46.	AN UNFAIR SONG	141
47.	A NEW BOW	143
48.	ICE	147
49.	BAPTISM	148
50.	MY NAME	150

51. HOOTER AND WORSE 153

52. MY QUEST 158

53. BROTHER 161

54. BETWEEN BREATH AND BREATH 162

55. HARES AND ANGELS 166

56. POTS OF TEARS 170

57. THE HALF=DEAD KING 171

58. LADY ALICE AND MY TAILBONE 173

59. GRACE AND TOM 177

60. FIFTH SON 187

61. THE GOSHAWK 188

62. THIN ICE 192

63. DEVIL'S BERRIES 196

64. ROT AND BAD BLOOD 198

65. THE ART OF FORGETTING 200

66. HOT AND IMPORTANT 202

67. THE GATES OF PARADISE 203

68. WORDS FOR LUKE 206

69. DESPAIR 208

70. THE MANOR COURT 210

71. BUTTERFLIES 221

72. MERLIN AND THE ARCHBISHOP 223

73. THE ACORN 226

74. SPELLING 227

75. THE POPE'S PROCLAMATION 229

76.	NOTHING'S NOT WORTH HIDING	233
77.	FOUL STROKE	237
78.	NOT YET	244
79.	THE ARCHBISHOP'S MESSENGER	246
80.	THE KNIGHT IN THE YELLOW DRESS	250
81.	TANWEN'S SECRET	254
82.	KING JOHN'S CHRISTMAS PRESENT	261
83.	NINE GIFTS	264
84.	THE SWORD IN THE STONE	266
85.	SPLATTING AND SWORD-PULLING	269
86.	RIDING TO LONDON	275
87.	CHRISTMAS	277
88.	SIR KAY	286
89.	FOURTH SON	288
90.	THE TURNING OF THE CENTURY	291
91.	LIGHTLY AND FIERCELY	293
92.	THE WHOLE ARMOR	296
93.	KING OF BRITAIN	298
94.	BLOOD-TRUTHS	303
95.	THE SON OF UTHER	310
96.	BLOOD ON THE SNOW	314
97.	UNHOODED	319
98.	AT ONCE	322
99.	WHAT MATTERS	326
100.	SONG OF THE NORTH STAR	330
	WORD LIST	331

ARTHUR AND MERLIN

Tumber Hill! It's my clamber-and-tumble-and-beech-and-bramble hill! Sometimes, when I'm standing on the top, I fill my lungs with air and I shout. I shout.

In front of me, I can see half the world. Far down almost underneath my feet, I can see our manor house, the scarlet flag dancing, the row of beehives beyond the orchard, the stream shining. I can see Gatty's cottage and count how many people are working in the two fields. Then I look out beyond Caldicot. I gaze deep into thick Pike Forest, and away into the wilderness. That's where the raiders would come from, and where Wales begins. That's where the world starts to turn blue.

When I'm standing on top of Tumber Hill, I sometimes think of all the people, all the generations who grew up on this ground, and grew into this ground, their days and years. . . . My Welsh grandmother Nain says the sounds trees make are the voices of the dead, and when I listen to the beech trees, they sound like whispering spirits — they're my great-uncles and great-great-aunts, my great-great-great-grandparents, green again and guiding me.

When I climbed the hill this afternoon, I saw Merlin already sitting on the crown, and the hounds bounded ahead of me and mobbed him.

Merlin tried to swat them away with the backs of his spotty hands, and scrambled to his feet. "Get away from me!" he shouted. "You creatures!"

"Merlin!" I called out, and I pointed to the sky's peak, towering above us. "Look at that cloud!"

"I was," said Merlin.

"It's a silver sword. The sword of a giant king."

"Once," said Merlin, "there was a king with your name."

"Was there?"

"And he will be."

"What do you mean?" I demanded. "He can't live in two times."

Merlin looked at me. "How do you know?" he asked, and his slateshine eyes were smiling and unsmiling.

I don't know exactly what happened next. Or rather, I don't know how it happened, and I'm not even quite sure it did happen. First, Tempest pranced up to me with a rock in his mouth; I grabbed the rock and pulled it, and Tempest growled, and the two of us began a tug-of-war. Tempest was so strong that he pulled me over, and I slithered across the cropped grass.

When I let go and looked round again, Merlin wasn't there. He wasn't on the crown of the hill, and he wasn't in the little stand of whispering beeches, or behind the old mound and the raspberry bushes. There was nowhere for him to go, but he wasn't anywhere.

"Merlin!" I shouted. "Merlin! Where are you?"

Merlin is strange and I sometimes wonder whether he knows some magic, but he has never done anything like this before.

High on the hill I felt quite giddy. The clouds tossed and swirled above me and the ground heaved under my feet.

+ 2 +
A TERRIBLE SECRET

"I won't tell anyone," I said.

My aunt Alice snapped off the head of a flower. "Now look what I've done," she cried. "An innocent cowslip!"

"I swear by Saint Edmund," I said. "I won't tell anyone."

"I should never have told you," my aunt said in a low voice. She twisted one of her light brown curls, and then she tucked it under her wimple. "You're too young."

"I'm thirteen," I protested.

"You must try to forget I ever told you."

A bumblebee, the first of the season, droned into our herb garden and threshed the air in front of us. Its wings glittered.

I shook my head. "It's dreadful," I said.

"I can't tell anyone else at all," Lady Alice said. "If people ever found out, there would be terrible trouble. You do understand that?"

"Will you and Grace and Tom be all right?" I asked.

Lady Alice closed her eyes, which are the color of ripe hazelnuts, and breathed deeply. Then she opened her eyes again, smiled, and stood up. "I must go or it will be dark before we get back to Gortanore," she said.

My aunt took both my hands between her small hands, and kissed me on the right cheek. Then she looked solemnly at me, turned, and hurried out of the herb garden.

I wish there had been more time to tell Lady Alice

3

about how Merlin disappeared from the top of Tumber Hill. And I wish I could have asked her whether she knows anything about my father's plans for me. What I hope with all my head and heart is that he does mean me to be a squire, and that he will send me away into service. Nothing in my life matters as much to me as this.

+ 3 +
into the bullring

My mother says I'm clean enough to come back into the house, but I can still smell the manure.

My little sister Sian says she can too. "You stink, Arthur!" she keeps shouting.

This afternoon my brother Serle and I went over to the Yard, wearing our mail-shirts and carrying lances.

"Three times round," said Serle. "And this time, no shortcuts!"

There's a track right round the Yard, behind the archery butts at each end, and it has five obstacles. There are two ditches, one shallow, and one really deep with steep sides, and that's the muddy one; there's a low hurdle made of wattle, and a gravel pan that's almost always full of water; and worst of all, there's an upright ladder with nine rungs, and big gaps between them. You have to climb up one side and down the other.

It's difficult to run round the track wearing a mail-shirt. As soon as I'm at all off balance, its weight pulls me farther sideways or forward. And when I'm carrying a lance as well . . . Mine isn't at all heavy but unless I'm holding it exactly right, it drags behind me or swings in front of me, or the point sticks into the ground.

It was very hot, and I started to sweat before we reached the starting post.

Serle smiled his curling smile. "You're useless at this," he said. "God made a bad mistake with you."

I showed both my fists to Serle, and my mail-shirt squeaked and clinked.

"How much start do you want?"

"None," I said.

"Because I'll beat you anyhow."

"Stop it, Serle!" I shouted.

What stopped Serle was a distant roar. Then a scream and yells.

"The fallowfield," said Serle. "Quick!"

We pulled off each other's mail-shirts, and ran back to the stone bridge, then down to the church and across the green.

Wat Harelip was looking over the hedge into the fallowfield. So were Giles and Joan and Dutton, still holding their scythes and twig-brooms.

Then I saw for myself. Somehow, both our bulls had got into the same field, and Gatty was standing between them. I could see she was talking to Harold — he's our old bull — but I couldn't hear what she was saying. She kept shaking her head, and the curls of her fair hair jumped and danced like impatient water.

"Gatty!" bawled Wat Harelip.

"Come on!" shouted Dutton. "Come out!"

Harold ignored Gatty. He was glaring at Brice, our other bull, and Brice was glaring at Harold. Both bulls roared, and began to scrape the ground. Then they charged at each other. Their horns clashed, and they rushed past each other so that Gatty was left standing between them again.

"Look!" cried Joan. "Harold's got a rip over his right shoulder."

6

"Gatty!" shouted Wat Harelip again. "Wait for your father."

"The bulls won't wait," said Joan.

"He was here in the field, Hum was," said Wat. "I saw him take off his jacket. Go on, Dutton! Go and find him. I can't run no more."

Dutton gave one last look at Gatty and the bulls, and then he barreled off across the green, calling for Hum.

"Lankin was here too," said Wat Harelip.

"I saw him sneak off," Joan said. "The thieving weasel!"

"What's he up to now?" said Wat. "He should be in there, herding the cows."

Our whole herd of cows are folded in the fallowfield, but they were standing well out of harm's way, some on their own, misty-eyed and mooing, some jostling each other, stamping and farting.

Gatty turned her back on Brice, and walked past Harold, and started talking to him again. Then she held up her father's maroon jacket, the one my father gave him on the day he appointed Hum reeve of Caldicot Manor.

Harold didn't like the sight of it at all. He lowered his horns and charged, and everyone gasped. But at the last moment, still holding up the jacket and waving it, Gatty stepped to one side. Harold caught the jacket; he drove one of his horns right through it; then he shook his head and tossed it away.

At once Gatty picked it up, she ran after Harold and twenty paces beyond him.

"What's she up to?" asked Giles.

"What does it look like?" said Wat Harelip.

"She's drawing him away from Brice," I said.

7

That didn't work, though, because Brice didn't want to be left out. Suddenly he came charging up behind Harold and butted him in the rump. Harold roared to heaven, and I saw that Gatty would never be able to separate the beasts on her own.

"Serle," I said in a low voice. "We must help."

"Are you mad?" said Serle.

"But we must."

"You'd be ripped to pieces."

"We must, though."

"It's not your duty," Serle replied. "And it's not my duty."

"I know," I said, "but I have to help Gatty."

"Fieldwork," said Serle contemptuously. "Squires and pages don't tangle with bulls."

"Squires and pages *are* young bulls," murmured a voice at my shoulder. "Aren't they?"

"Merlin!" I cried. "You've come back. Gatty needs us."

Serle shuffled and planted his feet more firmly on the ground. But then I felt the flat of Merlin's hand in the small of my back, gently encouraging me.

"I will then," I said loudly. And I ran along the hedge to the stile, and into the fallowfield.

"That's the boy!" shouted Joan.

"Careful, Arthur!" yelled Wat Harelip.

God's bones! I ran straight into it, a sloppy pool of first-day dung. I slithered, I slipped and fell flat on my back.

Seeing this, Harold at once trotted over to have a closer look. Still lying on my back, I saw the strings of saliva hanging from his mouth, and the points of his horns. Then Gatty came running past Harold. "Get up!" she panted. "Get up!" She pulled me to my feet, and at once Harold lowered his head. He pointed his horns at us.

I think I closed my eyes. Then I heard the thunder, and I felt it. And when I dared to look again, Harold had charged right past us, and Wat Harelip and Joan and Giles and Merlin were clapping and cheering.

"Now get out!" shouted Gatty.

"No!" I yelled.

Gatty looked at me with her river-green eyes, and they were shining.

"Come on! You come out!" I said, and I clutched at Gatty.

"Keep your hands off me," said Gatty, grinning.

Then she looked at her father's jacket. She found the tear Harold had made, pulled it apart, and ripped the whole jacket in two.

"You do Harold," she said. "Keep him in this corner. I'll do Brice."

I walked towards Harold, slowly. His right shoulder was bleeding and his rump was bleeding. His eyes were bloodshot.

"Come on then, Harold," I heard myself saying. "Are you coming?"

Harold looked at me. He looked at the red half-jacket. Then I did what I'd seen Gatty do. I flexed my knees, I raised the jacket and waved it, and as Harold ran at me, I stepped to one side.

I could hear more clapping and cheering and shouting from the hedge.

"Again!"

"Go on, Arthur!"

Gatty, meanwhile, made short work of Brice. First I

saw her draw him across to the far side of the field, and then she waved him right into the bullpen. As soon as she had closed the gate, she ran back across the field to join me.

"Come on!" she gasped.

But now that Brice was in the bullpen, Harold completely lost interest in Gatty and me. He snorted and turned away, and then tried to look at the wound on his right shoulder.

Gatty and I staggered across the fallowfield to the stile.

"Disgusting . . . you . . ." she gasped.

"Why were they both in the field together?"

"I fenced the pen wrong," said Gatty. "Brice barged out. My father will be furious."

"And mine," I said.

Gatty was right and she didn't have long to wait because Hum, followed by Dutton, came running down to the fallowfield while we were still talking. Hum was upset at Harold's wounds; he was angry when he saw what remained of his precious red jacket; and he was furious with Gatty for being careless.

Hum glared at Wat Harelip and Dutton and Giles and Joan. "And I suppose you lot encouraged them," he said.

"No," said Merlin. "We encouraged the bulls."

First Hum cuffed Gatty's right ear. Then he grabbed Dutton's twig-broom, told Gatty to bend over, and thrashed her six times.

Gatty didn't make a sound. Slowly and stiffly she stood up, and she looked at me. Her eyes were glistening. Then she lowered her head. I could tell Hum was minded to say something to me as well, but he must have thought better of it because he just glared at me.

"I told Arthur not to," Serle said. "I told him."

Hum said nothing to Serle either. He just turned his broad back on both of us. "Come with me!" he told Gatty and, without lifting her head, Gatty slowly limped after him.

"That man!" said Wat Harelip darkly.

"I'd like to break every bone in his body," Dutton said. "He weren't fair to Gatty, and he's never fair to us."

After that, I walked over to the millpond on my own, and my legs were shaking. I washed off as much of the filth as I could, but my clothes were still soiled, and my hair was sticky.

My mother was waiting for me in the hall, and as soon as I walked into the house, she ordered me straight out again.

"Go on!" she yelled. "Get your clothes off! Into the moat! Wash yourself all over, you horrible dung beetle!"

That's just like my mother: She's Welsh, and often sounds much more angry than she really is.

I took off all my clothes and slipped into the cold water. Then Sian and Tanwen, my mother's chamber-servant, came out of the house with a whole pot of soap and clean clothing.

"Wash your hair!" Tanwen called out. "Wash yourself all over."

"You dung beetle!" cried Sian joyfully. "How cold is it, Arthur?"

The mutton fat smelled bad but the wood ash smelled good, and both smelled much better than the cow glue.

But now my mother has allowed me back into the house, I can smell the manure again.

"Serle has told me what happened," said my mother.

"He doesn't even know," I said indignantly. "I'll tell you."

"I've heard quite enough," said my mother. "You can tell your father, and he will punish you. He'll talk to you tomorrow."

I pressed my lips together.

"Well?"

"Yes, mother."

"That's better. Always acknowledge your parents when they speak to you."

"Yes, mother."

"Serle says you left your lance and mail-shirt in the Yard. Run and bring them in before dew falls."

"Let's run together," Sian said. "Three-legged. You stink, Arthur!"

✦ 4 ✦
my black king-finger

From all this writing, my left hand aches. The tip of my king-finger is black.

Our priest Oliver says my father wants me to have a good writing-hand, and that I must practice for one hour each day. When I asked him what I should write, he replied: "That's obvious! It's quite obvious."

"Not to me," I said.

"No," said Oliver. "One person glimpses paradise while another stares at a field of thistles."

"What do you mean?"

"We read in the Book each morning, don't we? Today it was Abner and Ner and Ishbosheth and Joab and Asahel, who was as light on his feet as a roe. You must copy out your reading."

I don't want to write about Abner and Ner and Ishbosheth and Joab and Asahel, especially not in Latin. I want to write my own life here in the Marches, between England and Wales. My own thoughts, which keep changing shape like clouds. I am thirteen and I want to write my own fears and joys and sorrows.

I can hear snoring down in the hall. That will be my grandmother. When she starts snoring, the whole house trembles.

ᴅuᴛy

"But if I hadn't helped her, Gatty might have been killed."

"Maybe," said my father. "But firstly, Arthur, your duty is not to talk but to listen."

"But . . ."

"Secondly, it's not up to pages to play among cowpats. You shouldn't humble yourself. You know that."

"No one else lifted a finger. Wat Harelip and Giles and Joan, they all kept shouting, but they didn't help."

"What you did was wrong," said my father, "but for the right reasons. I know you were being loyal to Gatty, and you were extremely brave. No one wants to go into a field and face two angry bulls. But I want you to understand: Each one of us here in this manor of Caldicot has his own duties. What are your duties?"

"To learn to tilt and parry and throw and wrestle and practice all the other Yard-skills; to dress my lord, and serve at table, and carve; to read and to write."

"Exactly," said my father. "No one can learn these skills for you. In just the same way, Hum and Gatty and Wat Harelip and everyone in the manor have their own duties. They must be accountable for them — to me, and to God."

"Yes, father."

"In fact, it's the same for each man and woman and child on middle-earth: Each has his own place, his own

work, his own obligations. If we all start taking one another's places, where will we be?"

"Is it wrong, then," I asked my father, "to do what your
gut tells you to do?"

"Well," replied my father, "our instincts never lie to us,
but they do sometimes instruct us to do things we should
not do. And your tongue, Arthur, often says things it
should not say." My father walked right round the chamber, and poked with his left forefinger at one of the little
horn-window-slats which had slipped out of position. "The
next time Serle and I go hunting," he said, "you will stay at
home. That is your punishment, and the end of the matter.
Now! It must be a moon-month since you dressed me."

As he spoke, my father started to undress. He unlaced
his tunic and took it off, and threw it on the bed. He
kicked off his boots. Then he pulled off his shirt and
rolled down his hose. Soon, he was wearing nothing but
his breeches. "What can you remember about the skill of
dressing your lord?" he asked me.

"First," I said, "I invite my lord to stand near the fire."

"Or . . ."

"Sit by the fire."

"Go on, then."

"Sir," I began, "will you come and stand by the fire? Or
sit on this stool? It's warmer here."

"I'm warm enough," said my father.

I picked up my father's shirt and turned it the right
way out. "Your shirt, sir," I said. And I held it up so that he
could put his arms into it.

"And now," I said, "your red tunic. It's well aired, sir."

"And still in one piece, I see," said my father.

"Father," I said, "Gatty was really brave."

"Arthur!"

"May I lace your boots for you, sir?" I asked.

"No, Arthur. You're not concentrating. My hose first."

"Yes, sir."

When I had finished dressing my father, I went over to the window ledge, but the comb wasn't there with the mirror.

"Well, what are you going to do about it?" my father asked.

"Sir, will you wait here while I find it?"

"There's no need," said my father. "Not today." And he ran both hands through his long black hair. "But we do need another comb in this house."

"I cut one for Sian," I said.

"I know," said my father, and he smiled. "But what's lost is only hiding. It will show its teeth again at the next spring cleaning."

"Father," I said. "You know I'm thirteen now?"

"I do."

"Serle was twelve when he went into service."

"You are in service."

"I mean, when he went away into service."

"Aren't you learning enough with me?"

"Yes, but I mean . . . most pages go away when they're thirteen."

"Some do. Some pages become squires to their own fathers."

"But Serle went away."

"You're not Serle."

"Can't I go to Lord Stephen as well?"

My father shook his head. "I think one de Caldicot was quite enough for him," he said.

"Some pages go into service with their own uncles, don't they?" I asked.

"Yes."

"I could serve your brother."

"Sir William?" exclaimed my father. "You?"

"Why not?"

"He's very much older than I am," my father said. "He's sixty-four. And he's away from home half the time."

"Lady Alice would be glad if I did. I know she would."

"You do, do you?" my father replied. "It's not up to her. A squire serves a knight, not a lady."

"I mean, wouldn't I learn even more if I were away from home? Oliver says boys learn better from teachers than from their own parents."

"Hang Oliver!" said my father in a slow dark voice.

"But . . ."

"That's enough," said my father sharply. "At present, you're a page here in this manor. In good time, and before long, I'll tell you about my plans for you."

+ 6 +
coeur-de-lion

We heard bad news today.

Just before dinner one of Lord Stephen's riders galloped in. My father gave him leave to speak, and he told us King Richard has been badly wounded. A French arrow went in through his left shoulder at the base of his neck, and came out through his back.

Then we all started asking questions at the same time, and the messenger did his best to answer them.

"In the southwest of France, ma'am . . . a castle on a hilltop . . . Chalus . . . I don't know, sir . . . one of Count Aimar's . . ."

"Will he live?" asked Serle.

"Lord God gives life and Lord God takes it away," my father observed.

"Lord Stephen says you will know what to do," said the rider.

"Indeed we do," said my father. "We'll light candles. We'll get down on our kneebones. Every man jack living in this manor."

My grandmother Nain slowly sucked in her breath.

"What is it, Nain?" asked my father rather wearily.

"What is it with your kings?" my grandmother asked in her singsong Welsh voice. "Harold first. An arrow through his right eye. Then Rufus, nailed to his own saddle. And now, Coeur-de-Lion."

"If King Richard dies, it will be three times the worse

18

for us," said my father. "A new king means a new tax. Remember what we had to pay so Coeur-de-Lion could fight Saladin for the kingdom of Jerusalem. The Saladin tithe!"

"You Englishman!" cried my mother, flaring up like a candle that hasn't been properly trimmed. "Your king is dying and all you do is talk about money."

"I didn't know the Welsh cared much for King Richard," said my father, smiling.

My mother's eyes filled with tears. "He brought home a piece of the Holy Cross, didn't he?"

"Sir William taught me a poem about that," said Serle:

"Hot wind! Flags and banners streaming!
Helmets shining, broadswords gleaming!
Who can stop him, Coeur-de-Lion?
Cry Coeur-de-Lion! Jerusalem!

But thirty thousand Saracen troops,
Some alone, some in large groups,
Hoot and jeer him, Coeur-de-Lion.
Cry Coeur-de-Lion! Jerusalem!"

"You see, John?" cried my mother. "He's no king of mine, but he roared and rattled the gates of the Saracens."

"Which is more than his younger brother will ever do," said my father. "Prince John's not half the man his elder brother was."

"That often happens," said my mother.

I could feel Serle was staring at me, but I didn't look back at him.

"Far better King Richard's nephew became king," my father said. "Prince Arthur."

"Arthur!" I exclaimed.

"But he's only a boy," my father continued. "I fear for England if John is crowned king. And especially, I fear for us here in the March. The Welsh are like dogs. They can always smell a weakness."

"Did you hear that, Nain?" my mother asked.

"Speak up!" said Nain.

"John says there'll be trouble."

"Double?"

"No, mother. Trouble! Welsh trouble."

"It's the English who cause trouble," Nain said sharply. "Years and years of it. Generations!"

This afternoon, the sky bellowed. The day darkened and quivered but the rain never came. It would have been better if it had.

Then Sir William's freeman, Thomas, rode in, and he brought the same news. The same but different. He told us King Richard had ridden up to the hilltop castle at Chalus with a dozen men, right up to the portcullis, and that one of the king's own crossbowmen, supporting him from behind, fired short. "His bolt fell short of the battlements," said Thomas, "and it pierced the top of the king's back. It came out through his neck. . . . No! Not a French arrow. It was Norman or English. It was loyal fire!"

Which story is true? Is either of them true?

Oliver, my teacher, says it is better to record important messages. "Written words," he says, puffing up his chest, "are more reliable than spoken ones, because some messengers have very rich fancies and some have very poor memories."

my Tailbone

The bone at the bottom of my spine sticks out a bit. Sometimes it aches and sometimes it feels as if it's about to burst right through my skin, and grow into a tail.

In the church, there's a painting on the wall of Adam and Eve and a grinning devil. The devil has a tail as long as a grass snake, and he's holding it in his left hand and twirling it.

"Do devils always have tails?" I asked Oliver.

"Always," he replied.

"What about humans?" I asked.

Oliver harrumphed and shook his head. "Never," he said. "Not unless they're devils in disguise."

"And what if they are?"

"Their devil's parts begin to grow, until they can no longer hide them."

"And then?"

"Then," said Oliver darkly, and he put his right forefinger across his throat. His eyes gleamed. "Why, Arthur? Have you got a tail?"

"Of course not," I said.

Firstly, I need to find out whether my tailbone is growing, and until then I must be extremely careful that no one at all finds out about it.

And then I need to know why it sometimes aches, as it has done all today.

Last night, I kept thinking dark thoughts. I thought

21

that I don't care whether or not King Richard dies. Why should I? After all, he doesn't like the English. He has only come to England twice and never to the March. All Coeur-de-Lion wants from us, my father says, is money and more money. So what does it matter if he does die?

I'm not quite sure yet but I'm beginning to suspect that dark thoughts like these make my tailbone ache. But what if it's the other way round? What if it's my devil's part that causes me to have these dark thoughts?

little luke and
pigeon pie

Little Luke coughed and wailed from dark until dawn, a wretched cry as thin and cutting as the new moon. My mother and Tanwen and my father and I and even Serle tried to comfort him, but it made no difference.

My father says it's likely half the children in the kingdom cried last night to warn us that King Richard is dying.

"Babies can tell great births and deaths before they happen," he said. "Sometimes they rise and bubble, as they've never done before; sometimes they sink deep into themselves."

But Serle thinks Luke cried because it's such strange weather, hot and damp. "On days like this, we all feel wrong with ourselves," he said. "Even the dogs have their tails between their legs."

"Nonsense!" said Tanwen. "A baby cares only for one thing, and that's himself. What's wrong with Luke is somewhere inside him. Something he ate yesterday."

My mother didn't say what she thought, but I could see she was remembering how baby Mark began to wail one night early last year. No one knew why, and no one could stop him. None of Johanna's medicines made any difference, he just wasted away.

So no one got much sleep last night except for Nain, and that's the advantage of being deaf. Maybe this is what

Merlin meant when he told me that everything contains its opposite.

This morning, though, our cook Slim cheered us all up at dinner by serving a surprising pie. The pastry was shaped like our own dovecote, and there was a feather sticking out of the top of it.

Slim bowed to my father and set the pie on the table in front of him. "Sir John," he said, "do me the honor."

Well, when my father cut open the crust, there was a great commotion inside the pie. My mother and Sian squealed and stood up. Then a pink-eyed pigeon poked out its head and flapped its wings.

We were all showered with bits of crust, and the pigeon flew up to the gallery. Everyone clapped, and then Ruth, who helps Slim in the kitchen, carried in the real pie.

+ 9 +

tumber hill

My father took Serle hunting with him again today, but I had to stay at home because I helped Gatty to save our two bulls from killing each other.

After studying with Oliver, I saddled Pip and rode him round the Yard ten times. Except I didn't ask him to climb the ladder. Not even horses should be asked to do that.

My uncle William told me how he and his reeve once played a practical joke on one of their neighbors. They hoisted one of his cows into the hayloft and then removed the ropes and pulley to make it look as if the cow had climbed the ladder, but when he got home, the neighbor was very angry because he couldn't get his cow down again; he had to kill and butcher her up in the loft.

While I was in the Yard, I saw Gatty and Dusty stagger behind the butts with sacks of mast and bean-squelch for the pigs. So I rode over to them.

"Go on, Dusty," said Gatty. "I'll catch you up."

Dusty grinned at me.

"Go on!" said Gatty more sharply.

But Dusty still didn't move, because he doesn't understand words, and isn't any good at doing things on his own.

So then Gatty pushed him and his bean-squelch a few steps in the direction of the pigsty, and I dismounted.

"Are you all right?" I asked.

Gatty shrugged. "Same as usual," she said.

"I mean, he beat you with a twig-broom."

"Better than a stick. A stick he's got sometimes."

"My father uses willow rods," I said.

"Or a whip," said Gatty. "My father's got a whip."

"Without you," I said, "one of our bulls would have been killed."

"Harold," said Gatty.

"Yes. And I told my father how brave you were."

"Your brother didn't do nothing," said Gatty.

"Exactly," I said. "We got the bulls apart, and we got punished. It's Serle who should have been punished."

"Gotta go," said Gatty suddenly. "Dusty's no good on his own."

"I haven't forgotten our expedition," I said. "Upstream. This summer we'll do that."

"What about the fair then?" Gatty asked, and she lowered her eyes. When she does that she looks quite pretty because she has long eyelashes, and they tremble.

"That too," I said. "We'll go to the fair at Ludlow."

"You'll get beaten," said Gatty.

"So will you," I said. "But it's worth it."

At the end of the afternoon, I went up onto the hill with the hounds, Tempest and Storm. As soon as you're past the orchard and the copper beech, the ground arches its back. The hill makes my calves and thighbones ache. I'm stronger than it is, but I'm always panting by the time I get to the top because I try to get there as fast as I can.

The light was so strong and bright that away beyond Pike Forest and the wilderness, I could see violet hills. And beyond the violet hills, I saw — or thought I saw — the shadowy dark shapes of the Black Mountains. I have never traveled that far west, and my father says it would be dangerous to ride so deep into Wales and that, anyhow, there is no reason to go there. But each time I stand on Tumber Hill and stare, I think there is a reason, and I know that one day I'll ride west; I'll climb the violet hills and cross the Black Mountains, and gallop beyond them until I come down to the western sea. I would like Gatty to come with me, but I don't suppose that is very likely.

Today Storm chased a doe rabbit, and actually caught her. When he brought her back to me, she was still screaming, so I wrung her neck.

Later, I gave the doe to Slim.

"What about baking two pies with crusts like rabbit hutches?" I asked him. "One for his doe, and one with Sian's white rabbit alive inside it."

"I never boil the same cabbage for pigs twice!" Slim replied rudely.

While Tempest and Storm raced around, I sat down on the crown of the hill. I thought about my tailbone a bit, and then about Serle. He pretends he likes me when we're in company, but he's mean to me whenever we're alone. Sometimes he twists my arm behind my back until I have to get down on one knee and my arm almost breaks, but mainly he hurts me with what he says. I know Serle tells on me as well, especially to my mother, and she doesn't stop him because he's the apple of her eye.

After a while, I began to think about my father's plans for me. What are they, and why won't he tell them to me now? When I talked to him, he didn't say I could go away into service. He didn't promise I could be a squire at all. Is this because I'm not good enough in the Yard? Or because of something I don't even know about?

Everything is difficult now in my life but, all the same, I was more happy when I ran down Tumber Hill than when I climbed it. It helps to ask questions, even if I don't know the answers.

When I reached the bottom of the hill, I saw my father had come back from hunting, and he and Merlin were sitting under the copper beech. My father was out in the soft sunlight, but Merlin was dapple-dressed with yellow spots and purple patches of shadow.

"Too much sunlight turns today into tomorrow," said Merlin. "And it pickles the brain."

I know Merlin and my father were talking about me because they stopped talking as soon as they saw me.

"That's a fat doe," my father said.

"Storm caught her."

Then Storm began to bounce, and that made Tempest bounce.

"So," said my father, and that meant he was getting impatient.

"I'm going," I said.

"You were saying, John," said Merlin. "Your brother . . ."

"Sir William!" I exclaimed.

"Arthur," said my father. "How many times do I have to tell you?"

"I thought . . ."

"I don't mind what you thought. I'm talking to Merlin, not to you."

Then Merlin winked at me. He winked so fast that I wasn't quite sure whether he had winked or not.

"Yes, father," I said.

"I do know an old charm," said Merlin, "which makes second sons vanish."

"Huh!" exclaimed my father. "You must teach it to me."

What were my father and Merlin talking about when I interrupted them? I don't think my father can know what I know. What Lady Alice told me. Because she said she would never tell anyone else at all.

the sleeping king

I like my Nain's stories. Everyone does. And after supper last night she told us a new one.

"About the dragon," she announced.

The dragon was her husband and a Welsh warlord, but he died so long ago my grandmother can only just remember him.

"No," said Sian. "A story about our mother."

"Or," suggested Nain, "a story about the Sleeping King."

"The worstest thing our mother did when she was a girl," insisted Sian.

"The Sleeping King, Nain," I said. "You've never told us that story before."

There was a knocking at the door: Then the latch lifted.

"Merlin!" my father called out. "Nain's beginning a story."

"How did I know?" said Merlin.

I don't know how he did. But he often does.

"I'll sit with my friend here," said Merlin. And he promptly sat down beside me.

My father was in his chair, and Luke was in his cradle, asleep; the pair of hounds were under the table; and Tanwen and Sian were sitting on the little wall-bench with Serle wedged between them. So only my mother was not there, and if she had been, Nain's story would probably have been spoiled because she and my mother always argue.

For the last three nights, Luke has woken up and started to wail, and my mother is tired out with trying to feed and comfort him. At supper she kept yawning and, as soon as it was over, she greeted us all and withdrew to the chamber.

"Where was I?" asked Nain.

"At the beginning!" my father replied. "Sit on the floor, Sian. There's not enough room on that bench for you as well as Serle and Tanwen."

So Sian slipped down onto the rushes, and at once Spitfire miaowed, and came over and sat on her lap.

"Before I was born," said Nain, "a boy living here on the March went scrambling."

"Where?" I asked.

"Some say Weston or Panpunton Hill. I say Caer Caradoc. This boy found a cave he had never seen before, and inside the cave there was a dark passageway. It led right into the hill."

"But how could he see if it was dark?" demanded Sian.

My father cleared his throat. "Who is telling this story?" he asked.

"He lit a brand, didn't he," said Nain, "and walked right in under the hill. Halfway down the passage, the boy saw a bell, a huge one hanging and blocking the passage. He had to get down on his hands and knees, and he squirmed under it.

"Then he went on down the passage, it was damp and chill, and it grew wider and wider." Nain spread her black arms and flapped them like a crow. "The passage became drafty and the boy came to a flight of stone steps leading down into a grotto."

"What's a grotto?" asked Sian.

31

"A stone hall," said Nain. "And you know what? First he saw the grotto was full of shining candles, and then below him he saw men in armor. One hundred warriors, sleeping. They were lying in a great ring, all surrounding one man. And this man was dressed in scarlet and gold, and holding a naked sword."

"The king!" cried Sian.

"He was asleep," said Nain.

"Who was he?" asked Sian.

"The boy didn't know," Nain replied. "And even now no one knows. Some people call him the Sleeping King, some say the King Without a Name.

"The boy laid down his brand and crept down the steps. He picked his way between the sleeping warriors. He stared right down at the Sleeping King . . . his wrinkled eyelids, his generous mouth, almost smiling . . . his great sword with serpentine patterning on the blade.

"Then the boy saw a heap of gold coins lying beside the king. He bent down. *Just one,* see. Then quickly he passed through the ring of sleeping warriors, back up the stone steps. But the boy's flaming brand had gone out, and he couldn't see his way down the dark passage. First he scraped his knuckles on the walls, and then he bumped into the bell. Its tongue wagged. It boomed and shivered.

"At once all the warriors in the grotto woke up. They leaped to their feet. They ran up the stone steps and along the passageway. They chased after the boy, whooping and yelling.

"'Is it the day?' they called out." Nain stood up and flapped her black wings again. "'Is it the day?'"

"What about the king?" Sian demanded. "What did he do?"

"I don't know," Nain said. "He went on sleeping. But the warriors' whoops and yells echoed all the way down the passage. How the boy wished he could stop them, but he didn't know the old words, see. He didn't know the magic words that swallow every sound. He knew what to do, though. He could see the light at the end of that passage — a needle of hope — and he ran as fast as he could towards it.

"The warriors followed the boy, he could hear their footsteps and their loud breathing. But he got out before they could catch him, and not one of them came out into the light. Not so much as a footstep.

"So the boy, panting and trembling, he escaped. And he still had the gold coin in his right hand.

"Who was the king?" cried Nain. "And who were the warriors? Were they men of the March? Were they the British warriors who fought long ago against the Saxons?"

Nain paused and fixed each of us with her dark stare. "And when will the day come? When will the warriors wake and march out of the hill?

"The boy took his coin home, and of course he told people what he'd seen, and all the men and boys living on his manor went up onto the hillside with flaming brands.

"But you know what? They couldn't find the passage at the back of the cave. Not then, and never since. They searched and searched. It was there and it was not there."

Nain sighed and then she suddenly reached out and pointed through the darkness. "You," she called out.

"Who?" said Serle.

"Me?" asked Sian.

"You, girl! What's your name?"

"Tanwen."

33

"What does it mean?"

"I am white fire," said Tanwen in a low voice.

"Speak up!"

"White fire."

"That's what it means," said Nain. "Yes, and it's dangerous to play with white fire."

"What are you talking about?" my father asked.

"Names," said Merlin. "Names have power."

"Is that the end of the story, Nain?" asked Sian.

"Until the Sleeping King wakes," said Nain.

"Holy smoke!" exclaimed Sian, and everyone laughed.

jack-words

What Merlin says must be true. Names do have power.

Last night, I couldn't get to sleep for thinking about Nain's story, and wondering who the Sleeping King is and when he will march out of the hill, and which hill it is, and what the magic words are that will swallow sound. I did try to count the clouds crossing the sky inside my head, but the more I counted, the more awake I was. And it was just the same with sheep coming out of a pen. . . .

Then I began to think about the word Jack, and all the Jack-words I know.

There's Jack Frost, who scrawls and scribbles all over the horn-windows, and sometimes on the outsides of walls as well. There's Jack-Daw, and he's no friend of ours: He helps his friend Crow eat our green wheat. Jack-Straw! That's what Sian and I play. Her fingers are more quick and delicate than mine, and she usually beats me. And what about Jack who killed a giant? I wish I had a cap like his. As soon as he put it on, he knew the answers to everything.

Then there's Jack-o'-Lantern, glowing and scowling on Hallowe'en, scaring away warlocks and witches. Jack-o'-Lantern. His white face on fire . . .

I think this is when I fell asleep.

+ 12 +

fever

Sir William's messenger, Thomas, rode in again today — the same man who told us King Richard had been shot by one of his own crossbowmen. I thought he must be bringing us more news of King Richard, but he had come to say that Lady Alice and my cousins Tom and Grace will not be able to stay with us next week because they are ill.

My aunt says they all have a hot, dry fever and it is three days since they ate a mouthful, but they are drinking milk and lots of willow-bark soup.

When he heard the news, my father said, "Well, I can't say I mind. We're planning to shear the sheep next week, so Hum and I will be very busy."

I mind, though. I was looking forward to seeing Grace. We both think that our parents mean us to be betrothed, and I promised to take her up Tumber Hill, and show her my secret climbing-tree. It's best at this time of year, when all the new beech leaves have opened their hands, because then you can look out but no one can see in.

When Grace and Tom stay with us, my father doesn't make me study or practice. But we all go to the Yard anyway. Each of us can choose one skill, and Grace is the judge. Sian is her assistant.

Serle always makes us tilt at the quintain, and that's what I'm worst at. The sandbag has hit me on the head so often I'm surprised it hasn't knocked out my brains. Tom likes swordplay best, and I choose archery because it's the one skill I know I can win at. Then it's Grace's turn to choose, and last time she made us balance our lances, and aim their points, and run at the ring.

I was looking forward to seeing Lady Alice as well. I want to be sure she hasn't told my father our secret. If he does know, there's no point my asking him again whether I can serve Sir William. He'll never agree.

Tom and I worked out something strange. Serle is double Sian's age, because he's sixteen, and Lady Alice, who is Sir William's second wife and Grace and Tom's stepmother, is double Serle's age, but her skin's still as soft as a peach and she doesn't look as old as that. And then Sir William is exactly double Lady Alice's age.

Thomas told us Sir William is away from home. No one knows where. He is meant to be visiting his estate in Champagne but, for all my aunt knows, he may be fighting at the siege where King Richard has been wounded.

"The man's never at home for one month on end," said my father. And he gave my mother a long look, and then cracked his fingers.

"Ask Slim to give you something to eat before you go," my mother told Thomas.

"Quite right!" said my father. "And drink as much ale as you like."

I can see my father likes and trusts Thomas, and I think he wishes Thomas worked at this manor and not at Gortanore.

+ 13 +
KNOWING AND UNDERSTANDING

The verses of the Bible that I read with Oliver are often tedious, and so is the way he talks. He uses twice as many words as anyone else, and pretends to know everything. But all the same, I quite enjoy my lessons with him.

Our church is like the cave at the back of Tumber Hill. When it's hot outside, it stays cool. And when it's bitter outside, it's not quite so cold inside the building. All the same, my toes grow numb when I have to sit for hours in the vestry. One of Oliver's lessons was so terribly long that I made my head twitch and my teeth chatter. Oliver was worried then. He shut the Book and sent me straight home.

Today, I brought Oliver a rabbit — the second one Storm has caught, and this time it was a buck — but he told me to leave it on the porch.

"The crows will get it," I said.

"How are rabbits wise?" Oliver asked me.

"Their bodies are weak but they make their burrows among the rocks."

"How are ants wise?"

"They are weak, too, but each summer they lay in stores for the winter."

"And how are spiders wise?"

"Because they know how to use their hands, and some of them are courtiers, and live in kings' palaces."

"Who says so?" asked Oliver.

"The Book of Proverbs says so."

"What are proverbs?"

"Sayings to teach a young man knowledge and understanding."

"Exactly," said Oliver. "And the two are not the same, are they. First we learn a fact, then we learn what that fact means."

"Serle is my brother," I said.

"That is a fact."

"And my brother means different things: unkind as well as kind; enemy and friend."

"And that is an understanding," said Oliver.

"Serle says second sons matter less than firstborn," I continued.

"That is not true," said Oliver, and he puffed himself up, as a cock robin does after his dust bath. "No, that's not true at all. Some of us are men and some are women. Some of us are firstborn and some of us are not. In fact, most of us are not! But it doesn't matter. Men or women, firstborn or not, we are all equal in God's eyes."

"You've told me that before," I said, "but it can't be true. A few people in this manor are rich but most are poor. A few have plenty to eat, but most have almost nothing. That's not equal."

"Remember the Book," said Oliver. "'The poor are with you always.' Yes, Arthur, they always have been and they always will be. That's how things are. Poverty is part of God's will."

"How can it be?"

"We need a king, don't we: to rule over us?"

"Not King John, my father says."

"The country needs a king to rule over it, and the king needs Lord Stephen and his other earls and lords. Lord Stephen needs your father, Sir John, and all his other knights. And your father needs the men and women in this manor to plow and sow and reap. It is God's will."

"But it is not equal," I repeated.

"Arthur," said Oliver, "one boy may have more talents than another, but a good father should not love him more because of that. He should love all his children equally. That is how it is with God. We are all equal in God's eyes. Now! All this chatter! It's time you started your reading."

Then Oliver lurched across the vestry, pulling his greasy key-thong over his head. No! He never has to worry where his next meal is coming from; he always has plenty to eat, even if it is mainly oatmeal porridge and pease pottage; and he has his own land, and everyone has to give him a tenth of their crops and their chicks and lambs.

Oliver turned the key in the creaking chest, and took out the Bible. "In the name of King Richard," he said, "your reading is the twentieth psalm. The twentieth psalm and then the twenty-first psalm."

" 'We will wave our banners,' " I began to read in Latin, and then to translate, " 'in the name of God. Some men trust their horses and some their chariots: But we will remember the name of the Lord our God. We trample our enemies: They lie in the dust, but we rise and stand upright.' "

"You see?" said Oliver. "If you're going to fight, horses and chariots are all very well. Horses and chariots are necessary, but they're not enough. King Richard knows that. That's why he defeated Saladin at Arsuf. That's why he has saved for us the kingdom of Jerusalem."

"But doesn't Saladin worship God too?" I asked. "Don't Saracens worship God?"

"They worship a false prophet," said Oliver. "They're not true believers. Saracens are infidels."

"Sir William says that's what Saracens call Christians," I replied. "Infidels!"

Oliver snorted. "They don't understand the Book. They don't even read it."

"Aren't Saracens and Christians equal in the eyes of God then?"

"They are not!" said Oliver. "Of course they're not! In the eyes of God, all Christian people are equal. But you can be sure hell's mouth is wide and waiting for heathens and heretics and infidels."

"Sir William fought in Jerusalem," I said, "and he doesn't believe that. He thinks . . ."

"Sir William is a knight. He is not a priest," Oliver replied.

One reason why I quite like my lessons with Oliver is that I am allowed to argue with him, and find out new things. It's like climbing Tumber Hill inside my own head: The further I go, the more I see; and the more I see, the more I want to see.

"How many books are there?" I asked Oliver.

"Where?"

"In the world. Altogether."

"My dear boy! You expect me to know everything! Well, now! Each church in England has its Bible . . ."

"I don't mean copies of the same words," I said. "I mean different words."

Oliver pressed the palms of his hands over his stomach and gave a long, gentle sigh. "It is impossible to say," he replied. "There are books in Latin and in French, and a few in Hebrew and in Greek. I don't know! Twenty books, or even thirty, have been translated into English, and I have heard that one or two have even been written in English."

"Sir William says there are Saracen books too. About the stars, and medicines . . ."

Oliver shook his head. "You see?" he said. "If only they were Christian! No, Arthur. It's impossible to say. But I know you. You won't be content with that." Oliver paused and slowly nodded. "I think . . . I think there must be more than one hundred books altogether."

Another reason I like my lessons is that no one else in my family can read properly. My father can only read very slowly, and my mother can't read at all. Serle had lessons while he was in service with Lord Stephen, but he can't read as well as I can, and he doesn't know how to write.

Nain thinks there is no reason whatsoever for a page to learn to read and write. "Your father didn't learn much," she said. "And the dragon certainly didn't. Think what will happen if you start to depend on writing. Your memory will soon weaken. If something's worth knowing," she said, "it's worth remembering."

When people are as old as my grandmother, they don't like new ways of doing things. They soon start talking about their own childhood, and say that wise people leave the world as it is.

I would like to see how books are made: how the hide is scraped and dried and pumiced and chalked. I'd like to find out which plants make the different-colored inks.

Oliver says he will talk to my father about taking me to visit the priory at Wenlock. He says there is a writing-room there, and two monks and two novices work in it each day, making copies of the Bible and other books.

"It is hard work," he said. "Very hard."

"Sometimes my writing hand aches," I said.

"Then pray for scribes," replied Oliver. "Aching wrists and aching elbows; aching necks; aching backs. Their eyes water and grow dim. But make no mistake: Each word written to the glory of God is like a hammer blow on the devil's head. That's what the blessed Bernard said."

What I cannot work out is why my father wants me to read and write so well. I like reading. I like writing. And I would like to see the scribes in their writing-room. But not instead of serving as a squire. A squire, like Serle, and then a knight: That is what I want to be.

+ 14 +
jumpers and
my writing-room

A staircase climbs out of our hall. A flight of fourteen oak steps winds you round and lifts you up to the gallery.

The gallery is a good place to stand if you want a lot of people to be able to see you. When the guisers come on Hallowe'en, and when all the villagers crowd in at Christmas and the hall is packed, my father goes up there, and rings his handbell, and speaks to everyone.

Musicians sometimes play and sing from the gallery. Last year, a man with a cymbal and stick climbed up without our noticing him while his wife was singing a song about how a wicked knight seduced and then abandoned a miller's daughter. "Wicked!" cried the woman. And her husband up in the gallery clashed the cymbal with his stick, and gave us all a great shock. There's not enough room up there for dancers or mummers, though, because it's only one pace wide.

Two little rooms lead out of the gallery. They are like nests under the eaves. The first room is stuffed with barrels of wheat and barley. My father thinks it's prudent to keep some food stored inside the house, in case the Welsh raiders do come and stop us getting out to the kitchen or the barn. But our mice and rats don't like waiting. Our meal for tomorrow is their meal today. "Grab it! Scoff it!" That's what they squeak.

If they hear what happened to the jumpers, the raiders won't be in a hurry to come. They may not risk coming at all. It was last November. Just before dawn the jumpers tried to climb into our chamber through one of the little windows. But my father heard them. He rolled out of bed and picked up his sword. Then he crept over to the window and stood to one side of it and raised his sword.

As soon as the first man put his head through the window, my father brought his sword down. He cut the jumper's head right off.

"Quick!" said a muffled voice outside.

Then the second jumper gave the first one's twitching legs a push, so that the rest of him fell into the chamber.

"Go on!" said another voice. "Quick!"

So the second jumper heaved himself up and stuck his head through the window. Then in the gloom he saw . . . and at once he tried to jerk himself back. But his friends outside were holding onto his legs and trying to push him into the chamber. Then the jumper yelled and my father crashed the sword down for a second time.

"His head was still yelling after I had sliced it off," my father said.

I don't think that can be true, because our words and sighs and screams and farts are all made out of air — the air we breathe in through our mouths and down into our lungs. Merlin has got a whole skeleton folded up in a chest, and he got it out once and explained this to me.

When the men outside heard their friend yell, they ran away, and we don't even know how many of them there were. But after that, my mother wouldn't sleep in the chamber for a long time.

The bodies of the two men were buried in the same pit

45

in the north corner of the churchyard, while their heads were buried in a hole in the south corner.

"And that way," said Oliver, "their ghosts won't be able to trouble you."

Then Tanwen got Ruth from the kitchen to help her. They took out all the chamber-rushes and burned them. They even washed the clay floor with wet cloths. Then they brought in fresh rushes, and laid them, and laced them with sprigs of rosemary and tansy and thyme.

After that, my father asked Oliver to say prayers of purification in the chamber.

Even so, my mother wouldn't sleep in there. She had the mattress of the Great Bed dragged into the hall, and that's where she and my father slept all through the winter.

After that, my father had the two little chamber-windows almost blocked in. They are just slits now, and Sian is the only one who can get her wrists through them.

The second little room off our gallery is empty. The inner walls are quite soft. If I so much as touch them, they sprinkle me with flakes and pale powder. The outer wall is made of stone, though, and sparrows often fly in through the wind-eye and pick and peck at the mortar, because they like the taste of lime. The gaps they have made between the blocks of dressed stone are homes for all kinds of little creatures. Sometimes, when I'm sitting in the window seat, I can hear whirring and humming and soft scratching and throbbing and buzzing and ticking all around me.

So the walls are alive and, up above me, the huge beams and the thatch are alive too. The nests of martins and swallows. Hanging bats . . . The thatch is old and grey, so it doesn't smell fresh, but it does smell comfortable. I think thatch-scent is a kind of medicine: It helps to soothe anger and cure fear. It makes me think summer thoughts, and sometimes it makes me sleepy.

For most of the time, this room's quite warm because of the heat rising from the hall. But in winter that wind sometimes blows from the north, and then it whistles in the thatch and pours through the wind-eye.

When our old apple tree fell down, I sawed off a big slice of the trunk, and Gatty helped me to haul it up here. I perch my inkwell on it.

So I sit in this little window seat with my knees up. And if I press my back against one side of the alcove and my feet against the other, there's just enough space.

Here is my quill. My cream page. This is my writing-room.

15

NiNE

Merlin and Oliver often argue, and Oliver sometimes gets angry.

I walked several times round the moat with them today, and they began by agreeing that the complete and flawless number is nine. But then they disagreed why.

"The reason, Merlin," said Oliver, "is perfectly obvious. Lord God is our Father. He is the Son and he is the Holy Ghost. Three-in-one and one-in-three."

"And three equals nine," said Merlin.

"No, Merlin! Three does not equal nine."

Merlin waved his hands impatiently. *"Constipatus!"* he muttered.

Oliver took no notice. "Three is the divine number, and threefold three is nine," he went on. "So nine is the flawless number. *Quod erat demonstrandum.*"

"I get the idea," said Merlin.

"You get . . ." snapped Oliver, and he blocked one nostril with his right forefinger and blew snot from the other onto the ground.

"I'll tell you nine," said Merlin quietly. "The nine spirits, each with a bottomless chalice . . ."

"That is blasphemy!" said Oliver loudly.

"Nothing of the kind," replied Merlin.

"Do you deny Christ?"

"Not for one moment," said Merlin.

"It's as well for you," said Oliver.

"Are you threatening me?" asked Merlin.

Oliver glared at Merlin. "Your own tongue is your enemy," he said.

"My tongue is my servant."

"And it often leads you into mortal danger. There is no room in the house of Christ for nine spirits."

"One person sips from the chalice of poetry," continued Merlin, "and shapes poems for us. Another person sips from the chalice of song, and delights us."

"Cow dung!" shouted Oliver. "A load of cow dung! And you know it!" And he turned his back on us, and flounced off.

"Who are the other spirits?" I asked.

"I will tell you," said Merlin, "in a little while and soon. In the meantime, you must find your number."

"What do you mean?"

"Each of us is born under one star, and it guides us. In each of us, one element is most powerful. Each of us is true to one number, and it is time for you to find it."

three sorrows, three fears, three joys

I have worked out that I have three sorrows, three fears, and three joys, so my number may be nine.

My first sorrow is Serle, who is unfair and mean to me. My second sorrow is my tailbone. I am almost sure it is growing. My third is the secret Lady Alice told me, and the pain she feels. These are the sorrows of my heart and body and head.

My first fear is that my father will never agree to let me go into service away from home. And my second is even worse. I'm not all that good at my Yard-skills, my tilting especially, so what if my father doesn't mean me to be a squire at all? I know Grace likes me and I do hope that we will be betrothed. But my third fear is that my parents may want her to be betrothed to Serle and not to me.

My three joys. The first is to go out and about with Gatty, and Tempest and Storm. They're my companions; I am their leader. My second joy is my skill with the longbow. I am the best at that, and have even beaten my father. My third joy is my reading and writing, and what I learn when I talk to Oliver and Merlin.

+ 17 +

tempest's teeth

As I walked into the hall, Tempest came running out with some teeth between his teeth. They looked like a row of spikes: like the long, pointed teeth of the witch, Black Annis.

I called Tempest back and made him open his jaws, and what fell out was the comb I carved for Sian for her last birthday! I don't know where it had been hibernating, but I thanked Tempest for finding it and washed it in the moat. Then I gave the comb back to Sian and told her to use it sometimes. "Otherwise," I said, "Black Annis will come in the night and eat you."

"Not just for that!" said Sian. "Would she?"

51

just jack

Slim cooked mutton stew today, and my mother complained he put too much spice into it.

"I can't taste the meat at all," she said, "or the onions. Only the cinnamon."

She liked the honey custard, though, and so did I. At dinner, I told everyone my Jack-words. Jack-Daw and Jack Frost, Jack-Straw. "And there's Jack-o'-Lantern," I said.

"There is!" cried my mother. "And the uglier the better!" Then she screwed up her eyes. I should have remembered that baby Mark died on Hallowe'en last year.

"Go on, Arthur," my father said.

"That's all I know."

"I know another," my father said, "and so should you, Serle."

"I do," said Serle. "Jack. Just jack."

"What is it?"

"A kind of coat," said Serle. "Without any sleeves. I think jacks are made of leather, usually."

"They are," said my father. "Cloth or leather."

"With small iron plates sewn into the lining," said Serle. "We wouldn't wear them. Foot soldiers wear them."

"Very good, Serle," said my father.

19

NAIN IN ARMOR

Lying beside the hall fire last night, I started to think about the names for different pieces of armor. Then on the far side of the hall, Nain began to snore. And then I connected them:

And her shoes are connected to her shin guards,
And her shin guards are knotted to her knee joints,
And her knee joints are tied to her thigh plates,
And her thigh plates are thonged to her mail-shirt,
And her mail-shirt's strapped to her neck flap,
And her neck flap's fastened to her helmet,
And her helmet's bolted to her nasal,
And her nasal's what covers Nain's nose!

✤ 20 ✤

OBSIDIAN

I was halfway up Tumber Hill when I heard a shout and saw Merlin climbing up behind me. He has never done that before.

When we reached the top, he asked me whether I had ever thought about crossing-places.

"You mean fords?" I said.

"Fords, yes. Bridges! And the foreshore, where the ocean tries to swallow the land, and the land tries to dry up the sea."

"I've never seen the sea," I said.

"You will," Merlin replied. "Look over there, beyond Pike Forest. Where England ends and Wales begins."

"It's trembling," I said.

"Exactly!" said Merlin. "Between-places are never quite certain of themselves. Think of dusk, between day and night. It's blue and unsure."

"New Year's Eve is a crossing-place," I said.

"It is," said Merlin. "Between year and year. And this year, between century and century." He snapped a piece of grass, then wrapped one hand around the other, and stretched the blade between the joints of his thumbs, and blew on it so that it whistled.

"And the king is dying," said Merlin. "You see? Strange things will happen."

"How do you know he is?" I asked.

Merlin didn't answer my question. What he did was

unfasten his cloak, and pull out of an inside pocket a dusty saffron bundle. Then he slowly began to unwind the cloth.

"What is it?" I asked.

"A gift," said Merlin.

Inside the cloth was a flat black stone. It was four-cornered, and its span was just a little larger than Merlin's outstretched hand. One face of the stone was lumpen and covered with little white spots and patches, but when Merlin turned it over, the other side was smooth and glossy. It flashed in the sunlight.

"Take it!" said Merlin.

When I stared at the stone, I could see myself inside it. It was black of black, and deep, and very still. Like an eye of deep water.

"A mirror," I said.

"Not really," said Merlin.

"What is it?"

"A gift."

"I mean, what is it for?"

Merlin shrugged.

"What kind of stone is it?"

"It is made of ice and fire," Merlin said. "Its name is obsidian."

"Obsidian?"

"It's time for you to have it," Merlin replied. "It's time for me to let it go."

"What is it for?" I asked again.

"That depends on you," Merlin said. "Only you can tell. It's like your number."

"Nine," I said. "I think it's nine."

"It's like that," repeated Merlin. "The stone is not what I say it is. It's what you see in it."

I turned the flat stone over and over between my hands.

"The shape," I said. "It reminds me of something. Lots of things. A wolf skull, almost. Or look! The spread of the manor lands below us. I don't know. The big bruise on the face of the moon."

"It is for you," Merlin said gravely.

"But what . . ."

"What I can tell you is this," Merlin said. "From this moment, here on Tumber Hill, until the day you die, you will never own anything as precious as this."

I held the stone with both my hands. "What if it breaks?" I asked.

"It won't," said Merlin. "Not if you drop it! But you must guard this stone. No one must know you own it . . ."

"Why not?"

". . . or see it, or learn anything about it."

"Why not?"

Merlin smiled gently. "You must keep the stone to yourself until you discover its power. Until you understand its meaning. Otherwise, it will not be of much use to you. Come on now — down into the world again!"

In my writing-room, snails and beetles and spiders and lice live in most of the little gaps and cracks between the blocks of dressed stone; but there is one gap which is empty, and a fingerspan wide, so that is where I have decided to hide Merlin's gift.

No one comes up here except for me. And even if they did, they wouldn't notice a dusty cloth bundle stuffed deep into the wall.

My rough-and-shining stone! My dark halo! My strange obsidian!

lance and longbow

"It's not meant to be easy," said my father.

"It's impossible," I said.

"Your cousin Tom can do it, can't he?"

"Yes, father."

"Well! He's only a year older than you."

"I could do it left-handed," I said.

"No boy in this manor will do anything left-handed. It's not natural. You know that."

"I could, though."

"I'll show you again," my father said. "Nothing worthwhile is ever easy." Then he set off for the marker, polishing the shaft of his lance against his right thigh. Before he turned, he rubbed the palm of his right hand on his tunic, and scraped the ground with his right foot. Then he raised and bent his right arm, balanced the lance, and ran up to the ring. At the last moment, he raised his left arm to steady himself, and then he thrust the lance forward to catch the ring.

"God's teeth!" exclaimed my father, releasing the ring from under his left shoulder.

"Nearly!" I said.

"Nearly is never good enough," said my father. "Do as I say, not as I do! Don't run up to the ring too fast, otherwise you'll never balance your lance. But don't be too careful either; don't let your feet stutter. Do you understand that?"

"Yes, father," I said. "Why did you rub your hand on your tunic?"

"To wipe off the sweat. You can't grip a lance with a damp hand. Now before you thrust the lance, bring your left shoulder right round, so that you're running almost sideways to the ring, with your eyes looking along the line of your left shoulder."

"Yes, father."

"Go on then!"

Six times I ran in from the marker where my father was standing, and then another six times from the marker on the other side of the ring, but it was no good. I couldn't catch the ring, though I did once graze the outside of it with the tip of my lance, so that it rang and danced on its silken string.

"You're not using your left arm," my father said. "Raise it to steady yourself as you take aim with your right arm. And arch your back a little."

"Yes, father."

My father pursed his lips and sighed. "I don't know whether we'll ever make a squire of you," he said.

"I'll practice," I said. "I promise."

"All right," said my father. "Let's see you shoot now. You're better at that. Though if you can see straight enough to shoot, I don't know why you can't catch the ring."

"If I could use my left hand . . ." I began.

"Arthur!"

"Yes, father."

"Right! We'll shoot three ends of three. That will be enough for me to see how you're coming on. Then I must talk to Hum. Grey's gone lame again, and Hum thinks she may need a splint."

"That's the third time," I said.

"And the last time I buy from Llewellyn. Bloody Welshman!"

"Longbows came from Wales, though," I said. "The first ones."

"Who told you that?"

"You did!"

My father sniffed. "In that case," he said, "you had better watch out. Your bow may soon go lame."

My father is better at talking than listening, and when he says we've discussed something, he means that he has made up his mind, and there's no point my trying to change it. But when we're alone, he really does listen to me. And laughs. He tells me all kinds of things about the life of a knight, wonderful things that no one else tells me.

I laughed. "No, not lame!" I said. "But Serle says it's too small for me."

"Let me have a look."

When I planted one end of the stave on the ground in front of me, I could easily see over it. In fact, I could almost tuck the top end under my chin.

"It's much too small," exclaimed my father. "Have you grown that much this year?"

"Can I have one made of yew?"

"You know that's against the law. When you're seventeen . . ."

"Serle's only sixteen."

My father sighed. "He's in his seventeenth year, and when you are in your seventeenth year, you shall have a yew bow too. Anyhow," he said, "I'll ask Will to measure you up and cut you a new one. And some new shafts as well — with fine flights! How about that?"

"Thank you, father," I said.

"These butts," said my father. "How far apart are they?"

"Two hundred and twenty paces," I said.

"That's it! So what would happen if you were shooting at a much closer target?"

I have tried doing this. Gatty and I both tried, except she wasn't strong enough to pull the string right back, and she was amazed when I shot one arrow right through the barn door.

"Yes," continued my father. "I've heard some Welsh bowmen cornered twelve of King Henry's horsemen inside a churchyard. They shot at them there, and some of their shafts stuck into the plaster of the church walls, and one shaft went right through an Englishman's mail-shirt, right through his mail-shirt and through his thigh. Then the shaft pierced his saddle and wounded his horse."

"Blood of Sebastian!" I cried.

"Yes," said my father. "That's how fierce these long-bows are."

"Did the English get away?"

"Not that time. The shafts killed seven of them, and wounded the other five. Then the Welshmen closed in and finished off the wounded men with their knives. Now! Come on, Arthur!"

I shot the first end quite well, and the second end as well as I am able.

"You," said my father, as we pulled my three shafts out of the target, and picked up his from the grass, "you could shoot an apple off a king's head."

"Father," I began, "you know I asked if I could go into service with Sir William?"

My father looked at me.

"And you said he's sixty-four and away from home half the time."

"Well?"

"That's what I want to do."

"What someone wants and what is right are not always the same thing," my father said.

"Couldn't I begin with Sir William?" I asked. "And if that doesn't work, I could go to Lord Stephen. Serle did."

"I think one of my sons is quite enough for Lord Stephen."

"But . . ."

"Arthur," said my father. "We've already discussed this. I've said that in good time, and before long, I'll tell you my plans for you."

At this moment, a misty rain began to fall — rain so fine I could scarcely see it — and then Hum came striding out into the Yard.

"I'm sorry, Sir John," he said. "A messenger's come in."

"What does he want?"

"You, Sir John. Says no one else will do."

"We'll come in," said my father. "You're shooting well, Arthur. I'll ask Will about a new bow."

"Thank you, father," I said.

"And you did say . . ." added Hum.

"Yes, Hum," said my father briskly.

"Grey's hobbling, Sir John."

"As soon as I've heard this messenger, I'll come over to the stables. Wait for me there!"

If my father doesn't want me to go away into service, why won't he say so? Perhaps he doesn't want me to be a knight.

22

LONG LIVE THE KING!

The messenger was waiting in the hall with my mother.

"Sir John de Caldicot?" he inquired.

"I am."

The messenger raised his right hand, and I saw he was holding a red wax disk. It was stamped with a knight riding a trotting warhorse, and brandishing a sword.

"The king is dead! Long live the king!" proclaimed the messenger.

My father got down on his left knee. "Long live the king!" he repeated in a loud voice.

My mother bowed her head. "Long live the king!" she murmured.

Then my father gestured to me, and nodded.

"Long live the king!" I said.

"Who sends you?" my father asked.

"King John sends me," the messenger replied, and he raised the disk again. "The king has sent out seven messengers to the lords of the March, and this is his message: The king is dead! Long live the king! King John bids the earls, barons, and knights of England pray for him; and the king's archbishop, Hubert, bids the priest of each parish in England to say seven masses for King Richard's soul. King John ordains that all the church bells in his kingdom must be muffled until noon on Sunday next, and in the afternoon swung again."

"Is that all?" asked my father.

"King John," said the messenger, "greets his loyal earls, lords, and knights, who are the strength and health of his kingdom, and he will send a second messenger within a month to report on the revenue of England, and to bring news of new forest laws. Long live the king!"

"Ah!" said my father. "So the worst is still to come." Then he looked at me and his eyebrows bristled. "You'll see," he said. "First the new king has overridden the claims of Prince Arthur, his young nephew, and now he's turning his attention to his loyal subjects."

"Where have you come from?" asked my mother.

"London," said the messenger. "I rode for three days to Lord Stephen. And Sir Stephen instructed me to ride out to you and nine other knights. He said you would direct me to Sir Josquin des Bois."

"You won't get there tonight," my mother said. "It's half dark."

"You can stay here," said my father. "Anyone who comes in peace is welcome here. Even King John's messenger!"

"Thank you, sir," said the messenger.

"Where's Serle?" my father asked.

"I thought he was with you," my mother replied. "With his new falcon, I expect. He can't keep away from her."

My father grunted.

"Tanwen too," said my mother. "Where is she? I haven't seen her all afternoon."

"Serle's hunting rather too much these days," my father said darkly.

At this, my mother reached out and threaded both her hands round my father's right arm. "Well, then," she said, "he's his father's son, isn't he."

My father sniffed. "Serle's only sixteen," he said.

"Nain!" said my mother suddenly. "We must tell her."

"What's the point?" my father asked. "How many kings has she seen come and go? Stephen. Then Henry, and Richard. Now John! One king more or less won't matter to her."

"Sir John . . ." the messenger began.

"I'm going over to the stables," said my father. He glanced at the messenger under his eyebrows. "Yes," he said in a steel-cold voice. "I do know, messenger. I'll ensure every man and woman in my manor hears the king's message."

the messenger's complaint

King John's messenger won't forget his visit to us.

During the night, he had to go out to the latrine five times, though I only heard him when he cursed and woke little Luke, and then cursed again.

"Ugh!" he exclaimed. "God's guts!"

In the morning, his face was as grey as ash. "What do you eat out here?" he said. "In the Marches."

"Are you all right?" I asked him. "Slim could boil you some eggs, and mix the yolks with vinegar."

The messenger groaned. "You know how it is," he said. "The first time was so sudden I didn't think I'd get there — in the dark and all. These candles of yours, they're rotten, too. And the second time doubled me right up with cramp. I didn't know which end it was going to come out of. The third time was worst, though. I thought it was turning me inside out."

"Like Lip!" I exclaimed.

"What?"

"Lip, the Welsh warrior. He used to pull his upper lip over his head and his lower lip down to his navel. Like armor. To protect himself."

"Disgusting!" said the messenger. "The fourth time felt like I was burning. Burning! It took my breath away. The fifth time was just curds and whey. After that, I couldn't stop shivering."

The messenger looked at me strangely, and then he gasped and clutched his stomach. "God's guts!" he exclaimed, and he turned and half-walked, half-ran out of the hall.

24

ROYAL BROTHERS

"Ugh!" said my father. "That messenger! worse than a dung beetle."

I held out the bowl, and my father dipped his hands into the water, then watched as the clear beads dripped back into it from the ends of his fingers.

"No wonder King Richard said he'd be glad to sell London — the buildings, the river, and all the scum who live there. He said he'd sell the lot if that would raise the money to pay for another crusade."

My father took the cloth hanging over my right forearm and thoughtfully dried his hands. "Did you hear how he spoke to us? As if we were March blockheads? And did you hear him try to teach me my duty?"

"John . . ." my mother began.

"And then he spends the whole night souping up our latrine," said my father.

"John!" my mother said again.

Then my father looked round and saw that everyone was standing at their places, so he replaced the cloth on my forearm. "Thank you, Arthur," he said. "Right! *Benedictus benedicat. Per Jesum Christum dominum nostrum.* Amen."

We sat down and Slim at once brought over a large covered dish from the side table, and planted it in front of my father. "Herbolace!" he announced.

"Herbolace! Really!" exclaimed my father. "You mean to say we eat delicacies like this out in the March? I thought we only ate . . . only . . . Well, Sian? What's the worst thing to eat?"

"Squirms!" said Sian. "I did once. No! Toads!" And she bunched up her right hand and hopped it off her trencher.

"That's what he was," said my father. "One of King John's toads. Yes, Helen. I know. I'm keeping you all waiting." Then my father lifted the dish lid, and helped himself to a large dollop of scrambled eggs and cheese and herbs, while Slim brought over another dish from the side table.

"Collops, Sir John," he announced.

"Very good, Slim," said my father. "Fit for a king! And too good for King John."

As soon as my father had finished eating, and we had just begun, he exclaimed, "It was insulting! That message! It insulted King Richard. Not one word of praise, not one word of sorrow. And not one lean word about King John's own plans. Just — ring bells! And more bells! Does he think we're all fools?"

"Surely," said Serle, "the new king wants to please his earls and lords and knights. He wants them to like him."

"If that's what he wants," replied my father, "he would do best to tell us what's what. To be fair and to be straight. I don't need covering with a coating of slime."

"You're judging the king by his messenger," said my mother.

"I am not," said my father. "I am judging him by his words. And his words were all fat."

"Erk!" exclaimed Sian. "There's a squirm in this cheese!"

"Put it on the floor!" my mother said.

"Another one!" wailed Sian. "Look!"

"Just give it to the dogs," said my mother. "Don't fuss so!"

"There's the difference," said my father. "Two men. Two brothers from the same pod, but as unalike as you can imagine. Do you know why his men followed King Richard to the kingdom of Jerusalem? Because he was open with them. Tough? He was very tough! But he never asked them to do anything he would not do himself."

"Sir William told me," I said, "that the leader of the Saracens . . ."

"Saladin," said my father.

". . . Saladin sent King Richard a basket of fresh fruit when he heard Richard caught the red fever."

"There you are!" said my father. "His soldiers loved him and his enemy admired him. Saladin sent King Richard pomegranates and grapes, lemons, cucumbers: rare fruits almost as costly as jewels."

"Oliver says the Saracens worship a false prophet," I said.

"They do," replied my father.

"And he says Hell's mouth is waiting for Saladin."

"I doubt it," said my father. "Saladin and Coeur-de-Lion! They were both fighting a holy war. One called it a jihad, the other a crusade. From all I've heard, Saladin was a noble man. Far better than King Richard's own brother."

My father looked at Serle and picked his teeth. "This is not the first time our new king has told his earls and lords and knights what he thinks they want to hear," he said. "Not so long ago he made us all false promises in the hope of stealing his brother's crown, and that was while Coeur-de-Lion was fighting for Jerusalem. You understand that, Serle?"

"Yes, father."

"King John does not always mean what he says. And he says one thing and does another."

"Fickle!" said my mother.

"When a man gives his word," my father said, "you should be able to rely on it. You can't rely on King John's word. Our Welsh friends will soon smell this out."

"Will they attack us?" I asked.

"Listen!" said my father. "If the Welsh can find a way to capture the lands held by the Marcher lords, you can be quite certain they'll do it."

"Capture?" said my mother. "No! Recapture! These lands are Welsh lands."

"What if King John promises the Earl of Hereford he will support him with soldiers," my father asked, "but then fails to do so? It won't take us long to hear about it, and it won't take the Welsh long either. Then we'll all be at risk. Hereford, Shrewsbury, even Chester, let alone the little castles and manors like our own."

"However!" said my mother, half-smiling.

"However," my father said, "your mother is Welsh. Nain is Welsh. And your grandfather, the dragon, he was a warlord."

"Red!" said Nain unexpectedly. "Red to the roots of his hair."

"The reason why your mother and I married . . ." my father began, "the main reason why our fathers arranged our marriage was to make peace in this part of the March."

"Must I be betrothed?" asked Sian.

"Ssshhh!" said my mother. "Your father's talking."

"When?" demanded Sian.

"I don't know. Eleven. Or twelve. I was twelve."

"Erk!" said Sian. "Do I have to?"

"That's enough, Sian," said my father.

"I used to think half the English were drunkards and the other half robbers," my mother said. "That's what I used to think." Then she smiled at my father and put an arm around his shoulders and kissed him on the cheek.

"The Welsh have strange notions," said my father. "But not as strange as the people who live in Greece and Sicily."

"Why?" asked Serle.

"Sir William was there with Coeur-de-Lion," my father said, "and he helped King Richard rescue his sister, Joan. In Sicily, they took a number of hostages, and do you know what some of them asked Sir William? They asked him what he had done with his tail." My father pushed back his chair and threw back his head, and laughed. "Can you believe it? They thought every Englishman had a tail. And the Greeks! They thought the same. Well!" said my father, "the English have their weaknesses, but they haven't got tails. The only people with tails are those the devil has chosen. He enters their heads and hearts and deforms their bodies."

"What happens to them?" I asked. "Those people."

"They try to hide it," my father said. "They know that if anyone finds out, they'll be tried and burned at the stake."

ice and fire

I can see myself quite clearly in the black face of the stone Merlin has given me. My mother says that when God made me, He had a spare blob of clay which He put on the end of my nose. I can see that, and my red ears which stick out more than Serle's or Sian's.

I like the rough-and-silky feel of the stone, and I like the way it quickly warms between my hands. But what is it for? And what did Merlin mean when he said it was time for me to have it, and time for him to let it go? "Until the day you die," he said, "you will never own anything as precious as this."

Serle always keeps an old arrow-tip in one of his pockets; he says it protects him from ever being wounded by an arrow. And Oliver has a coin from Jerusalem strung on the greasy key-thong around his neck. "The pope has blessed it," he says, "and I wear it day and night. It drives away dark spirits."

Is my stone like this? A kind of charm? Or does it have some other power? My obsidian! Merlin said it is made of ice and fire.

26

MERLIN

I cannot remember when I didn't know Merlin. He lived here before I was born and when I look at his strange, un-lined face I sometimes wonder whether he'll still be here after I'm dead.

I can see Merlin in one of my earliest memories. I am two, that's what my mother says, and Merlin is holding up a large square of golden silk. When he shakes it, it waves and floats like a flag or a banner. Or a gonfanon! I like that word. It's got air inside it. I keep reaching up to catch this silk, and it brushes the tips of my fingers. I strain and squeal. But I still can't catch it. Then Merlin wraps the silk right round me; it winks and shimmers, and I feel much too hot.

Each Sunday, my mother invites Merlin to eat dinner with us, and I know she and Nain like him. My father likes him too. He listens to Merlin and even asks his opinion. Sometimes they walk and talk together.

Merlin isn't a lord or a knight, but he isn't a priest or a monk or a friar. He isn't a manor tenant or a laborer; he doesn't do any days' work for my father. And he isn't a reeve or a baker or a brewer or a beadle. So what is he? Has he always lived here, next to the mill? Why doesn't he ever talk about his mother or his father? Has he any brothers or sisters? How is he able to pay for meat and bread and ale? I realize I know almost nothing about Merlin.

"It's obvious, Arthur," said Oliver. "Merlin has something to hide."

"What?" I asked.

"I'm sorry to say it but he's hiding something. That's why he never talks about himself — his childhood, his family, where he's come from. People with nothing to hide are open about these things."

"But what is he hiding?" I asked.

"Have you ever thought," said Oliver, "why Merlin prefers shadows to sunlight? What does that tell you?" He lowered his voice. "Some people say he's the child of his own sister."

"What do you mean?"

"Work it out, Arthur. His father was his father and his mother . . ."

"Who says that?" I exclaimed.

"And some people think his mother was a nun . . ."

"But nuns . . ."

". . . and his father was an incubus."

"What's an incubus?"

"A demon," said Oliver between his teeth. "An evil spirit! It comes during the night and enters a woman while she lies asleep."

"You don't think that?"

"I don't know what to think, Arthur. But when I hear what comes out of Merlin's mouth . . . His delusions! His dangerous opinions!" Opinions! Oliver spat out the word with such force that he sprayed me with saliva.

"Merlin's an infidel!" he exclaimed. "He's not true to the three-in-one and one-in-three. I'll tell you something: Your father shields Merlin. Were it not for him, Merlin would be in mortal danger."

"You mean . . ."

"I mean people with false beliefs must admit their mistakes. Otherwise, they're cursed. Last year, in Hereford, an old woman went around telling people she was the Virgin Mary. She said she'd been sent back to earth by her son to tell people to repent."

"What happened to her?"

"She was tried," said Oliver darkly. "And then she was walled up."

"Alive?" I exclaimed.

"She defiled the name of Our Lady," said Oliver. "And believe me, the same fate would befall Merlin but for your father. I can't think what Sir John sees in him."

Until I talked to Oliver, I didn't realize how much he hates Merlin. But can what he said be true? Merlin's own sister and his father . . . or a nun and an incubus?

I think I will ask my father about Merlin — and my mother too. And maybe Serle knows something. There's not much point in asking Merlin himself because he'll just smile, and answer a question with another question. I don't believe Merlin is dangerous or cursed, but it's true there's something strange about him.

muffled

King John's messenger told us to muffle our church bell until next Sunday, so Oliver has climbed the belfry and tied a kind of leather hood over the clapper of the church bell.

"Your father's doves," Oliver told me, "are so pea-brained they seem to think my belfry is their cote. They've painted the whole place white. The walls are streaming. And I had to be careful going up the steps because they're so slippery."

So when Oliver tolled the bell for Vespers this evening, it sounded very far away and lost in a thick fog.

"If memories had voices," my mother said, "the sad ones would sound like muffled bells."

the peddler

A peddler walked in yesterday afternoon, and he had come all the way from Sir Josquin des Bois. That's fourteen miles.

"I've got something here for each of you," the peddler said, and he delved into his dirty sack and pulled out colored silken threads, and leather pouches, and little cushions for pins, and linen kerchiefs, and a black leather belt, and gold-thread tassels, and two nightcaps.

"These will keep you ladies warm," said the peddler. Then he put a pointed, cornflower-blue cap on my mother's head and a rust-brown cap on Tanwen's.

"Gogoniant!" exclaimed Tanwen — her mouth is full of strange Welsh words like that.

"Glory be!" exclaimed my mother. "We look like two of the little people!"

They both laughed and hugged each other.

My mother bought the two nightcaps, and also a little pot of ointment for sore breasts; and before supper, my father decided to buy a square clay tile with a strange face on it: a wide-eyed man with a face as long as an almond, and a mess of hair, and an unkempt beard, and leaves sprouting out of his nose and ears.

"He is beautiful and horrid," my father said.

"Just horrid!" said Sian.

"Both," said my father. "As we all are. And something

else: If you move, the man's eyes move too. His gaze follows you. He's always looking at you."

"Threepence!" said the peddler.

"Never!" said my father. Then he bargained with the peddler, and in the end he bought the face for one penny. "We'll feed you well," my father said, "and you can sleep in the hay barn."

When we woke up, the peddler had already gone. But so had Sian's cat, Spitfire. She didn't come in for dinner, and she has never missed dinner before.

"Why did he take her?" wailed Sian.

"Her white fur," said my father.

"What for?"

"That'll make a pair of mittens."

Then Sian banged her forehead on the table and howled.

"That's quite enough, Sian," said my father. But my mother put an arm around her, and Sian buried her face in my mother's lap.

After dinner, Sian and Tanwen hunted for Spitfire everywhere, even in the stables. I kept hearing them calling for her, and Sian went right round the village asking if anyone had seen her.

"Pointless!" said Serle.

"No," said my mother, "she may not find her, but it's not pointless, Serle."

When we were alone, I asked my mother about Merlin.

"He came to live here soon after you were born," she said. "Twelve years ago now. Your father made an agreement with him, and rented him his cottage and croft."

"Where did he come from?"

"Merlin keeps himself to himself," my mother said, and she shook her head.

"What about his family?"

My mother shook her head again. "I don't know much of his story," she said.

"Oliver hates him," I said. "He says Merlin may be the son of his own sister. Or a nun and an incubus!"

My mother screwed up her eyes. "Shame on him! That's dangerous talk, and he doesn't know anything about it."

"You like Merlin," I said.

"So do your father and Nain. Merlin's Welsh and wise, and he makes me laugh."

"And me," I said.

"He has always cared for you," my mother said.

"Why?"

"I don't know. You're always asking questions and they're as hard as nutshells."

"Mother," I began, "do you know what my father's plans are? For me? He does want me to be a knight, doesn't he? He will let me go away into service. . . ."

My mother gave her quick little nod which doesn't mean yes and doesn't mean no, but means she is listening very carefully. Then she spread her right hand like a comb and ran it backwards through my hair.

"He hasn't got another plan, has he?"

"Arthur!" said my mother, and gently, quite firmly, she pressed her warm hand down on the top of my head.

"Will you ask him to talk to me?" I said. "Please will you?"

luke

"The most precious gift in our lives," Lady Alice said once, "is good health."

She told me she used to have stiff fingers and stiff toes, but now she always keeps a hare's foot in one pocket, and each day she rubs it along the joints.

So when Merlin gave me my ice-and-fire stone and said it's the most precious thing I will ever own, was he giving me good health?

If so, I wish I could share it with Luke. Today is his name day but he blew bubbles and whimpered all morning. Saint Luke was a physician, and he must have had good health himself because Oliver says he lived for eighty-four years, but he doesn't seem to be able to hear our prayers for my brother.

+ 30 +

POOR STUPID

"I'll help you," I told Gatty. "I don't mind."

I do mind, though. I mind Serle's hot words and my father's cold silences. I mind the way my father doesn't understand me. I mind how a pig's eyelashes go on twitching.

But I think it's unfair of Hum to make Gatty do all the mucky work, like debloating the cows and shoveling up the afterbirths and digging out the latrines, so that is why I sometimes offer to help her.

First, our pig-man Dutton tied a rope to one of Stupid's back legs, and Stupid snuffled and snorted because he thought Dutton was taking him to root for beech mast. Dutton always puts the pigs on long tethers because otherwise they might stray too far into the forest.

But when Dutton and Giles took hold of his collar and led him in the wrong direction, away from the forest, Stupid sensed something was wrong and began to squeal. He didn't want to cross the ford, so while Dutton and Gatty tried to drag him, Giles and I shoved him from behind, and we all got wet.

"Bones!" said Dutton. "He's just as cussed as his brother was. Shove, Arthur! Shove!"

When we had half-pushed and half-dragged Stupid to the yard behind the barn, Dutton told Gatty to run over to the kitchen and bring back the large mallet and three wooden bowls. "And this time be quick!" he said.

As soon as Dutton saw Gatty coming back, he knelt

down and grabbed Stupid's front legs, and tried to get him to kneel down too; and then Giles took the big mallet.

"Come on, Stupid!" gasped Dutton. "Say your prayers!"

But Stupid stamped and squealed, and then he lurched out of Dutton's grasp and ran off across the barnyard.

"The rope!" shouted Dutton.

I pounced on the rope tied to Stupid's back leg, and Gatty got hold of it too, and when the tether was at full stretch, we gave it a jerk. That stopped poor Stupid in his tracks.

"Right!" panted Dutton. "Giles! You ready?"

Giles grunted and Stupid squealed louder than ever. He knew! He's not as stupid as all that.

Then Dutton squatted and reached out and wrapped both arms round Stupid's forelegs and brought him to his knees, and at once Giles raised the big mallet and thwacked Stupid on the top of his head.

Stupid gave one short, sudden, hoarse woof. Then he simply dropped his dripping snout onto his chest, and slowly settled back onto his haunches, and all at once the yard seemed a very quiet place.

Dutton let go of Stupid's forelegs and stood up. "Right!" he said. "Ready?" And he cut Stupid's throat.

As soon as Gatty, Giles, and I had filled the three bowls with blood, Dutton rubbed the bristles on the top of Stupid's head and Stupid's sandy eyelashes faintly flickered and twitched.

"Good pig!" he said. "Right, you three! Get those bowls into the kitchen before the flies drink the whole lot. And be careful! If you spill a drop, Slim will slice up your guts for sausages and chitterlings!" Dutton guffawed at the thought of it. "He'll skin you alive," he said. "Look at the three of you! So worshipful! Like you're celebrating Easter Mass, and holding up the sacrament."

"No, Dutton," I said. "You shouldn't say that."

"Says who?" asked Dutton. "Fat Oliver? You coming back, Arthur?"

"If Gatty is, I am," I said.

"A good thing too," said Dutton. "All the skinning and butchering — that needs four of us."

"It needs four of us," said Giles.

"Yes, Giles," said Dutton. "I just said that."

Then Gatty and Giles and I walked slowly across the yard, carrying our bowls of blood.

"What's it for?" asked Gatty. "All this!"

"Black pudding," I said. "Slim adds vinegar and spices to it, and whips it with a sprig of sage to stop it from curdling. And after he's salted all the joints — the neck and the shoulders and the ribs, the belly and the loin and all that — he'll make black pudding."

"Never tasted it!" said Gatty.

"Slim says he's making it for Hallowe'en," I said, "so I'll save you a piece for when you come guising. You too, Giles."

"What's it made of?" Gatty asked.

"Stupid!" I said. "Mainly! And fat and spice. And onions. You mix it all up, and pour it into the gut, and poach it. Slim showed me."

Serle must have heard us because he came bursting out of the kitchen and met us just outside the door.

"Serle!" I exclaimed. "What are you doing here?"

"What's that?" demanded Serle.

"It's Stupid! His lifeblood."

"You! You, doing yardwork?"

"I'm helping Gatty."

"First fieldwork! Now yardwork!"

"Arthur's a helper," said Giles. "That needs four."

"It does, does it?" said Serle, and he stepped up very close to me. "I've been looking for you everywhere. Where have you been?"

"I've told you," I said.

"Father's waiting. He's at the mill."

"What for?"

"Us. He told me to find you."

"Why?"

"I don't know," said Serle, and then he shouldered me. I gripped my bowl but it was so slippery. It slopped and then it slid out of my grasp, and I dropped it. The blood splashed all over my tunic and my leggings.

"You cack-hand!" crowed Serle. "You can't even carry a bowl of blood without dropping it."

"You saw what happened," I said to Gatty and Giles.

"They saw you drop it," said Serle in a measured way, and he stared at Giles and Gatty. "You saw him drop it," he said. "Didn't you?"

"Yes, sir," said Giles.

"Didn't you, Gatty?"

Gatty looked at Serle, and she said nothing.

"Didn't you, Gatty?" said Serle, much more loudly.

Gatty carefully dipped one little finger into her bowl. Then she reached out and made the sign of the cross with it on my forehead. I felt it, cool and wet; I felt it burning into me.

"What do you think you're doing?" Serle demanded. "You fleabag! How dare you?"

Gatty said nothing. She just stepped through the kitchen door, and Giles followed her.

"Come on!" Serle said. "He's waiting."

"I must explain," I said. "I must tell Slim."

"He's not here," said Serle.

"Or Ruth . . ."

"No! No one's here!"

But Serle was lying, and I knew he was, and he couldn't stop me from stepping into the kitchen. Tanwen was there. She was standing on the other side of the table and holding a pestle so tightly I could see the whites of her knuckles. Her face was flushed.

"Tanwen!" I exclaimed. "Are you all right?"

"Come on!" insisted Serle in a hoarse voice.

So I went with my brother, though it was the last thing I wanted to do.

"You're covered in blood," jeered Serle.

"Leave me alone."

"How many times has our father told you that pages shouldn't humble themselves?"

"Slim will be furious," I said. "Oh Serle! If only . . ."

"What?"

"Don't you care? Don't you understand?"

"What?"

"I know what my duties are. My Yard-skills. My reading and my writing. I keep working at them. But why should Gatty do all the mucky work?"

"Why?" exclaimed Serle. "Because she's . . . who she is. Hum's daughter. Gatty has her duties, and you have yours."

"Is that what you really think? In your guts?"

"Everyone does. Lord God gives each of us our duties on middle-earth. And our first duty, Arthur, is to obey Him."

For a little while we walked along the stream in silence, matching stride for stride.

"What were you doing in the kitchen?" I asked. "You and Tanwen."

"Nothing."

"You were."

"That's enough, Arthur."

"Her face and eyes were hot."

"I've warned you, Arthur."

I could tell Serle was feeling nervous, because he had started to threaten me.

"It's all right," I said. "I won't tell."

"There's nothing to tell," said Serle.

"I won't, anyhow."

"No, you won't!" snarled Serle. Then he shouldered me again. He shoved me so hard that I staggered sideways and fell into the millpond.

When I surfaced, I could hear Serle shouting, "Hogwash, and you know it! Pig swill!"

When I had splashed back to the bank, Serle offered me his outstretched hand, but I refused it. Smiling his thin smile, he stood there in his oatmeal tunic; I stood below him, dripping, daubed with millpond mud, stained with poor Stupid's blood.

I wouldn't mind if Serle had pushed me into the millpond, laughing; and I would have tried to push him back. But it wasn't like that. It wasn't what my mother calls horseplay, and it never has been.

Why has Serle never liked me? He is the firstborn, and

he's almost seventeen. Serle is a squire and will soon be a knight, while I'm only a page and may never be a squire. And he's much stronger than I am. So why does he sneer at me and shoulder and shove me?

I could never tell Serle one of my secrets because he would only keep it for so long as it suited him. He doesn't know about Lady Alice's secret and he never will because I promised her I would never tell anyone. But he must never know about my tailbone either, or else I could be in danger. And if I tell him about my obsidian, that might take away all its power.

the seeing stone

Something very strange has happened.

I woke up at green dawn and I felt rinsed. I felt fresh. Yesterday's mud and blood and angry words and stony silences had all dissolved. Somehow, I felt ready. I felt as keen as the edge of my jackknife when I have just ground it.

It was quite warm in the hall but it's cool in my writing-room, so I wrapped myself in my house-cloak and put on my rabbitskin cap, and then I crept upstairs. The fourth and fifth stairs creak, and so do the ninth and tenth, so I haul myself up and over them.

Over my wind-eye a spider had woven its web, and it was trembling and shining. It was silver unless it was gold.

I reached into the dusty gap between the blocks of stone, and pulled out the saffron bundle. I've done that each day since Merlin gave it to me.

First, I warmed my obsidian between the palms of my hands. Then I scratched one of the white spots on the lumpen side, but I couldn't dig it out. The stone is very hard. I can't mark it at all.

Then I turned the stone over and stared into its dark shine. Its deep eye that never blinks. I stared into it and, after a while, I had a strange feeling that it was staring back at me.

At first, all I could see was what I've seen before. Me! My ears and my blob nose. My rabbitskin cap. But then my stone began to glow. Slowly its darkness cleared. Day dawned in my stone.

I can see a man sitting on a grassy bank. He's wearing a crown. There's another man standing beside him, but I can't see his face because he's wearing a dove-grey hood.

"Dig the ground!" this man calls out in a deep voice. "Dig the ground!" I know that voice. I'm sure I do. But I can't think where I've heard it before.

Beneath the bank, there's a shallow pit. Many people are shoveling earth and rocks out of it and, as they do so, the pit begins to fill with water. The water wells up out of the ground. It covers their feet, their ankles, it climbs their shins until they can no longer dig. It washes around their waists.

"Drain the pool!" calls the hooded man in his deep voice. "Drain the pool!"

Then all the people wade and splash out of the pit. They cut canals from its four corners, and the water in the pool sluices out and away.

At the bottom of the pit I can see two caves. Two open, dark mouths. Out of one writhes a dragon with scales as white as lily spathes. Out of the other writhes a dragon with scales as red as quick, fresh blood. The moment the dragons see each other, they snarl. They pant. They throw spears of flame at each other.

First the white dragon forces the red dragon back until he's at the very edge of the soggy pit. Blood oozes out from between his scales, and he's spattered with mud. He snarls, his chest heaves. Then the red dragon raises his head to heaven; he roars and wraps the white dragon in flames. . . . The smoke! All the smoke! My eyes cannot see. But the hooded man, I can hear his deep voice again.

But what is he saying? I can't make out his words.

". . . the king who was . . . and will be . . ."

All the people are shouting, and I can't make out the hooded man's words.

Then the smoke in my stone began to clear. It drifted; it cleared. But the king and the hooded man had gone. The dragons and the people and the pit: They had all gone. All I could see was myself again.

✤ 32 ✤

ON MY OWN

As soon as I'd finished my Yard-skills, I came back up here. It is almost dark now, so I have sat in this window seat for a long time. In fact, I feel as if I have been sitting here all my life.

I know my parents and Serle think I am strange because I like to be on my own sometimes, but I need time to work things out. To write down my thoughts and feelings.

"On your own half the time," Nain complained to me. "It's unnatural! You're not one of us."

I need to talk to Merlin. I need to tell him what happened this morning. But he has ridden to the fair at Ludlow and last year he didn't come back for four days.

I have never heard of a seeing stone. But that's what my obsidian is. I looked into it. I saw through it. And it spoke to me.

Why now? Was it because of the way I held it? As soon as I came up here, I unwrapped my stone again; but although I turned it round and turned it over, and held it in my left hand and my right hand and in both hands, and looked deep into it, it was dark and silent. So how did I hold it and will I ever be able to see into it again? Why were the dragons fighting? And who was the king? Who was the hooded man?

"The king who was . . . and will be . . ."

What does all this mean?

33

NUTShells and
GOOD EARTh

Earth-frost! The first of the autumn.

A tide of cool air flowed through my wind-eye and washed my face and wrists. It flowed through the copper beech and hundreds of leaves broke loose. A whole fleet of them, staggering and spinning. Drowning in air.

Some of the leaves fell into the fishpond, and that always happens if the wind blows from the north. It annoys my father because he likes to watch our perch and waving trout and little golden fish silently nosing around their kingdom.

"They can't answer him back," Serle told me once. "That's why he likes them."

When most of the leaves have fallen, my father gives two of the villagers, Brian and Macsen, day-work, and they wade into the pond up to their chests, and rake off as many leaves as they can. But although the pond is stepped, the bottom is uneven and sticky, so usually one of them falls right in.

Brian and Macsen also rake up the leaves around the base of the tree. Last year, they made a huge pile, and Sian and I tried to go to sleep in it. We got too cold, though, and couldn't stop shivering even when we hugged one another. So when the Swan glittered right over us, and Arcturus was already low in the west, we gave up and went back into the hall.

Through my wind-eye I watched Sian skipping and waving, and Nain hobbling after her. Sian tried to catch the leaves falling from the copper beech before they touched the ground, and her legs kept getting in each other's way. Three times she fell over!

I don't know how many leaves she managed to catch, but enough anyhow to stuff into her pillow and save herself from sniffs and snuffs for the whole of this coming winter.

If only little Luke was old enough to catch leaves too! Each evening my mother dips his feet in hot water, and then holds his soles close to the fire until its heat has dried them. After that, she rubs garlic and Stinking Roger into them. But Luke still coughs and shivers, and he whimpers for half the night, and my mother is afraid for him.

Then, through my wind-eye, I saw Merlin! Merlin coming out of the orchard, eating an apple! I put down my pen and levered myself out of my alcove; I ran down the stairs and met him outside the hall door.

"Merlin! Where have you been?"

"Where I always am," said Merlin.

"What do you mean?" I said.

"With myself."

"I mean . . ."

"I know!" said Merlin, smiling, and he took another bite of his apple.

"I need to talk to you."

"And it can't wait," said Merlin.

I led Merlin away from the hall, past the fishpond and

93

into the herb garden, and there was no one there. We sat down on the coping of the well.

"Heigh-ho!" sighed Merlin, and he began to warble:

> "Now the rose withers
> And the lily is spent
> That both once bore
> The sweetest scent
> In summer, that sweet time . . ."

"Merlin!" I said.

"Leaf-eaters!" said Merlin accusingly. "Look at all these holes! Do you know what to do if you want to get rid of caterpillars?"

"I need to talk to you."

"You have to take them to church and sit them on a cabbage," said Merlin, grinning, "and invite them to listen to Mass. . . . Ask Oliver! He knows all about it. Now, Arthur. What is it?"

"The stone! My obsidian!"

"Yes?"

"Its darkness . . . it cleared."

"Ah!" said Merlin slowly, and he took another bite. "Very sour, this apple! It needs more straw ripening."

"It cleared. There was a king. I think he was a king. He had a crown. And a hooded man. And a crowd of people digging out a pit. There were dragons, and they started to fight. One was red and the other was white."

"Yes," said Merlin. "The red dragon of Wales — Wales and all the Britons! The white dragon of England."

"They were fighting to the death."

"Who won?" asked Merlin.

"I don't know! The dragons opened their jaws and threw flame-spears at each other. But their smoke blinded me! And when the smoke cleared, the stone was dark again."

"Begin at the beginning!" Merlin said.

I told Merlin everything. And I asked him all the questions I had already asked myself. Who was the king? And who was the hooded man? Who were the dragons and why were they fighting?

Merlin's eyes were shut. He always closes them when he is listening carefully. "Questions! Questions!" he said.

"Who was the king?" I asked again.

"What if I said he was Vortigern?"

"Who? Where was his kingdom?"

"You see. The answer to that question leads to more questions; and you have to know the answer to them before the first answer means anything. Vortigern was king of Britain."

"When?"

"After the Romans left Britain in peace. Before the Saxons broke that peace."

"How do you know?"

"I've heard an old story," Merlin said, "very old, that Vortigern wanted to build a tower, a fortress. But he was unable to do so because each night the earth swallowed up the foundations laid by his masons on the previous day. So the king summoned a wise man, and the wise man told him, 'Dig the ground!' And when the king's people dug the ground below the foundations, they unearthed a pool . . ."

"That's it!" I cried.

"Many questions," Merlin said, "are like nutshells — with their nuts still inside them."

"That's what my mother says," I said.

"We all echo each other," said Merlin. "You asked me who the dragons were, and why they were fighting. But haven't you heard of the red dragon of Wales and the white dragon of England? Why, the Caldicot coat of arms has a red dragon in one quarter because of your mother's blood. And the Welsh and the English have always been enemies, haven't they? Sometimes they fight; sometimes they lick their wounds and get ready to fight again."

"I see," I said.

"But you must see for yourself," Merlin said. "That is what you must learn. That's what I told you up on the hill."

"But you've told me about Vortigern and the dragons," I said, "and now I understand."

"It's right to hear the old stories," said Merlin, "and to learn from ancient books. But what use is knowledge? It's dry as dead leaves; it's no use at all unless you're ready for it."

"I am ready," I said.

"Mmm!" said Merlin, as he dropped the core of his apple into the well. "Has Oliver told you about the man who sowed seeds? He strewed some by the wayside and the birds ate them. He dropped some on stony ground, and they soon withered. He threw some among thistles which sprang up and choked them. But some seeds the sower planted in good earth. . . . That's it, Arthur. You have to be that earth. You have to ready yourself."

"I am ready," I repeated. "I want to be."

"You want to be," said my father in a loud voice. "What do you want to be?"

Merlin and I stood up.

"It doesn't matter," said my father, shaking his head impatiently and advancing towards us. "What matters, Arthur, is that I can never find you when I want to speak to you. What matters is that you're so disobedient. You didn't come to the mill yesterday . . ."

"Sir, I was coming . . ."

". . . and Serle says that instead of practicing your skills . . ."

"It was Serle's fault I couldn't come," I said fiercely.

"Merlin!" said my father pleasantly, and he took Merlin's right hand between both of his own. "Welcome home!"

"Greetings, Sir John!" said Merlin.

"Ludlow, was it?" my father asked. "I want to hear. But not now! Hum is waiting for us in the hall. Come on, Arthur!"

Merlin looked at me and raised his eyebrows. "Unless you behave," he said, without the flicker of a smile, "I'll turn you into a caterpillar. And you know what will happen to you then, don't you."

My father turned on his heel and I followed him out of the herb garden. "First the bulls!" he said over his shoulder. "And now Stupid!" He stopped and turned right round. "No, Arthur! I won't have this. I've told you before what your duties are."

"But I do practice," I said. "And I study with Oliver, and I write. And anyhow, Serle has kitchen duties, doesn't he? I saw him in the kitchen."

"Stop talking nonsense!" said my father.

In the hall, my father took his chair and Hum and I stood across the table, facing him.

"Now, Hum!" said my father, wagging his right forefinger, "I've reminded Arthur of his duties. He understands what they are. He is not to work in the fields or the sties or the stables or anywhere else unless he has my permission."

"It's my Gatty!" said Hum, shaking his head.

"No," said my father. "We are all responsible for our own actions. Isn't that so, Arthur?"

"Yes, father."

"I trust Arthur to obey me," my father said. "And I trust you, Hum, to tell me if he does not."

"Yes, Sir John."

"All right!" said my father. "The three of us understand each other."

34

ᐁesire

The wind has dropped. So my writing-room isn't too cold and I can smell the thatch again. It hangs round my shoulders like an old cloak, out of shape and stinking, but comfortable all the same.

Our sparrows have been pecking at the mortar. This morning my seat in the alcove was covered with grit and my apple tree stump smeared with white paste, still slimy. But now Slim has given me a shaggy towel and I'll hang it from the spike above the wind-eye when I am not there. That should keep the birds out.

Almost as soon as I stared into my stone, its darkness cleared. The hooded man! I saw him again. And I heard his deep voice. But the king was not the same king I saw before. Vortigern . . . And the people were not the same people who dug the ground and drained the pool.

Dukes and earls and lords! In a high hall, each man stands next to his own squire, and many of the squires look the same age as I am. Some of the noblemen have brought their wives, their children with them, and each of them waits on the king.

The king is tall and well-built. He has a ruddy complexion and a sandy beard, but he's bald as an egg.

"Nine daughters!" he says to the earl kneeling in front of him. "Nine daughters, is it? Talk to my wise man! He has a powder made from the hairs of caterpillars."

Now the earl stands up, rather stiffly, and the herald blows his trumpet.

"Gorlois, Duke of Cornwall!" announces a chamberlain with a neck like a plucked chicken and a very loud voice. "King Uther will greet the Duke of Cornwall and his wife, Ygerna."

A handsome man with a mane of dark hair steps out of the crowd, and the most beautiful woman in the hall follows three steps behind him. She has violet eyes and her lower lip is slightly puffy, as if it has been stung by a bee. Her shoulders are gentle slopes. First Ygerna and Duke Gorlois look at each other, then very slowly get down on to their knees.

King Uther leans forward. "Gorlois," he says in a cold, hard voice.

Gorlois stares at the king.

"Greetings at Easter!" says the king.

"Greetings!" says Gorlois, and he inclines his head.

Now the king leans forward again, and lightly brushes the woman's wrist with his sandy fingertips. "And you, Ygerna," he says quietly. "I am very glad to see you." But Ygerna's head is bowed. She kneels beside her husband, and her eyes do not meet the eyes of the king.

Now the herald gives seven short blasts on his trumpet, and at once stewards and panters and kitchen boys wade in with dishes and platters. One steward bears a roast peacock in his arms, with all its feathers stuck back into its body. One carries a strange-looking beast with a front half like a capon but a back half like a sucking-pig. And here's another with a front half like a sucking-pig but a back half like a capon!

At the feast, Gorlois, Duke of Cornwall, sits on the king's left and Ygerna, his wife, sits on the king's right.

Eel pasties! And now a dish of meat surrounded by crayfish tails! Blancmange with minced chicken and chopped almonds! The longer the feast goes on, the more King Uther talks to Ygerna and the less to her husband Gorlois.

"Pears in cinnamon and honey!" exclaims the king. "Sweetness and spice!" And with that, he almost completely turns his back on Gorlois, and starts to pat Ygerna with his sandy paws, and offers her wine from his own gold goblet.

But Ygerna shakes her head.

"Wood is unworthy of you," Uther says, and he hiccups. "You can't drink from wood. Silver's not good enough for your lips."

Ygerna sits very still. She does not look at the king.

"I desire you, Ygerna," says the king. . . .

Mist in my stone! It rose like October mist that often dips and lifts over Nine Elms and Great Oak and Pikeside. Its white silence spread across the stone's shining face. But I looked. I still looked. And after a long time the mist thinned, and cleared again.

The king has gone. All the feasters have gone. I can see no one but Duke Gorlois and his wife Ygerna.

"Outrageous!" shouts Gorlois.

"He insulted me," says Ygerna, "with all his honeyed words, his bumbling and fumbling. He insulted me by thinking I would not be true to you."

"He insulted us both," says Gorlois coldly.

"If you care for me and our marriage," Ygerna says,

"take me away from this place. Away from London! Away from this Easter feast!"

"I will take you home," Gorlois says. "But when Uther hears we have gone, you can be sure he'll be angry. He'll send messengers and order us to return."

"What will we do then?"

"Ignore them! You'll be safe at Tintagel. No one and nothing can touch you there."

"And you, Gorlois?"

"I'll go to Castle Terrible and prepare for a siege. King Uther will sit outside the walls and try to starve me out."

"My husband," says Ygerna. "I will wait for you. . . ."

Waves in my stone! Washing and swelling! I have never seen the sea but I have seen the lake under Gibbet Hill, the nine waves and their daughters, rolling, then slowly folding into themselves, creaming and sparkling, and that's what I saw in my obsidian.

White waves! They rolled and rose and broke, and when my stone began to grow calm again, I could see King Uther and the man in the dove-grey hood, sitting in the hall, with a large bowl of apples and nuts between them.

"I helped Vortigern, your father," the hooded man says, "and I will help you too."

"How dare he leave court without my permission?" the king demands.

The hooded man sighs. He takes a nut from the bowl and rolls it between his right thumb and forefinger. "Fear," he says, "fear and anger sometimes make a man very bold."

"I am wild for that woman," says the king.

"We will follow them to Cornwall," says the hooded man.

"Gorlois will take her to Tintagel," the king says.

"No one and nothing can stand in the way of great passion," replies the hooded man. "And great passion can cause amazing things to happen."

The king stands up. "I am on fire!" he shouts.

"I will help you," says the man in the dove-grey hood.

"Gorlois!" says the king in a dark voice. "He's a pest! A Cornish pustule! I will swaddle him in his bright coat of arms and paint a black cross on his forehead."

"And I," says the hooded man, "will bury him in the earth, a mile deep."

a flyting

I could hear them shouting from inside the vestry, and as soon as my reading lesson was over I hurried out. Gatty was sitting on the church wall with a boy on either side of her.

"Over here!" yelled Gatty.

I zigzagged across the churchyard between the gravestones.

"What's going on?" I said.

Gatty was grinning from ear to ear. "It's a flyting," she said. "You can be the judge. The first to laugh is the loser."

Jankin and Howell are the same age as I am. They groom the horses and muck out the stables, and Jankin and Gatty are going to be betrothed next year.

"Now . . ." said Jankin, and he leaned forward and turned to look at Howell with his bright blue eyes, "you walking, talking scrot of fungus!"

Howell's eyes danced. "You bluebottle!" he said. "You crock of mucus!"

"You bubble-butted bullfrog!"

"You herring-pouter!"

"You! You clucking clinchpoop!"

Howell grinned and snuffled, but he didn't laugh. "You . . . pismire!" he said.

"You, Howell! You pulpy stew! You rotten flap-mouthed maggot!"

"You!" shouted Howell. "You, Jankin! You hairy embryo! You bird-slime soup!"

"You piddle-scum!"

"You greasy bladder! You ghastly crow!"

"You, Howell. You . . . you humming weasel! You bug-eyed horseradish!"

As soon as Jankin said that, Howell waved his hand in the air and snorted. Then he brayed like a donkey.

"Stop!" I exclaimed. "Jankin, you're the winner. Into the water, Howell!"

Then we all ran over to the pond, and Howell waded straight in and fell flat on his face. After that, Jankin grabbed squealing Gatty and threw her in as well. "Come on, Arthur!" he shouted.

"I've got to practice in the Yard," I said.

So Jankin waded into the pond after Gatty and Howell, and left me high and dry on the bank.

For a while, the three of them splashed and staggered around the scummy pond, and as soon as they got out, Jankin and Howell lolloped off, dripping and laughing.

"Go and put some dry clothes on," I said to Gatty. "I'll wait."

"Can't," said Gatty.

"Why not?"

"I haven't got none."

"What do you mean?"

"Only got these, haven't I?" said Gatty. "Doesn't matter."

So Gatty and I hoisted ourselves back up onto the churchyard wall.

"When you signed that cross on my head . . ." I began. "You know, with Stupid's blood . . ."

Gatty nodded.

"Well . . . Why?"

"I saw Serle, didn't I. He shouldered you. He made you drop the blood."

"Yes, but why the cross?"

"Just came into my head. I thought as you were a Crusader, like them Crusaders you told me about. Serle's a Saracen."

I put one arm round Gatty's sopping shoulders. "Thanks, Gatty," I said.

"Where is Jerusalem, anyhow?" asked Gatty.

"A long way. A very long way from here."

"Is that further than Chester?" asked Gatty.

"Oh, Gatty!" I said, and I laughed.

"Is it?"

"Much, much further," I said. "Why?"

"Why's because I want to see where Jesus was born. Instead of Ludlow Fair, let's go to Jerusalem."

"Gatty!" I said. "You can't walk to Jerusalem."

"I can and all," said Gatty.

"You can't," I said. "Only a magician could. It's across the sea."

Gatty lowered her head and looked at the ground. "I didn't know that," she said in a quiet voice. She sniffed, and then she drew in her breath, and sneezed.

hallowe'en

To begin with, the only people in the hall with me were Nain and Sian.

As soon as the fire began to crack and spit orange sparks, Nain told us to sprinkle water onto the rushes around it. "Keep it damp," she said.

"Spitfire's ghost is inside that fire," I said.

"Really?" exclaimed Sian.

"If you look into the flames," I told her, "and keep looking until your eyeballs burn, you may see her tonight."

"If that's all we had to fear . . ." Nain began. "The walkers are out and about tonight. So are the witches, riding to meet Old Nick."

"What's that?" asked Sian.

"The devil," said Nain. "Are the turnips by the door?"

"Yes, Nain."

"You carved one?"

"Arthur did too."

"And they're burning?"

"Yes, Nain."

"So they should be. I'll tell you what happened one Hallowtide . . . before my father died. Our little housegirl Gweno always used to lay out the washing to dry on the church wall; but one time, when she came to collect the clothes, she saw someone sitting on the grave, wearing a white nightcap. Gweno thought it was one of the village lads, trying to scare her. You know what? She went right up to him, and snatched the nightcap off his head.

"'You stop trying to scare me!' she exclaimed. And with that, she ran back into our hall.

"When Gweno looked at the white nightcap, though, she saw it was all dirty and earthy on the inside, and it smelled of death." Nain shook her head. "Next morning," she said, "the someone was still there. Sitting on the gravestone. His head was bowed."

I could feel Sian leaning into me. That's what Tempest does when he wants me to fuss over him.

Nain waved her stick. "My father told Gweno there was nothing for it. 'That's a specter,' he said, 'and you must put the cap back on its head. He'll trouble us all year long otherwise.'

"Little Gweno was very scared. My father went with her to the churchyard gate, and then she ran up to the specter, and jammed the nightcap down onto his head. 'There!' she shouted. 'Are you satisfied now?'

"At once the dead man leaped to his feet. 'I am!' he shouted. 'And you, Gweno. What about you?' Then he raised his left fist and thwacked her on the top of her head."

The hall door creaked and swung open, and Sian and I both took a step backwards. But it was only my father and Serle.

"It's dark, almost," said my father.

"Listen, father!" cried Sian.

"Poor little Gweno," said Nain. "The dead man gave her a great thwack and she fell to the ground. My father ran through the churchyard, but by the time he reached

Gweno, she was already dead. And the specter, he just flowed back into his grave."

"Yes," said my father. "I've heard that one. Oliver's on his way."

"The Seven Sisters are up," said Serle.

"Who?" asked Sian anxiously.

"The Seven Sisters," Serle repeated. "Stars, stupid!"

"And the Black Sow's on the run," said Nain. "Snuffling and snorting."

"What does she do?" asked Sian.

"Follow guisers as they hurry through the dark," Nain replied. "She nips at their heels! That's what she does. And heaven help the stragglers! The Black Sow always eats her fill before daylight."

"The lanterns," said my mother as she walked into the hall from the chamber. "Are they burning?"

"They are," said my father, and he crossed the hall and put an arm round my mother's shoulders. "One for each of us. Six lanterns, burning."

"I was looking in the mirror," my mother said.

"Whom did you see?" Nain asked.

"Mark, my baby," said my mother in a low voice. "I saw him peering over my left shoulder. He was beckoning. Then I held the mirror to little Luke's face." My mother stared at my father. "There was no reflection," she said. Then at once she buried her face in my father's shoulder, and I could see her whole body was shaking.

"As God wills," said my father gently.

"No!" cried my mother. "Not again. Why does He will it?"

"You must ask Oliver that," my father said.

By the time Oliver walked in, though, my mother had gone back into the chamber. But I don't think human beings can say what is in God's mind, any more than horse-flies can say what is in human beings' minds. No one can. Not even Oliver.

My father greeted Oliver. "Have you seen Merlin?" he said. "As soon as he's here we can bob for apples. Where is he?"

"Oh! Flying around somewhere," Oliver replied. We all laughed at that, and Oliver laughed the loudest.

"I've brought the snails, anyhow," said Oliver. Then he reached into his surcoat pocket and pulled out a whole cluster.

"Let me see!" squeaked Sian.

"I've laid them on the altar and blessed them," said Oliver. "Each of you must take one — except you, of course, Sir John."

"Why?" demanded Sian.

"Now stick your snail to the wall," said Oliver, "and by tomorrow morning, its slime will tell you who you're going to marry."

"Dear God!" exclaimed Nain.

"How can it?" said Sian.

"The shape, of course. It will trace the first letter of your husband's name."

"I can't read," said Sian.

"Then Arthur will read it for you," said Oliver. "Ah! Merlin. How long have you been standing there?"

"O is for Oliver," said Merlin.

"Here's your snail," said Oliver.

"What is it?" asked Merlin.

"It is a snail, Merlin," said Oliver in a dry, flat voice.

110

"Not a caterpillar?"

"No."

"But you're going to make it vanish."

"No, Merlin, I am not going to make it vanish. You are going to make it talk. It will tell you the name of your future wife."

"Are you going to marry?" asked Sian.

"Most certainly not," said Merlin. "Unless you, Sian . . ."

"Erk!" exclaimed Sian.

"Come on, Merlin!" said my father. "Stick your snail to the wall."

But Merlin's snail was on Merlin's side. It refused to stick to the wall, or to anything else. And when I inspected the snails this morning, Sian's and Serle's and mine had scarcely moved at all; but Oliver's snail had traced a glistening zigzag while Nain's snail had made itself dizzy going round and round in circles. Nain and Oliver? That's impossible!

"Right!" said my father. "I'll go and get the apples. You tie them up, Merlin." He threw Merlin a bundle of pieces of string, the same ones we have used for as long as I can remember.

"It's Merlin who's tied up," Oliver said, "with all his tangled ideas."

"What are brains for?" Merlin replied. "Some people have subtle minds, some have simple ones."

By the time my father came back into the hall bringing my mother with him, Serle and Sian and I all had our hands tied behind our backs, and were kneeling in front of the tub.

"Good!" said my father, smiling. "And the tub's full."

Then my mother dropped three apples into the water, and at once Serle and Sian and I started nosing and terriering for them, splashing and snorting and choking and spitting, gasping and yelling, jostling and banging heads, weaseling and snapping, blinking and coughing, half-blind with the water in our eyes, half-sick with the water up our noses.

Sian was the first to catch an apple. That's because her teeth are so sharp. And I was the second. So Serle had to duck his whole head underwater and stay down for as long as he could hold his breath. When he came up, he shook himself like a dog, and then he started laughing.

"Now!" panted Sian. "Bounce and Fly."

"No," I said. "Apple Twirl."

But at that moment there was a fierce banging at the door.

"The guisers!" we shouted — we all shouted. Even my mother. Even puffball Oliver. And my half-deaf, toothless Nain waved her stick in the air.

"Untie the children!" said my father, as he walked over to the door.

As soon as he had unbarred it and swung it open, a big nose poked into the hall. And spiked teeth! Then we saw staring eyes, waxen and red, and pricked cloth ears.

Sian stood behind me and wrapped both her arms around my waist.

All the guisers neighed then, all except one who hooted like an owl, and their horse started forward and lolloped into the hall. Its body looked as though it was made from the same material as the saffron cloth wrapped round my obsidian, and it was just as dirty. Two men were crouching under it, one behind the other, and all I could see of them was their legs.

Close behind the horse pressed all the guisers, carrying their scowling lanterns. Some men were wearing women's clothing and women men's clothing, and some boys were wearing girls' clothes and girls boys' clothes; and all the women with long hair had pinned it up and covered it; and everyone had blackened their faces and hands with soot. So, to begin with, it was impossible to say who was who. Each of the guisers was someone else, like a shape-changer. I couldn't even pick out Gatty or Hum.

"Helen!" said my father in a loud voice. "Tell Slim the guisers have come."

Slim was ready. He followed my mother straight back into the hall, and Ruth followed him, carrying oats for the horse, and a collop and a swig of ale for each guiser.

"For you, Sir John, and your family," said Slim, "there's black pudding."

"Very good," my father said. "And for Merlin and Oliver too."

"I'll lay it out on the table," said Slim.

When I climbed halfway up our staircase, I could see everyone at the same time. I looked and I thought how our roofbeams and old thatch were sheltering every man and woman and child who lives on our manor land — well, everyone who can walk. Three times I tried to count how many of us were in the hall, but each time the number was different. Forty-one, then thirty-nine, and then forty-two. My father says that altogether there are sixty people living at Caldicot.

Looking at all the people in our hall, I remembered King Uther's hall, and all the earls and lords and knights feasting there. I wonder whether Uther and the hooded man did follow Ygerna and Duke Gorlois back to Cornwall.

The first guiser I managed to recognize was Gatty, because she grinned at me. And the second was Tanwen, because I saw Serle edge right up behind her. She was wearing a kind of black shift and a white head-warmer, and I thought that in the flickering candlelight she didn't look quite human. Her eyes were sloe-black and her skin so pale I could almost see through it. I don't think Tanwen can be a changeling or anything like that, but here on the March we all live in between — that's what Nain and Merlin say.

When I saw Slim coming back into the hall, proudly carrying the black pudding on its lattice of willow twigs, I ran down the stairs again.

"Not as much as I hoped for, Sir John," said Slim. "You heard what happened."

My father nodded.

"A waste of Stupid," said Slim. "That's what I say."

"Yesterday is yesterday," said my father. "Anyhow, this looks good."

As soon as I had taken my piece of pudding, I pushed my way across the hall until I reached Gatty. "Here!" I said.

"What is it?"

"Black pudding. Remember?"

"Stupid!"

"I said I'd give you some — and Giles."

"You did and all," exclaimed Gatty, and she sounded quite astonished.

Then I broke my piece in two and gave her half, and she crammed it all into her mouth. A moment later, though, she spat it all out again.

"Waargh!" she exclaimed. She cleared her throat, and then she scraped her tongue on her front teeth. "You taste it," she said.

Gatty watched me nibble and chew and then swallow part of my piece. "See? You don't like it neither."

"I do," I said.

"I can tell," said Gatty.

Gatty was right, of course, but sometimes it's better to pretend. I used to pretend I didn't mind eating slimy kidneys, and now I quite like them. And most of the time I pretend I don't mind Serle's insults, because otherwise I think he would scent blood and try to hurt me all the more.

"Where's Giles?" I asked Gatty. "Can you see him?"

But before we were able to find him, my father and Oliver had climbed up to our little gallery, and my father rang his handbell. He welcomed the guisers and then he invited them to sing the song of the year, as he always does when manor people gather in the hall.

"January," called my father, and he struck his bell.

"By this fire we warm our hands," sang the guisers.

"February," my father announced. And he struck the bell again.

"And with our spades we dig our land."

"March."

"The seeds we sow grow into spring."

"April."

"And now we hear the cuckoo sing."

By now, the guisers were singing very loudly. By the time my father reached the end of the year, though, some of them were just bawling.

"November."

"Time to kill and salt our beasts."

"December," my father proclaimed. And for the twelfth time, he struck his little bell.

"And now we rest. And now we feast," chanted the guisers.

Much cheering and shouting followed the end of this song. Then Oliver stepped forward and raised one hand.

"We know they are here," said Oliver. "Tonight they are all around us. The enemies of God are everywhere. Keep your lanterns trimmed. Speak the old words." Then Oliver began to intone a sort of prayer-spell:

> "Dear Jesus, guard our doors tonight,
> Our roofs and windows, floors and walls,
> As Hallowe'en darkness falls."

Oliver stretched out both hands and called out in a loud voice:

> "Out Gurg!
> In Jesus!
> Out Gassagull!
> In Gabriel!
> Out Maledictus!
> In Benedictus!"

On Hallowe'en, the Devil rides around on his goat, and plays his bagpipes, and all the evil ones — the boggarts and goblins and broomstick witches — come out to meet him. When Oliver called out "Gurg" and "Gassagull," I knew the devil was somewhere near, and my tailbone began to ache.

"May the saints protect us," said Oliver. "Their souls are in the hands of God, and the torment of malice shall not touch them." Oliver paused. "Friends," he said, "now say the leaving charm with me."

Then all around me people began to mumble, and I joined in:

> "Here we are but go we must.
> In Jesus Christ we put our trust.
> May the Holy Trinity
> Save us from the enemy
> We recognize but cannot see."

"In the name of the Father," said Oliver, "and the Son, and the Holy Ghost. Amen."

After this, the guisers quietly took the door into the dark. Their horse with its wild eyes and pointed teeth, made from rusty nails, led them through the night, each of them grasping an angry-faced lantern.

"Come on, priest," said Merlin. "Go we must."

"Sleep in peace," Oliver said.

"He'll be safe with me," said Merlin, and he was grinning.

Nain sat down on the stool beside the fire; she gave a deep sigh, and for a long time she stared into the dying embers. Serle, meanwhile, unrolled the bedding for himself and Nain, but then for Sian and me as well. He almost never does anything like that, so there must be some reason when he does. I don't know what it is yet.

Before he barred the door, my father checked our six lanterns were still burning, and laid out collops and ale on the threshold for the dead. He took my mother by the hand and, when he opened the chamber door, I could hear the sound of sharp, thin wailing.

37

PASSION

My heart is beating and beating as though I'd rushed from here to the top of Tumber Hill. King Uther! Ygerna! I have seen them again. And the man in the dove-grey hood.

My stone was so cold when I unwrapped it. But while it was showing me the story, it grew very warm. Warmer than my own breath.

The king stretches out both his arms, as if he's hanging on the cross. "Ygerna!" he shouts. "Ygerna! Let this west wind hear your name. Let it carry my voice to Tintagel. Can you hear me? Ygerna!"

"Uther," says the hooded man. "Patience!"

Once again that deep voice, as thick and calm as cream. I've heard it before, I know I have.

"How can I be patient?" snaps the king, and he jams the sandy fist of his right hand into the palm of his left hand.

"I have helped three kings of Britain before you," the hooded man replies, "and I will help you. Now listen to me! You must keep Duke Gorlois here in Castle Terrible."

"I can keep him here for a year and a day. But what use is that? Will it bring me any nearer to Ygerna? Not one heartbeat."

"You don't understand me," says the hooded man. "I mean your life depends on keeping Gorlois imprisoned here. Your men must maintain the siege while you and I go to Tintagel."

"Tintagel! It's surrounded by cliffs that fall into the sea. The only way in is a rock bridge, and that's so narrow three men can easily defend it."

"True," says the hooded man. "No amount of force, no fine words . . ."

"Then how?" asks the king.

"If no power on earth can enable you to reach Ygerna," says the hooded man, "you must use an unearthly power. I told you before: No one and nothing can stand in the way of great passion."

"What power?" says King Uther, and he tugs his beard fiercely.

"If you are to have your desire," the hooded man says, "you must promise me my desire."

"I swear," says King Uther, "by Saint Matthew and Saint Mark, Saint Luke, Saint John."

"When you make love with Ygerna, she will conceive a child. You must give that child to me to bring up as I wish."

"I swear it by all the saints," says the king.

"I will honor your child and your child will bring you honor," says the hooded man. "I will help you, Uther, and I will help your child who was and will be."

Then the hooded man opens his right hand, and nestled in his palm there is a little circular bone box. He strokes it with his fingertips. "In this box, there is a drug. Soon after you take it, your appearance will change. You will look exactly like Duke Gorlois. I will take it too, and I will look exactly like Sir Jordans, the Duke's closest companion. And then we'll be able to enter Tintagel."

"Ygerna," says the king under his breath.

"When you reach her room, don't say too much to her.

I can give you Gorlois's body, but not his mind or memory. Just tell her how you've longed to see her — how you slipped away from this siege. Hurry her into bed."

"I understand," says the king.

"Now order your men to maintain the siege. Then we'll ride to Tintagel."

As I stared into my stone, I saw King Uther and the hooded man sniff the drug-powder, and saw their appearance begin to change. I saw them leave the siege and gallop up to the fortress of Tintagel in the dark, and saw the guards allow them to cross the rock bridge because they looked exactly like the Duke of Cornwall and Sir Jordans.

"I will wait here, outside her chamber," the hooded man says. And he winks at the king.

Then Uther lightly knocks and opens the chamber door; and there, in the candlelight, stands Ygerna wearing her white nightgown, stitched with white silk stars.

"Gorlois!" cries Ygerna, and she steps towards him.

Uther looks at Ygerna. His heart is beating. He is out of breath.

It is true, she is beautiful. Her face is almond-shaped. Her bare shoulders and bare arms are rounded and pale and slender, like stripped willow, curving.

"I've longed to see you," says Uther. "I slipped away from the siege at Castle Terrible."

"How?"

"In this dark. Come!" And Uther takes a step towards Ygerna. He puts his arms around her . . .

For a few moments, my black stone sparkled. It was like the night sky on a freezing winter night, full of hundreds and thousands of stars, each of them sharp as a thorn and sparkling. Then it flashed and flooded itself with white light, and I heard birds singing, a dawn chorus. And I saw Uther and Ygerna again. Lying in a storm of linen, side by side, still sleeping.

Now Ygerna begins to stir and Uther begins to stir, both at the same time, as if each knows the other is waking.

Uther opens one eye. At once he reaches up and pats the top of his head, and I know why. Gorlois has a mane of black hair, but he is bald, and he wants to be sure the drug has not worn off.

Ygerna opens her eyes. They are violet as the little wood-violets that grow round the fringes of Pike Forest.

"I have conceived a child," Ygerna whispers. "My body tells me so. We will have a boy, and he will be a great king."

Now there is a fierce rapping at the chamber door, and Uther and Ygerna sit up on their pillows. Then the hooded man, still looking like Sir Jordans, leads two messengers into the room.

"I'm sorry, my lord," the hooded man says, shaking his head and smiling, "but these two fools insist on speaking to Lady Ygerna . . ."

"Well, what is it?" Uther demands.

"Duke Gorlois!" one messenger exclaims.

"Is it you?" says the other. "I mean . . ."

"Get on with it!" says Uther.

"Lady Ygerna," says the first messenger. "We've ridden here from Castle Terrible with this message for you. Last night our lord, Duke Gorlois, saw King Uther ride away from the siege, and so he had the portcullis raised, and rode out with his men and few as they were, they attacked King Uther's men. Lady Ygerna," says the messenger, "Duke Gorlois was killed."

"Killed, was he?" says Uther.

"And after that," the messenger adds, "King Uther's men killed many of the Duke's men and captured Castle Terrible."

"Well!" says Uther, and he puts both arms round Ygerna. "I am not dead. As you see, I'm very much alive. The man you left for dead lying on the battlefield got here before you!" Uther closes his eyes and his whole body heaves in a sigh. "But you've brought bad news," he says. "Now that Uther has captured Castle Terrible, he will soon advance on us here. He knows he cannot force his way in, so he will try to starve us out. I must ride out as fast as I can, and rally my men, and make peace with Uther. It will be the worse for us, otherwise."

King Uther waves his right hand, the messengers bow, and the hooded man leads them out of the chamber.

"There's not a moment to be lost," says Uther, and he leaps out of bed and quickly dresses himself. Then he takes Ygerna into his arms one more time. "I will return to you very soon," he promises her. "And not as a dead man. As your husband."

"A boy," whispers Ygerna. "He will be a great king."

STRANGE SAINTS

Slim always cooks hare for All Hallows dinner.

"And it's a nice young one, Sir John," Slim said. "It's only got one hole under its tail."

As soon as dinner was over, Oliver rang the church bell and, one way or another, every person living on our manor came to church. Some people walked and the little ones ran, some staggered, some hauled themselves along on two sticks. Hum and Gatty carried Hum's old mother on a litter, because she hasn't walked since she broke her hipbone. And Giles and Dutton made a hand-chair for Madog because he has never walked. He's the same age as I am, and he just sits against the wall all day, and shakes with laughter, and blows bubbles, and waves his arms.

First Oliver reminded us of the four Saint Edmunds painted on the church wall. "Our own parish saint," he called out, "and the saint of all England."

Then he held up a little bone box, and it looked very much like the hooded man's box — the one in which he kept the magic powder. "Saint Edmund's fingernails," Oliver proclaimed. "His nails went on growing for years after he died, and the shrine warden used to clip them. Pray to Saint Edmund to intercede for our souls!"

After this, Oliver said prayers for All Hallows and then he asked each of us to call out the names of our favorite saints.

Serle chose Charles of Apple Orchards, I don't know

why, though I've noticed that he sometimes goes out to our orchard, and sits under an apple tree on his own. Slim called on Saint Laurence, who was roasted on a spit, and Gatty named Isidore the Farmworker because his sickle sharpened itself. Nain recited the names of eleven Welsh saints I have never heard of before: Tysilio and Cadoc and Ffraid and Tanwg . . . I can't remember the others. And then Sian made us laugh when she called on Cushman, saint of happy betrothals. I think she is still wondering whether Merlin was serious when he offered to marry her.

I expect Oliver thought I would call on Saint John the Divine, because he is the saint of writers. But I named the angel Raphael, saint of lovers, and then Gerard, who watches over pregnant women.

"What very strange choices, Arthur," my mother said to me as we walked out of church. "Why did you call on them?"

"They interest me," I said.

But of course I couldn't explain about Ygerna and Uther.

My father stared at me. "The things you know," he said. "You could be a schoolman."

UTHER EXPLAINS

I know I can't keep asking Merlin about my seeing stone. I know I have got to work out things for myself. My head is crammed with questions. Is there a place called Tintagel? And a fortress there? And is there really a drug that changes the way you look? I can ask Johanna in the village about that.

When the hooded man said, "No one and nothing can stand in the way of great passion," I think he meant that what happens in our lives depends on how determined we are, and how much we believe in ourselves. If so, I may be able to persuade my father to send me away into service, even if he doesn't want to.

Time in my stone sometimes runs slower, sometimes faster than the sun chasing shadow round our sundial. When I looked into it this afternoon, I could soon see that Ygerna was already six months gone. She and King Uther were married, and they were in London, sitting in the same huge hall where Uther had held his feast.

"Your baby," says the king. "Whose is it?"

"Whose but mine?" Ygerna replies.

"I mean," says the king, "whose child are you carrying?"

Queen Ygerna lowers her head.

"Tell me the truth," Uther says. "Don't be afraid. I won't love you any the less for it."

Ygerna hesitates. "I will then," she replies. "The night my husband, Duke Gorlois, died, a man came into my chamber at Tintagel. He looked exactly like Gorlois and spoke like Gorlois. I thought he was Gorlois. My own husband, safe from the siege at Castle Terrible. I opened my arms to him."

"That is the truth," says the king. "Ygerna, I was that man."

"You?"

"I am the father of your child."

Then I heard Uther tell Ygerna how the hooded man gave him a drug to change his appearance, and took the drug himself so that he would resemble Sir Jordans. At first, Ygerna wept for the loss of Gorlois; then she smiled, in relief. . . . She placed both hands over her baby, and embraced the whole world.

"Our son," she calls out.

"But I have made a promise," King Uther says. "I have promised the hooded man I will give him our child to bring up as he wishes."

"No!" cries Ygerna.

"He will honor our child and our child will bring us honor. I have sworn it by Saint Matthew and Saint Mark, Saint Luke, Saint John."

+ 40 +

schoolmen, scribes, and artists

"What is a schoolman, exactly?" I asked Oliver.

"First things first," said Oliver. "You can't bring those hounds into the church, and you know that perfectly well."

"Why not?"

"Because they're beasts."

"So is Serle."

"They have no souls," said Oliver.

"If you bring in caterpillars, why can't I bring in Tempest and Storm?"

"That was to curse them and get rid of them," Oliver said. "Do you want me to curse Tempest and Storm?"

So I called the hounds to heel, and shooed them out into the porch. Then I slowly shut the oak door in their faces.

"That's better," said Oliver. "Outside are the hounds and sorcerers! Now, Arthur, what were you asking?"

"A schoolman?"

"Schoolmen are thinkers. They build bridges between us and our Lord."

"Are they monks?"

"They teach in cathedral schools, sometimes in monasteries. Yes, they are monks. Why?"

"Because my father says I could be a schoolman."

Oliver rubbed the end of his nose and gave me an owlish look. "He does, does he?"

"Has he talked to you about his plans for me?"

"No."

"I don't want to be a schoolman."

"Have you heard of Pierre Abelard?"

"Who?"

"Or Pierre Lombard? Or John of Salisbury?"

"You know I haven't."

"They were all great schoolmen. You see. How can you tell what you will or won't be when you don't even know what you are talking about?"

"Does my father know about them?" I asked.

"I very much doubt it," Oliver replied.

"Anyhow," I said. "I don't want to be a schoolman."

"That," said Oliver, "is rather like a clod of mud wheezing that it doesn't want to be a star. Or a cat miaowing that it doesn't want to be a queen. Now come on! It's time we began."

"It's still All Hallows tide," I said.

"So?"

"So will you show me Saint Edmund's nails?"

"I did, yesterday."

"Will you open the box?"

"Certainly not!" said Oliver indignantly.

"All right!" I said. "Will you explain the four Edmunds painted on the wall?"

"That is a better question," replied Oliver. And he turned on his heel, and led me up the north nave. "Red lead," said Oliver. "Malachite. Arsenic salts. All kinds of colors!"

"What do you mean?"

"I told you to pray for scribes," said Oliver, "with their aching wrists and elbows, their aching necks and backs."

"I do," I said.

"Is that why you called on — who was it?"

"Raphael, the angel."

"Is that all?"

"Saint Gerard."

"Ridiculous," said Oliver. "Are you pregnant?"

"No."

"You are. Your head is pregnant with ideas it should never have conceived. Now! You pray for scribes and you should pray for artists too. Mixing their paints. Decorating their manuscripts. Teaching us on the walls of our churches. Think of all the work. Grinding and mixing the paints. Building the scaffold. Priming the wall. Pricking out all the curves with compasses, all the circles and diagonals. All this before the artist even started painting. All this," said Oliver rather grandly, *"Pro amore Dei et Sancti Edmundi* — for the love of God and Saint Edmund."

I tilted back my head and stared up, and with their large, quiet eyes, the four Edmunds stared down at me.

"Who painted our Edmunds?" I asked.

"Strangely enough, a man called Edmund." Oliver pursed his lips. "A very strange man too, if that's what he was. His hair hung down to his waist, and his whole body was covered with hair. He grunted like a beast. He ate like a beast. But he painted like an angel."

"Did you know him?" I asked.

"Dear boy! I'm not that old. Our Edmunds are four generations old. When your father's father's father was a boy . . . that's when they were painted."

"I think you could be a schoolman, Oliver," I said.

Oliver's eyes gleamed. "You think so?" he said.

"I do."

"Do you think so or know so?"

"Oh! Oliver," I said. "Not this afternoon."

"Are you practicing your writing?" Oliver asked.

"Yes."

"Each day?"

"Yes, Oliver."

"With your right hand."

"With both hands."

"Just because you can write, you mustn't neglect your memory. On the contrary, memory and writing support one another. Many things do not need to be written; they can easily be remembered."

"Yes, Oliver."

"What is the difference between length, depth, and width? Can you remember?"

"Imagine a spear pierces the top of a man's skull," I said, "and comes out of his arse. That is length."

"That measures length," said Oliver.

"If the spear goes in through a man's chest and out through his back, that measures depth. If it goes in through one rib cage and out through the other, that measures width."

"Right, Arthur! That will do for today."

"Oliver," I said. "Have you heard of Tintagel?"

"What?"

"Tintagel."

"What is it?"

"Oh! It doesn't matter," I said.

"What does it mean? Tintagel?"

"I don't know," I said.

131

mouthfuls of air

"Oliver says, Oliver says," grumbled my grandmother. "The trouble with our Oliver is that he gets in his own way. He only sees himself."

"That's like Narcissus," I said.

"Who?" said Nain.

"Narcissus. He was in Oliver's book about the Greeks. He fell in love with his own reflection."

But Oliver isn't really like Narcissus at all. He isn't young, and he certainly isn't beautiful. I think he just puffs himself up in case we don't notice him.

"And the trouble with you, Arthur," Nain continued, "is your writing. You're always writing or reading."

"Oliver says . . ." I began.

"There you go again," said Nain.

"I do practice remembering, Nain," I said. "Writing and reading and remembering."

"That you should!" said Nain sharply. "Do you know what happens each time you write a thing down? Each time you name it? You sap its strength."

"But I think . . ."

"Who are you listening to? Me or yourself?" demanded Nain. "You're as bad as Oliver." Nain gripped the side of the table and pulled herself up from the bench. Then she hobbled over to the door and opened it.

"Come over here!" she said. "What's the wind saying?"

I closed my eyes and tried to listen.

"How it praises God!" cried Nain. "On its way from yesterday to tomorrow. The spirits in the copper beech! The grumble and chuckle of stones. Listen! Our words must dance like they do. Mouthfuls of air, not dry ink." Nain sniffed and then she glared at me. "Oliver says, Oliver says," she grumbled. "You should learn to honor the power in things. You'd do better to listen to Merlin."

Poor Nain! It's her November now. She looks more stooped each day, as if she is growing into the ground.

I don't believe everything she says but I wish I could take her once to the top of Tumber Hill, and look out with her into the heart of Wales. I would remember every word she said.

+ 42 +
foster child

Ygerna moans. She sounds like little Luke when he is asleep, or half-asleep, and doesn't even know he is whimpering.

"Let me see," she pleads. And then again, fiercely: "Show him to me!"

The midwife holds up the baby and Ygerna reaches out for him. But Uther raises his right hand. "Wrap him in gold cloth," he tells the midwife.

Then Uther sits on the edge of the bed, and looks down at his wife, and Ygerna grasps the king's right wrist and digs her fingernails into it. "It is not what I wish," the king says gently. "It is what I promised."

King Uther walks out of the chamber, carrying the baby, and my stone goes with him. He strides down a corridor. The pale oak floorboards creak. The walls are painted with hounds and wolves, hares and cats, owls, blackbirds, and other birds and beasts.

Now the baby begins to wail, as if he knows he is being taken away from his mother.

Footsteps and cries . . . in the corridor, they bounce from wall to wall, ceiling to floor. The whole world is full of beating drums and flashing knives.

The king unbolts a door and, outside, the hooded man is waiting. For a moment, the two men say nothing. They just stand there, on either side of the threshold.

"Ygerna . . ." the king begins. But that's all he says, because it is useless to say anything. He shakes his head.

"I said I would help you," the hooded man says. "I never said there would be no price." Then he looks at the baby, wrapped in gold.

"Will I see him again?" asks King Uther.

"He will be safe," the hooded man replies.

"That is not what I asked."

The sorcerer looks at the king. "Some questions are better not asked," he says. "A knight and his wife will foster your son. They are loyal to you, strict, and kind. They have a young son of their own, he is almost three. The woman will wean him and feed your baby with her own milk."

"What are their names?"

The hooded man says nothing.

"Where?" asks Uther. "Where are you taking him?"

"Away to the west," the hooded man replies. "He was conceived where sky and water meet. He is the child of crossing-places, and I will take him home."

"Home?" repeats the king.

"His foster parents will name him and have him christened. They will bring him up, and teach him to dress and serve his lord, to tilt and to parry, even to read and write. They will keep him at home until he is thirteen — and I will watch over him."

"And then?" asks Uther, King of Britain.

The hooded man takes the baby out of the king's arms. "I will come for him," he says, "when his time comes."

crossing-places

When the hooded man told King Uther that his son was the child of crossing-places, I remembered how Merlin said that between-places are always chancy. Our Marches and the foreshore and dusks and bridges: They're times and places where strange things happen.

My moon-bruise! My wolf-skull! In a way my obsidian is a kind of between-place: between me and everything I can see in it.

And what about Nain? She's a crossing-place, too, whenever she tells us stories.

It's only seven weeks now until this century ends and the new one begins. I don't think anything amazing will happen, like half the world breaking off, but I can feel things will be different; I just don't know how.

"Let little Luke get well," said my mother. "That's the change I want."

"We still got to eat, haven't we?" said Gatty, and she sucked her raw knuckles. "Things may change for you. Nothing won't change for me."

"Let things stay as they are," sniffed Nain.

"What kind of change?" Merlin inquired. "Without or within?"

+ 44 +
# luke's illness

My mother sat up in the great bed and hugged little Luke
to her to keep him warm, to give him some of her life.

"John and Serle were wrong," she said. "Luke wasn't
screaming because of King Richard, or because of the
weather. Tanwen's right. The evil's inside him: Luke was
born to die."

"God is merciful," said Nain. "He shows mercy when
He takes a child out of this mad world."

"Luke is suffering," my mother cries, "and I am suffering. I know it is all because of me. All I have done. All I've
left undone."

"At least John has an heir," Nain said. "You have given
him Serle."

Tears were streaming down my mother's face. She bent
over little Luke.

"Serle's strong and healthy," continued Nain. "You
should be grateful."

"Come here, Arthur!" my mother croaked. Then she
reached out with one hand and fiercely pulled me to her,
and for a while we huddled on the Great Bed, with little
Luke between us.

Late this afternoon, my mother called me down from
this writing-room, and asked me to go with her to see the
wisewoman, Johanna.

I'm glad she didn't want me to go on my own. I don't
mind Johanna's half-moustache and whiskers, or her hut

which smells like bad eggs, but her sudden rages scare me. One moment she is normal, the next she's glaring and shouting.

"Tomorrow's an evil day," Johanna said. And then she snapped, "Hear that? Woman?"

No one else would dare to speak to my mother like that.

"Yes," said my mother meekly.

"So do what you do tonight before midnight," Johanna ordered her.

Then Johanna told my mother to mix dried shepherd's purse with honeysuckle, and grind them both to powder. "Put the powder in warm red wine, and give it to Luke."

"He won't drink," my mother said. "Not honey-water. Not ale. He won't even drink my own milk."

"He'll drink this," said Johanna. "After that, undress him, and sit him on a stool with a hole in the middle. Drape a cloth over him. Boy!"

"Yes," I said, and my heart jumped.

Johanna glared at me. "You are to do this. Make sure the cloth reaches down to the ground. Light a little charcoal fire right under him, so the heat enters him . . . You understand?"

"Yes, Johanna."

"You don't. You don't understand anything."

"She is a terror," said my mother, as soon as we had left Johanna's hut, "but she does know recipes."

"I don't believe half of them," I replied.

"She healed my nipples when they were inflamed . . ."

"You said that was Saint Gerard."

". . . and Nain's oozing eyes," added my mother.

"Tanwen knows recipes too," I said.

"Yes," said my mother. "For enchanting."

"What do you mean?"

"It doesn't matter," my mother said.

"Mother," I began. "You know you said you would talk to my father."

"What about?"

"His plans. He does mean me to be a squire, doesn't he? He will let me go away soon? He doesn't want me to be a priest, or a schoolman?"

On the bridge across the moat, my mother paused and put her hands on my two shoulders, and looked into my eyes. "Arthur," she said.

"I can't be those things."

"I will talk to him," my mother said, "and ask him to talk to you. But not tonight."

Then she turned towards the hall, and I followed her.

+ 45 +

PAINS

Johanna was right. Luke did sip a little of the warm wine with shepherd's purse and honeysuckle in it; but when we sat him on the three-legged stool, and held him there, bare and upright, and kindled the charcoal fire under him, he screamed and threw it all up again.

Some of the fire's heat must have entered Luke, and risen right through him. But that hasn't done him any good either. All it has done is made Luke's bottom very red and raw.

Tanwen has given my mother a pot of ointment for burned skin. It smells quite disgusting, and is made of oil and dung beetles, and the heads and wings of crickets. When my mother rubbed it into little Luke's bottom, he screamed terribly.

My tailbone began to ache again while my mother and I were in Johanna's hut, and it still hasn't stopped. So it seems it doesn't hurt only when I have dark thoughts, but sometimes when I'm upset or afraid.

I could tell Johanna about my devil's part in case she has a cure for it. But I think that's too chancy. She might denounce me to my father.

46

AN UNFAIR SONG

If your baby never stops moaning
And whimpering and groaning,
Feed him with wine and shepherd's purse,
And light a small fire under his . . .
Pronounce a blessing or a curse.
That's Johanna's medicine.

If your baby never stops crying
And there's nothing left worth trying,
Brew him ointment from fish oil,
Dung beetles and crickets' wings,
And bring the mixture to the boil.
Then smear him, Tanwen says.

If your baby needs a new night nurse,
There cannot be anybody worse
Than Sian, my little sister.
All night she'll want to bolster-fight,
Royster-doyster, play the jester.
And that's Sian's treatment.

I know this song isn't fair, except about Sian; but sometimes I start to make one up without really knowing where
it is going.

It is true some herbs can help us, as long as we don't
pick them on an evil day when they have no power; and I

know Johanna and Tanwen have learned more recipes than anyone else on our manor. Tanwen has sometimes given me lemon balm to sweat out my fevers, and once she quieted my aching head with feverfew.

All the same, I know some of her and Johanna's recipes are completely useless, because Tanwen told me so herself.

"They're bogus," she said. "But we still sell them at Ludlow Fair. People pay for them."

"Why?" I asked.

"Fear, I suppose," said Tanwen. "When people are ill, they become afraid, and when they're afraid, they can be very stupid."

When Tanwen said that, I remembered what the hooded man told King Uther after Duke Gorlois and Ygerna dared to leave his feast.

"Very stupid," I said. "Or very bold."

47

A NEW BOW

My new bow! It is so beautiful.

I know I am meant to keep it in the armory with my father's coat of mail and the practice swords and spikes and everything, but I have brought it up here so I can keep looking at it.

Will bore it into the hall after dinner, and it's made of elm, but at first I thought it was made of yew.

"Not until you're seventeen," my father said. "I told you that."

It doesn't matter, though. My bow shines in sunlight and candlelight, and the stave's a fingerspan taller than I am.

"He'll grow up to that," Will said.

"He's grown two fingerspans during the last twelve months," my father said.

"Can I string it?" I asked.

"Not much use otherwise," my father replied.

So I noosed the hempen string round the bottom horn nock and planted the bow on the floor against the arch of my foot; then I grasped the middle of the stave, and reached up and pulled down the top until I could just slip the string over it. Lightly I pulled the string, and it popped and hummed. Then I slid one hand down the top half of the stave, the long slope of it, and felt how it flexed and swelled like a woman carrying her baby. "It is the most beautiful thing I've ever seen," I said.

Then Will looked at my father and my father looked at Will, and they both laughed because I was so pleased.

"With this bow," my father said, "you'll be able to shoot the full furlong. Make sure the butts are that far apart."

"Now?"

"Wait here!" said my father. He went into the chamber and came straight out again with a long linen bag.

"You'll need these," he said.

Then my father gave me the bag, and I opened it. Inside were the most wonderful arrows in the world. Their shafts were cut from pale ash-wood and their flights from peacocks' feathers, downy and blue and green.

"Where do they come from?" I cried.

"Lord Stephen keeps a pride of peacocks," my father said, "so I sent for some feathers."

One by one I rolled each arrow between my right thumb and forefinger: ten arrows! Each flight was bound to the shaft with red silk, and each nock was inlaid with little strips of horn. The heads were lean and very sharp, and I pressed each one into the ball of my thumb. When at last I looked up, my father and Will were still standing there, quietly watching me.

"May Will come too?" I asked my father.

"Down to the forest first," my father said. "That's right, isn't it, Will?"

Will nodded.

"Pike?" I said. "Why?"

"The wood come from Pike, didn't it," said Will. "Take some, give some!"

"Every bowyer and fletcher will tell you that," my father said. "Never take without giving. Otherwise the wood will turn against you."

So my father and Will and I walked out of the hall, and when we had crossed the bridge, we saw Oliver picking up fieldstones in the glebe.

"Come down to Pike," my father told him.

Oliver sucked his teeth, and looked up at the sky. It was full of rooks, sweeping upwards and hurtling downwards.

"Breaking their necks!" said Will. "There's a gale on the way."

"Or . . ." said my father. But he didn't finish what he had to say.

We walked right down to the edge of the forest: nothing in front of us but leaf-mold and tangled roots and clutching ivy. The darkness of the forest reached out towards us. Will pulled an old arrow from his belt and handed it to me.

"Give him one of the new ones," said my father. "Better be safe." Then he put a hand on my shoulder. "Careful!" he said. "You're not wearing a bracer."

I notched an arrow to the new hempen string, and drew the string right back to my cheek, and cocked my wrist a little so that the string wouldn't lash it. Then I fired the arrow upwards, deep into Pike Forest.

"That's it," said Will. "Wood to the wood."

So now I have nine arrows fledged with peacock feathers, and nine's my number.

"Good!" said my father. "Now let's see what you can do in the Yard."

Oliver made the sign of the cross over me and my bow.

"Peace be with you," he said. *"Pax tecum."* And as he walked away, he called out, "The stones await their master."

My father and Will and I followed Oliver, and when I thanked Will for making my bow, he lowered his head.

"I know a good bow doesn't make a good archer," I said.

"You're good already," my father said.

"And I know a good archer doesn't make a good squire. But father, this new bow will make me better at my other skills as well."

+ 48 +
ice

When I unwrapped my obsidian early this morning, it was cold as a lump of ice. I cupped it and rubbed it between my hands for quite a long time, but it still didn't grow warm, as it has done before, and its shine was a dull shine.

Why wouldn't it show me anything? What have I done wrong? I am sure I wrapped it up right, and I held it in the same way I always do, with the lumpen side and white spots pressed into my right palm. Or is my stone's silence saying something?

Ygerna's heart is ice. Her baby has been ripped away from her, and I don't think she will ever see him again. She is so frozen with grief she cannot even melt into tears.

49

BAPTISM

My stone's shine was dull again today, like the shine on one of Slim's cooking pots. I could only see the smoky shape of myself, not my eyes or my nose and mouth. The roll of my scarf made my neck as wide as my head. And my ears were the flaps of my rabbitskin cap, sticking out sideways. If I hadn't known who I was, I wouldn't have been able to recognize myself. In fact, I wouldn't even have been sure I was looking at a human being!

For a long time, I nursed my obsidian between my hands, as I did yesterday, and my blood warmed it. Then I heard words in it, and it must have been a priest speaking.

"Remember the words of our Lord," says the voice. "He said, 'Ask, and you will receive.' He said, 'Seek, and you will find. Knock, and the gate will be opened for you.' Listen to us, Lord. Let us who ask receive. Let us who seek find. Open the gate to those who knock."

At first, I thought this priest sounded quite like Oliver. But maybe that's because Oliver likes saying the same thing twice, or else priests saying prayers all sound like one another. To begin with, the words were a very long way away; and although I kept warming the stone, it still would not show me anything.

"Lord," says the priest, "we pray this baby will be blessed by your heavenly washing. Let him be an heir to the kingdom of heaven." The priest coughs. "Who speaks in the name of the child?" he asks.

"I do," booms a deep voice, and I recognize it at once. It is the hooded man.

"In the name of this child, will you renounce the devil and all his works?"

"I renounce them."

"Do you believe in the three-in-one and one-in-three?"

"I believe."

"Lord," says the priest, "bless this water. Let it wash away sin. Let the old Adam in this child die and be buried. Let the spirit live and grow in him."

"Amen," says the hooded man.

"Amen," say several voices. Who are they? They must be the baby's foster mother and his foster father. His elder brother. His whole family. I wish I could see them.

"Who names this child?" asks the priest.

"I name him," says the hooded man.

"Name him!" commands the priest.

But I can't hear what name the hooded man gives the baby because of the sip-and-slop and splashing of the water as the priest dips the baby into the font, and then the baby's yelling because the November water is so cold.

"I baptize you," says the priest, "in the name of the Father, and of the Son, and of the Holy Ghost. Amen."

50

MY NAME

At dinner this morning, my father was in a good mood, so I asked permission to speak.

"What is it, Arthur?"

"My name."

"Yes?"

"Who chose it?"

"Chose it?" said my father. "Your father, of course."

"What does it mean?"

"Mean? I don't know."

"But some names have meanings," I said. "Oliver told me about the three kings. He says Melchior means king of light . . ."

"What do I mean?" asked Sian.

"Trouble!" said my father. "Who said you could speak?"

Sian put her head on one side, and grinned her gap-toothed grin. She can get away with almost anything.

Nain turned to my father. "The boy is right," she said. "Of course names mean, and you know that very well. You, Helen, you mean the bright one. The dragon chose your name. And John means the favored one. Serle means armor."

"I chose that," said my mother.

"And Tanwen means white fire," added Nain. "Remember?"

"What about me?" demanded Sian.

At this moment, Tempest and Storm started to bark, and then there was a loud knocking at the door. My father and Serle and I all stood up.

"Who is it?" shouted my father.

"Thomas," called a muffled voice. "From Lady Alice."

So my father unbolted the door, and Thomas fell in. He looks quite like a hen, with his beaky nose and jerky movements, and this morning he looked like a very wet one.

"Devil's teeth!" he exclaimed, and he shook himself and sprayed us all with raindrops. "I've never known rain like it. Cold and biting."

"Warm yourself by the fire, man," my father said. "You'll soon dry out."

Thomas told us Sir William is staying at his manor in France, and is not expected home until Christmas, but that Lady Alice and Tom and Grace wish to visit us.

"Excellent!" exclaimed my father. "There's plenty to talk about."

It is agreed that our cousins will arrive in ten days' time, and stay for three nights. I am very pleased about this. I like them both and it is a long time since I have seen them, because they were ill and unable to come in August. I won't have to do lessons with Oliver while they are here, and I can use my new bow when we go to the Yard. And at last I can show Grace my secret climbing-tree.

Serle is always kinder to me when Tom and Grace visit us, and sometimes he makes us all laugh. He was quite friendly and laughed when we bobbed for apples on Hallowe'en, and I remember how he unrolled Sian's and my bedding, but for all of October and these first days of

November he has been strangely quiet, and sometimes he gets angry without good reason. I know he doesn't like me, but he doesn't seem to like anyone much.

If I can find a way to be alone with Lady Alice, I may be able to find out more about whether Grace and I are to be betrothed. And I want to tell her I have kept her secret about Sir William, and ask her whether she has told it to anyone else.

I still don't know what my name means either. The only other Arthur I have ever heard of is the prince of Brittany, the son of Coeur-de-Lion's younger brother Geoffrey.

"Geoffrey died thirteen years ago," my father told me, "and he was younger than King Richard but older that John, so the fact is that young Arthur has a better claim to the throne of England than his uncle John."

"Then why is John the king?" I asked.

"He snatched the crown," said my father.

hOOTER AND WORSE

This has been a very bad day because of what Serle told me. And all the worse because it began so well. "A very sharp morning!" said my father while we were breaking our fast with round bread and butter and smoked herring. "Today's the first day of the winter reckoning and Hum and I have plenty to do. But you, Serle. Why don't you and Arthur ride out and search for signs of Hooter?"

"What's Hooter?" asked Sian.

"Yesterday morning, Will told Hum he heard Hooter rattling in his chains," my father continued.

"What is Hooter?" demanded Sian.

"When the Vikings came to England," my father said, "they brought Hooter with them. A huge black dog. He has long black hair, and he's larger than a wolf, almost as large as a pony. His eyes are orange. Hooter's master died. He was killed in battle by the English east from Hereford. But Hooter's still alive, and searching for his master and howling."

Sian's dark eyes were as large and round as my mother's shoulder-clasps.

"Joan has found spoor," my father told us.

"What's spoor?" asked Sian.

"Footprints," said my father. "Along both headlands between Nine Elms and Great Oak. Hum doesn't know what to make of them. They're not wolf or bear — and certainly not boar."

"Why have Serle and Arthur got to search for him?" demanded Sian.

"He'll eat our hens and geese," said my father. "He may attack our sheep. If he's anywhere around here, we need to hunt him and kill him."

"I want to search for him," said Sian.

"That's quite enough," said my father, waving away Sian's words as if they were pestering flies. "Serle and Arthur will never get out at all."

My father has never once before suggested Serle and I should hunt alone together, and I felt proud and rather nervous.

First, we went to the kitchen for food. Slim was busy cooking dinner, but Ruth wrapped up pieces of boiled mutton for us in one shaggy towel, and oatmeal cakes in another. She filled two bottles with ale from the barrel, and stoppered them, and gave us each an apple and a pear.

I like Ruth, and I think she and Howell will be happy when they marry next year because they both laugh so much. Tanwen doesn't like her, though. She told me once that Ruth is a loudmouth, and can't keep secrets.

In the stables, I saddled Pip and Serle saddled Gwinam, and we put our food and drink in our saddlebags. Serle chose a short spear, and I tied my quiver of peacock arrows to my belt and slung my new bow over my shoulder. Then we rode out.

First we picked our way along the headlands to see the spoor for ourselves; it was very large, and splayed, more like a boar than any other creature. When I dismounted and looked at it, I felt a cold finger touch the back of my neck, and it wasn't Serle's.

The sun had still not burned away the ground-frost as we picked our way down Pikeside to the edge of the forest. Side by side we rode, and quite slowly, searching for signs, and all around us in the forest there were singing birds, bobbing rabbits, a jack-hare, chucklings and rustlings.

"This is a very strange quest," said Serle, "and it's like looking for one of our mother's hairpins in a barn full of hay, and it could last a lifetime. If we'd brought Tempest and Storm, they might have picked up Hooter's scent."

What did it matter, though? What mattered to me was riding out together, and the sharp edge of the morning.

Serle was quite friendly when we set out, but by the time we stopped to eat, he had become moody again.

"You know what Nain said about names?" I began. "What they mean. What Serle means."

"What about it?'

"I'm making up a song about Jack-Hare:

> Cat-of-the-wood and cabbage-patch stag,
> Squat-in-the-hedge and frisker,
> Sit-still and shiver-maker,
> Snuffler, twitching-whisker . . ."

"A hare's a witch," said Serle.

"I know," I said. "I'm going to say that too."

"You think you know everything," said Serle.

"I don't," I said.

"You do."

"The more I know, the less I know."

"What's that supposed to mean?"

"I do know I want to be like you," I said. "I want to go into service. I want to be a squire."

"That shows how much you don't know," said Serle, and he stuffed his mouth full of mutton.

"What do you mean?" I said.

"I mean . . ." said Serle, but his mouth was so full he couldn't go on.

"What do you mean, Serle?" I repeated.

Serle chewed and chewed and swallowed the mutton. "I mean two things," he said. "First, you're not good enough at your Yard-skills to be a squire or a knight. You're not, are you? All you're good at is archery."

"I'm getting better," I cried. "I keep practicing."

"Squires use swords," said Serle. "Swords and lances, not bows and arrows." Then he stuffed his mouth again, and chewed, and spat out a piece of gristle. "And this is the second thing," he said. "Our father doesn't mean you to be a squire."

"How do you know?" I cried.

"It stands to reason," said Serle, and he was half-smiling. "Haven't you thought about it? A man may have two sons, or three sons, or ten sons, but it's only the firstborn who inherits the manor."

"But . . ."

"Think about it, Arthur! The most you can hope for is a little land, with my agreement."

"Why with your agreement?"

"Because it could have been mine. Do you want to weaken our father's manor? Do you want to break it up?"

"But . . ."

"Is that what you want?"

"No! No, it's not!"

156

"And how can you make a good marriage without your own manor? Have you thought about that? You can't."

"I will!" I shouted.

"You can't."

"But Lady Alice said . . ."

"What did she say?"

"It doesn't matter."

"You're good at reading and writing, Arthur," said Serle, "and that's just as well. You must become a monk, or a priest if you want."

"I won't," I shouted.

"Or even a schoolman. Our father said you'd make a good schoolman."

"Why do you hate me?" I asked in a low voice.

For a while we sat in silence. All around us the birds sang, and the sun threw its spears between the tall trees.

"Everyone hates a cuckoo," Serle replied, "because it lays its eggs in another bird's nest. But I'm the firstborn, and I'm stronger than you are. You're not pushing me out."

Then Serle stood up, and he mounted Gwinam. He galloped away and left me and Pip in the middle of Pike Forest.

For a long time, I sat there on my own, and I felt so sad I wouldn't have minded if Hooter had come out of the forest, and rattled his chains, and swallowed me. Anyhow, I think Serle is more dangerous than Hooter.

52

MY QUEST

I woke this morning so sad because of my argument with Serle. I felt as if part of me had died, and I could never be happy again. Then I started to ask myself questions. Is it true my father doesn't mean me to be a squire? Does he think I am selfish, wanting to weaken his manor? But if I'm not a squire, how can Grace and I ever be betrothed? What if my father does want Serle to marry her?

Nobody was awake. I crept upstairs and missed out the creaking steps. In the half dark I stumbled into my writing-room. It's cold and bare, I know, but it is mine; I can warm it and fill it with my thoughts and feelings; with the pictures and stories in my obsidian.

When I pulled the saffron bundle out of the crevice, it glimmered in the dawn light. I unwrapped it and cradled the stone tight between my right palm and my heart.

I felt it grow warm, and then I looked.

There is a boy and he is alone. Kneeling in front of a huge tombstone in a forest clearing. I can't see who he is, though, because his back is turned to me.

For a long time he remains on his knees.

Then I see what is carved on the tombstone. Just one word. BROTHER.

I can hear hooves, and then two horses gallop into the clearing. One is riderless and the other carries a knight holding a black shield with a yellow star on it. Then a second horseman gallops into the clearing. It is the hooded man!

The knight and the hooded man dismount, and kneel down on either side of the boy. Ringdoves sing their throaty, three-note songs and rusty leaves spin down from the oaks and beech trees.

"What is your name?" the knight asks the boy.

"Arthur."

"That is right," says the knight.

"What does it mean?" asks the boy.

"One thing and many," says the hooded man.

"Each of us must grow into his own name," says the knight.

"What is your name, sir?" Arthur asks the knight.

"Pellinore," says the knight. "And I'm hunting the Yelping Beast."

"The Yelping Beast?"

"It's ten years since I last glimpsed him," Sir Pellinore says with so deep a sigh that his shoulders heave. "He has a head like a snake and a leopard's body, a lion's backside, feet like a hart."

"The strangest beast on middle-earth," says the hooded man.

"And strangest of all is the sound he makes," adds the knight. "He's not so very large, no larger than a pony, but when he yelps he sounds as if there are sixty hounds baying inside him."

"Why are you hunting him?" Arthur asks Sir Pellinore.

"Because he's my quest."

"What is a quest?"

"A long journey, with many adventures, many setbacks, many dangers."

"Where to?"

"Ah!" says the knight. "That's the point. That's what you have to find out. Then you'll grow into your name."

"Each of us needs a quest," says the hooded man, "and a person without one is lost to himself."

"Each of us must have a dream to light our way through this dark world," Sir Pellinore says.

"So, Arthur," says the hooded man in his deep voice, "what will your quest be?"

Then the hooded man and the knight take Arthur by the left arm and the right, and raise him to his feet. They bow to him, and give him the reins of the riderless horse. Then they mount their own horses and ride away, deeper into the forest.

Arthur is alone.

He turns round, very slowly, and I recognize him.

I am Arthur: Arthur-in-the-stone is me.

BROTHER

But how can I be in the stone?

Merlin told me once about magicians who can appear in two places at the same time, but this can't be like that, because Arthur-in-the-stone and I are not really the same person, and I'm not a magician.

When I woke this morning, I was already thinking about Serle. He's so unfair and unkind to me, and I think he would be glad if I fell ill and died. So is that why the one word on that tombstone was brother?

Or was the word because of Luke? He has grown very weak, and none of Johanna's medicines have helped him. He can only mew like a kitten, and I think he will die soon.

The way my stone glistens and fizzes with stars, and the way it looks deeper than the lake under Gibbet Hill! The way it shows and says! It is like a world inside my world.

BETWEEN BREATH
AND BREATH

I sat up with a start.

My father was kneeling beside my bed, holding a candle in each hand.

"Luke is dying," he said quietly. "Will you go and wake Oliver? Ask him to ring the Passing Bell."

I pulled on my drawers and rolled up my leggings.

"You can wear your house-cloak," said my father. "Leave the door unbarred when you come back in, and carry this candle through to our chamber. I'll wake Serle and Sian and Nain."

As I walked down the glebe, each star was sharp as one of the thorns in Christ's crown. I had to bang on Oliver's door seven times before he woke up, and by then I had woken every dog in the village, and some of the goats as well.

When I got back to the house, my mother and father and Nain and Serle and Sian were all kneeling round Luke's cradle, each holding a candle.

Sian stroked Luke's forehead with her right forefinger. "Little one," she said. "Don't die."

"He's not dying hard," said Nain.

My mother gulped, leaned forward, and nuzzled her face into Luke's body.

Nain was right. Luke didn't struggle; he didn't whimper. The pulse of life in him just faded. He reached out and up with both hands and, between breath and breath, he died.

Our candles shone in the darkness; they did not even flicker.

But suddenly my mother jerked and screamed, as if she had been pierced with a spear. She threw herself against my father, and tore at her long black hair.

"Arthur," said my father. "Hide the face of the mirror so it cannot trap him. Over there, on the ledge! And open the hall door. We must clear the way for him."

"My Luke!" keened my mother. "My Luke! My beautiful life!"

My father tried to draw my mother to him, but she tore herself away and banged her head against the ground, and gasped.

"Mother!" said Serle hoarsely. "Please, mother!"

Sian's eyes were quick and bright with tears. "He's not dead for me," she said.

We all stayed with little Luke through the watches of the night, and when dawn broke, my father sent Serle over to Brian's and Macsen's cottages. "Ask them to dig the grave," he said. "They know where."

Then Nain and my mother washed Luke's body. His skin was bluish-white, like milk after the second skimming, and his limbs had become very stiff. I held his cold right hand, and I wanted to squeeze it, but I was afraid I might break it.

My mother and Nain dressed Luke in his new nightshirt and little stockings, and my mother put on his head the cornflower-blue nightcap she bought from the peddler. Then they wrapped him from head to toe in a black winding-sheet. But when the time came to carry him down to the graveyard, my mother wouldn't let him leave the house.

"No!" she wailed. "He's mine! My life! My life!"

"Helen!" said my father, gently and steadily. And then he reached out for Luke, but my mother held him to her all the more tightly, and I don't think my father knew what to do.

Then Serle put his arms right round my mother — round her and Luke — and for a long while he held her without saying anything. Slowly my mother's passion and energy drained away. She sagged, and Serle had to hold her up. Then she began to shake without making a sound, and my father gently took Luke out of her arms.

Brian and Macsen had opened Luke's grave next to the little mounds where we buried Mark last year, and Matthew the year before.

"The Lord shows mercy to the children He takes away from this evil world," Oliver told us. "They are alive but in another place. They are angels."

Again my mother began to shake, and then to sob. She leaned over little Luke as he lay in his winding-sheet, cradled in my father's arms, and her warm tears splashed onto him.

"A child," Oliver said, "is flesh of his parents' flesh. It is natural to feel grief when he is taken away. But it's wrong to mourn as if there's no life after this life. Those who mourn lack faith."

As soon as my father and Oliver had lowered Luke into his little grave, Sian stepped forward and quickly dropped something on top of him.

"What was that?" demanded my father.

"My knucklebones," said Sian.

"Why?"

"He may need them."

My father looked at Oliver and Oliver shrugged his shoulders, but there was nothing they could do about it. You can put things into a grave, but you mustn't steal from the dead — not even a game of knucklebones.

"We brought nothing into this world," said Oliver, looking down his nose at Sian, "and it is certain we can take nothing out. The Lord gave, and the Lord has taken away." Oliver reached down and picked up a handful of earth, and gestured to us to do the same. "We commit Luke's body to the ground," he said, and he cast his handful of earth into the grave. "Earth to earth," cried Oliver, "ashes to ashes, dust to dust: in sure and certain hope of the Resurrection to eternal life. Blessed are the dead which die in the Lord."

Then we all cast our handfuls of earth over Luke, and after that Brian and Macsen filled in the grave with the soft earth. They used their spades as gently as I use this pen.

"Arthur," said my father. "You're our wordsmith. You must choose the words to be carved on Luke's tombstone. That's right, isn't it, Helen?"

My mother inclined her head.

"Will you do that?" my father asked.

I will; I'll do it for Luke. But I don't want my father to think I'm a wordsmith. I'm going to get worse at reading and at all the writing exercises I do for Oliver; and I'm going to get better, much better, at all my Yard-skills.

"Good," I heard my father say. "You find the right words, Arthur; and then I'll ask Will to cut them."

haRes anD anGels

Serle has a toothache and a stinking mouth. One of his molars is rotten, and Johanna says there are worms in it.

Last week, she pasted the tooth with purple periwinkle petals crushed in honey and vinegar, but that didn't help. And then she made Serle swill and swallow a mouthful of his own warm urine, but that didn't help either. The ache is even worse today, and Serle keeps groaning; he thinks the tooth will have to be pulled.

My mother says that when I was a baby and teething, I fretted and yelled so much that she asked Johanna for a medicine, and Johanna told her to boil a hare's brains in a little water, and rub them into my gums. And that is what my mother did.

Serle is right: Witches do turn themselves into hares in the daylight. Hum says they steal milk from our cows, and when she was pregnant, Wat's mother saw one hop into her cottage, and that's why Wat was born with a harelip.

But hares can help us as well, and not only with teething. My aunt Alice swears that the hare's foot she keeps in her pocket eases her stiff elbow and knees and ankles. I want to put all this into my hare-song; and I think Serle will like it then.

Merlin came back to the manor this afternoon. I was standing in the middle of the ford, trying to find the right words for Luke, when he came riding in from the east on Sorry, his old rounsey.

"Aha!" called Merlin. "Arthur of the crossing-places."

"Where have you been?" I shouted.

I told Merlin about Luke at once. I told him everything.

No one listens to me like Merlin. He keeps very still, and looks at me very calmly and warmly. He makes me feel he isn't interested in anyone or anything in the world except me.

But when I repeated what Oliver had told us — his words beside Luke's grave — Merlin frowned.

"Dead babies do not become angels," he said. "That's against the teaching of Holy Church."

"How do you know?" I asked.

"I have been away in Oxford," said Merlin.

"Oxford! Why?"

"Talking to schoolmen."

"Why?"

"Why does one usually talk to schoolmen?"

"I don't know," I faltered.

"Then guess," said Merlin.

"To learn their teaching?" I asked.

"And to teach them learning," said Merlin, half-smiling. "In any case, Oliver is wrong. He's a heretic, and I will tell him so."

"But Luke?" I said.

Merlin gazed at me and his blue eyes were unblinking. "Time and place and flesh and thought and feeling," he said. "All these things are our friends but also our enemies. Luke has escaped them. He is at peace."

"Sian said he's not dead for her," I told Merlin, "and that's what I think too. He's not dead in me, and he never will be."

167

"True," said Merlin, "and that is another kind of life."

"Merlin," I began. "My stone!"

"And that is a third!" said Merlin.

"I've seen myself in it."

"Your reflection."

"No. I've seen myself in its story," I said.

"Have you!" exclaimed Merlin, and he looked rather pleased.

"What does that mean?"

Merlin pushed out his lower lip. "I've told you before," he said. "The stone's not what I say it is; it's what you see in it."

"I was kneeling in front of a tombstone," I said, "and it had just one word carved on it: BROTHER."

"BROTHER," repeated Merlin.

"What did that mean? Did it mean Luke was going to die?"

"Maybe," said Merlin.

"Was it telling me what was going to happen?" I asked. "Or was the word for Serle? Was it because he hates me, and I've lost him as a brother?"

"Don't you remember what I told you about questions?" asked Merlin.

"What?"

"They're like nutshells . . . with their answers inside them. What if your stone is telling you whatever you need to know?"

"I see," I said slowly. "I think I do."

With this, Merlin clapped his hands and looked at the sky, and then he remounted. "Come on, Sorry!" he said.

But Sorry wouldn't even lift one hoof. Merlin clucked

and he neighed; he dug in his heels; he slapped Sorry's rump; but it made no difference.

"Well," said Merlin, "I'm not surprised. It's a long way from Tumber Hill to Oxford; and even farther back again. And clever as they are, those schoolmen do talk a lot of nonsense. How many angels can dance on a pinhead? I ask you!"

"Is that what you talked about?" I cried.

"Yes, and how can you free a human soul trapped in a mirror?" said Merlin.

"But that's important," I said.

"Though there were other matters," Merlin said thoughtfully.

"Tell me," I said.

"Is it the case," asked Merlin, "that the Christian religion hinders a full education?" First he nodded and looked extremely solemn; but then he shook his head and grinned like a naughty child. "Ah yes!" he exclaimed. "I'd still rather talk to a schoolman than anyone else."

"Why?" I asked.

"Because the greatest of all pleasures is insight into truth," Merlin replied. He patted Sorry's neck. "And the slowest of all journeys is aboard this stupid horse."

Then Merlin dismounted again, and at once Sorry set off for home. Merlin cursed, and trudged after him.

I watched them until they were both out of sight; then I paddled out into the ford again and went on looking for the right words in the water.

56

POTS OF TEARS

A gaggle of little children, little children and babies, some of them well-dressed and some of them in rags, came running up a long, straight path, running towards huge iron gates, and I knew they were the gates of heaven.

All the children ran past me, laughing and shouting, all except three, three tiny ones lagging far behind. They couldn't run, all they could do was stagger up the path.

"You three!" I called. "Why can't you run?"

Then I recognized them. They were little Luke, and Matthew, and Mark. Each opened the side of his cloak, and showed me a heavy, brimming metal pot.

"These are our mother's tears," Luke said.

"The tears she wept for us," said Mark.

"They weigh us down," Matthew said.

Then my three brothers turned away and staggered on up the path, and I thought they would never reach the gates of heaven.

This was my dream.

the half=dead king

King Uther's hall.

A knight and a squire are kneeling beside the king's bed, and Uther looks much older than when I last saw him. There are yellow-brown patches under his eyes, and he has shrunk; his skin is too large for his body.

Now King Uther slowly raises both arms, as if he were lifting two flat irons.

"I, Sir Ector, swear my allegiance," says the knight, and he looks like my own father.

"And I, his squire Kay, swear my allegiance," says the squire, and he looks exactly like Serle.

"You're still a squire?" the king asks.

"Yes, sir," says Kay.

"It's time you were knighted," says the king. And then he looks at my father. "And this is your only son?"

Sir Ector and Kay stare at each other.

"There is another," says Sir Ector. "But he is still too young."

"How old?"

"He's only thirteen," says Sir Ector.

"And he hasn't mastered his fighting skills," Kay says.

The king levers himself up on his pillows. "I need every boy in this kingdom," he says. "You know what our Saxon enemies call me, the half-dead king! Yes, and it's Octa and Eosa and their treacherous followers who are killing me, not my old illness. They torture my men and rape my women, they enslave my children; they torch my villages and cornfields. They destroy the whole body of my country."

"You can count on us," Sir Ector says quietly. "Thousands of us."

"And I will lead you myself," replies Uther in a hoarse voice. "I'll have my carpenter build me a litter."

"There's no need, sire," my father protests.

"Nothing comes of nothing," says King Uther. "We must fight. I'd rather die with honor than live in disgrace."

A young girl with hair as black as my own walks up to King Uther. "Father," she says. "It is time."

The king nods, and Sir Ector and Kay stand up and bow.

Before they have left the hall, the old, ill king has already fallen asleep.

+ 58 +
lady alice and
my tailbone

Lady Alice and my cousins Grace and Tom have just gone. For three days and three nights Caldicot Manor has been filled with laughter and activity, and now it seems very quiet.

My only chance of talking to my aunt Alice on her own was after we came back from church this morning. While my father went off to the stables with Grace and Tom to oversee the saddling of the horses, I asked her whether she would like to see my writing-room.

"You want to show it to me," she said, "and so I want to see it."

Because the wind has blown from the north during the past three days, my room was very cold. Not even its rough coat of thatch has managed to keep it warm. When I invited my aunt to sit in my window seat, she drew her orange cloak around her, and then took my right hand between both her small hands. "How are you able to write?" she asked. "Don't your fingers turn blue?"

"Up here, I write with my left hand," I replied.

"And that hand stays warm, does it?" asked Alice, and she laughed and took my left hand.

Although she was only teasing me, I believe Alice was telling the truth. My right hand often feels cold and stiff, but even in the bleak midwinter, my left hand almost never gets cold.

I thought of showing Alice my obsidian, but when Merlin gave it to me, he warned me it would lose its power if I showed it to anyone, or even told anyone about it. But I did show her something else. I hadn't planned to do so, and I'm not quite sure why I did, except that she's the only adult I know whom I can trust with a secret.

"You swear," I said.

"I swear," said Lady Alice. "You've sworn to keep a secret for me, and I swear to keep one for you."

"And it doesn't matter how bad it is?"

My aunt gently shook her head.

"Because I think it's very bad. In fact, I know it is."

"Tell me, Arthur."

I looked at my aunt, the curls of her light brown hair peering out from her wimple, and her wide-apart eyes, hazel and unblinking, and I realized I was almost out of breath.

"I'll show you," I said huskily, and I turned round and pulled up my house-cloak and pulled down my hose and showed Lady Alice my tailbone.

"You poor creature!" said my aunt. "You must rub ointment into it."

Then I told Lady Alice everything I have found out about humans who grow tails, and how they're like rotten apples in the loft that poison all the apples ripening around them; how they have to be rooted out and burned at the stake, or drowned.

"But this is a tailbone," said my aunt. "It's just a tailbone, not a tail." Then gently she pulled up my hose, and pulled down my house-cloak.

"You are sure?" I said.

"It's not unusual," said Lady Alice. "Maybe your mother or your nurse dropped you. Or did you fall wrong? On the ice? Or out of a tree?"

"I did," I exclaimed. "A tree."

"There you are," said my aunt. "And you dislodged your tailbone."

"Then why does it ache when I'm upset or think dark thoughts, and when Old Nick rode past on Hallowe'en?"

"I think I can explain that," said my aunt. "Some parts of our bodies feel things more quickly than others. Because your tailbone has moved, it is very sensitive. It's the first to feel things, and it feels them deeply."

"I thought I was growing a tail," I said.

My aunt smiled. "And what about my secret?" she said. "You haven't told anyone?"

"I swore not to," I said.

"Because there'd be terrible trouble. You know that?"

"Would Sir William . . . I mean . . ."

"Oh yes!" said Lady Alice. "Sir William would be tried and hanged."

"That's dreadful."

"Not only that," said my aunt. "The king would take control of our manor."

"Don't be afraid," I said. "I will never tell anyone."

"You serve me with your secrecy," Lady Alice said.

"I wish I could see you and Grace and Tom more often," I said.

"I know your secret wishes," said my aunt. "To go away into service. To be betrothed. To Grace."

"How do you know?" I exclaimed.

My aunt drew her knees right up and swung her legs down from my window seat.

"Because you haven't talked about them!" she said. "And because you have a mother and a father."

"They've told you?"

Lady Alice shook out her orange cloak. "Be patient!" she said. "What's worth having that isn't worth waiting for?" My aunt smiled at me. "I may see you again before Christmas," she said. "If Sir William comes back in time, the two of us may ride over."

"Why?"

"Because," said my aunt, "your father and mother have invited us."

"But why?" I asked.

"You're worse than Tom," said my aunt. "If I opened you up, I'd find you were full of questions." Then she stepped towards me and kissed my left cheek. "There!" she said. "A flower! *Une fleur de souvenance!*"

"What's that?" I asked.

"You must learn French for me," said my aunt.

So now they have gone. The hall is very quiet, and this writing-room is very cold. But my left hand is warm, and my left cheek is still burning.

GRACE AND TOM

The prettiest thing about Grace is probably her delicate, sloping shoulders, and the funniest is her little snub nose. But what I like about her most are the lights dancing in her blue eyes, and the very quick way she speaks and moves.

When I saw her in May, I promised to take her to the top of Tumber Hill and show her where England ends and Wales begins, and point out where the jumpers came from when they raided us last year, and climb my climbing-tree with her. And that's what we did, although not in the way I expected.

On the first afternoon, Serle and Sian and I climbed Tumber Hill with Grace and Tom and the dogs, but Serle didn't talk much because Johanna had pulled out his rotten tooth early that morning and his mouth was sore. It was damp and cold, so when Sian begged us to play hide-and-seek, we agreed so as to keep warm.

Sian was the first to hide, but it didn't take us long to find her half-hidden under a pile of leaves. I was the last and, while the others hid their faces in their cloaks and counted up to one hundred, I ran through the beeches to the little green glade just over the top of the hill, and quickly climbed my climbing-tree. There were few leaves left on it to hide me, but seekers seldom think of looking above their heads.

"How did you know?" I asked Grace after I'd pulled her up onto my high perch.

"I thought of it at once," Grace panted, "because you promised you'd show me your secret climbing-tree."

While Serle, Tom, and Sian sought us, and the hounds galloped between them, barking, Grace and I talked. She told me how her stepmother, Lady Alice, has begun to teach her French, and I told her how I'm going to get worse at my reading and writing lessons with Oliver in case my father wants me to be a monk or a schoolman, and she told me how Tom is no good at reading anyway, and I told her about Serle's unkindness, though not what he said about my inheriting only a little land, and she told me she often cries because her father is always away or going away, and I told her how I want to go away to serve as a squire, perhaps with Sir William, but I didn't say my father doesn't seem to like this idea.

"I'd never see you anyhow," Grace said dolefully, "because my father is never at home."

"Does your stepmother mind?" I asked Grace.

"She has to do all the lady's work, of course," Grace replied, "and half the lord's work too. She figures the accounts and, this autumn, she managed all the day-work, the ditching and dung-spreading and sedge-cutting and all that. She grows very tired, and that's when she cries."

Grace and I stayed up in my tree, and talked and talked, until it was the blue hour and our limbs were almost as stiff as the tree's branches. Then we shouted and called out for Tom and Sian and Serle, but none of them answered.

It was very quiet in the glade.

"Sometimes," I said, "you can hear the whispering spirits."

"What spirits?" asked Grace.

"The voices of the dead in the trees. That's what Nain says."

"You could cut Luke's name into this bark," said Grace. "Then it will become part of the tree."

"Come on!" I said. "We'd better climb down now."

From the top of the hill, I pointed out Pike Forest, but beyond that there was nothing but grey gloom, rising from the ground and falling from the sky. We couldn't see the violet hills or the shadowy shapes of the Black Mountains.

"Wales isn't there," I said, "but it is there."

"There's a word for that," said Grace, frowning.

"Paradox," I replied. "Something that seems to contradict itself."

Grace smiled. "You're a paradox," she said, and for a moment she took my arm. "Isn't there, but is there," she slowly repeated. "In that case, Wales is a matter of faith."

"Grace," I said.

"What?"

"Will you be betrothed?"

"I don't know," she said. "I think they're talking about it."

"Not Serle?"

"Serle! No! I won't marry Serle," said Grace fiercely.

"Would it be all right?" I asked.

"You and me?"

"Yes."

"I don't know. You're not too old, anyhow."

"I'm thirteen!"

"I know, but my other cousin had to marry a man who

was nearly forty and had a stinking mouth. My mother was twelve when she was betrothed, the same as I am, and Sir William . . ." Grace paused and counted on her fingers. ". . . my father was forty-four." There were daggers in Grace's eyes, and when she tossed her head, her hair sparked and flashed.

"The trouble is . . ." I began.

"What?" asked Grace.

I wanted to tell her what Serle had said — that my father doesn't mean me to be a squire, and that I can't make a good marriage without inheriting my own manor — but I was afraid to. "Come on!" I said. "It's getting dark. We'll be in trouble."

When we got back to the manor, we found Serle and Tom and Sian sitting beside the fire; the hall was very smoky, and they were cross with us for not shouting and calling out earlier, and Serle said we'd wrecked their game.

"No, Serle," said Grace. "We hid for as long as you had light to find us. But you gave up and left us to freeze to death."

While Grace and Tom stayed with us, my father excused my lessons with Oliver. It rained so hard all the next morning that we were unable to go to the Yard, but on the third morning we went out immediately after dinner. Sian wasn't allowed to come with us, though, because first she dribbled into her food, and then she was rude to my mother and said she looked like a bad mushroom.

"In that case, Sian," said my father, "you can stay in for the morning and sew."

Sian howled, and then my mother and my aunt asked my father to excuse her, but it didn't make any difference.

"There's only one way of learning," my father said, "and that's the hard way."

In the Yard, Serle had first choice, and he made us tilt at the quintain, so we all had to troop back to the stables, and I saddled Pip while Serle saddled Gwinam. Tom's horse was lame, so Serle offered to share Gwinam with him.

In the first round, I managed to hit the shield with my lance, but the sandbag swung round so fast that it swiped me on the side of the head, and I fell off my horse. I didn't ride the next two rounds because I was dizzy, so Grace pronounced that I was third and scored no points, and Tom was second and scored one point, although he never hit the shield at all; and Serle, of course, was the winner, so he scored two points.

When it was my turn to choose a Yard-skill, I opened my mouth to say "archery," but instead I said, "I choose swordplay."

"You choose swordplay," repeated Serle.

Tom grinned a slow grin. He knows he and I are on the same side and do things for each other. "Like a brother": That's what I was going to write.

"Are you mad?" demanded Serle.

"Right!" said Tom, and he spat into the palm of his right hand, and drew his short sword from its sheath.

"Wait!" cried Grace. "Put on your jerkins!"

"Our jacks," I said.

"This is swordplay, Arthur," said Serle, and he smiled a twisted smile. "Not wordplay."

First Serle beat me and then Tom beat me, as he always does; but he beat Serle too, by seven hits to four, and once he dashed Serle's buckler right out of his hand.

So after the first two Yard-skills, Serle and Tom had each scored three points but I had scored none.

It was Tom's turn to choose next. He scratched his head, and grinned, and then he licked his right forefinger and held it up against the wind, and then he sniffed the air and shook his head and sighed.

"Come on, Tom," said Grace.

Tom looked at me with his blue eyes, which are even brighter than Grace's because there are no flecks in them. "I choose archery," he said.

"You choose archery," repeated Serle. "You're both mad, then."

"That's really chivalrous, Tom," said Grace.

Tom stared at the ground and scraped it with his right boot.

"That's not chivalry," Serle said. "It's tit for tat."

I let Tom use my new bow and peacock arrows, but I still beat him easily, and he beat Serle. So after the third round, I had two points and Tom was in the lead with four points and Serle had three.

While we were standing at the far end of the butts, Gatty and her little brother Dusty came trudging out of the sites with two dripping sacks slung over their backs. The sacks were so heavy they could scarcely carry them.

"Who says you can take that?" Serle shouted.

Gatty tried to look up at him and staggered sideways.

"Stop!" called Serle. "I'm talking to you."

Gatty dropped her sack and walked up to Serle; there was a smear of manure across her right cheek and neck. Then Dusty dropped his sack and walked up behind Gatty.

"Who says you can take that?"

"Dunno," said Gatty.

"That's our manure. You're stealing it."

Gatty shook her head.

"Did Hum say you could?"

"Yes," said Gatty.

"Why didn't you say so?" demanded Serle. "Go on, then."

Gatty looked at me. I know she was waiting for me to say something, and I didn't. She looked at me again, and when she turned away, I felt my head drawing up all the blood in my body, and my face growing red.

"That's Arthur's friend," Serle explained to Grace and Tom.

Gatty crouched down and gripped the sack of pig manure with both hands, and then swung it round onto her back. My heart banged inside my chest.

"He helps her with fieldwork," Serle said.

"You don't," exclaimed Grace, and she smiled at me and put her hands on her delicate shoulders.

"And yardwork," added Serle.

"Stop it, Serle!" exclaimed Grace. "Stop teasing!"

"Fieldwork and yardwork," Serle said, "against our father's orders."

"It's not true, is it?" Grace asked me, her eyes wide open.

"Why should Gatty and Dusty — Gatty and Dusty and Giles and Dutton and Brian and Macsen and Joan and all the others have to do all the dirty work?" I asked. "Yes! I do help them sometimes."

Tom was frowning. He didn't say anything, but I could see he felt uncomfortable.

"At least I used to," I added.

"But now he's promised not to work in the fields or the sties or stables or anywhere else," said Serle.

"How do you know?" I cried.

"But they're not your duties, Arthur," said Grace. "I don't understand."

"Exactly," said Serle.

"Maybe they are my duties," I said.

"Maybe they are?" Serle repeated. "Only if you want to be a reeve, like Hum. Is that what you want?"

"You don't understand," I mumbled.

"It's you who don't understand," said Serle. "Or you do understand, but choose to disobey."

"Stop arguing," said Tom, and he sounded quite angry.

Serle glared at me and I glared at him.

"Anyhow," said Serle, "you can see what kind of friend Arthur is. He didn't say a word. He didn't defend Gatty. That's what I call a fair-weather friend."

"Come on!" urged Tom. "It's your turn to choose a skill, Grace."

"Well," said Grace. "I was going to choose wordplay . . ."

"That's not a Yard-skill," said Serle.

Tom shook his head dismally.

"Who says the competition is only for Yard-skills?" Grace asked.

"It is," said Serle.

"Who is the judge?" demanded Grace.

No one said anything.

"Who is the judge?" Grace repeated.

"You," said Serle in a quiet voice.

"And I say it's not," said Grace.

"Can't we run at the ring?" asked Tom. "We did that last time."

"What use are Yard-skills without manners?" Grace continued. "Anyhow, it's beginning to rain."

Inside the hall, Sian was sewing with Nain, but as soon as she saw us she jumped up, and Grace hugged her.

"Poor Sian has been in prison all morning," said Grace, "and we must cheer her up." And then Grace asked us to praise Sian in just eight words, one for each year of her life.

"Praise!" I exclaimed. "Can't we insult her?"

"Insults are not mannerly," said Grace. "Sian, you can be the judge with me."

"Sister black," said Serle, "and sister white, with hair like jet and whalebone teeth and keen eyesight."

"That's not eight words," said Grace.

"It will be when I've boiled it," Serle replied.

"What about you, Tom?" asked Grace.

"Erm!" said Tom. "How about, Sian is the daughter of a mushroom?"

"Sian is the daughter of a mushroom," Grace repeated solemnly, and then we all reeled around laughing, even Serle.

"Seven words," I said.

"Easy!" shouted Tom. "Sian is the bad daughter of a mushroom!"

"What about you, Arthur?" asked Grace.

"Hail, nightingale!" I said. "Nimble thimble! Moth-mouth! Climbing rhymer!"

"How do you like that?" Grace asked Sian.

"Best," said Sian.

"So do I," said Grace. "And Serle's second best."

So after the last test, I had scored four points and Serle had four and Tom had four, and only Serle was disappointed.

On our way down to church for Terce this morning, Grace nudged me and said under her breath: "Try to find out."

"What?"

"Betrothal."

"I will," I said, "but my father never tells me anything."

Lights were dancing in Grace's eyes. "We can't often see each other," she said, "but we can still be like Wales to each other."

"What do you mean?"

"A matter of faith," said Grace.

fifth son

We're not only made of clay; we're made of spirit as well.

But after that, what matters most? My name? The name of my family? How I loved my family and they loved me? My concern for other people, all the people living on this manor? Or is it that I'm loyal to the king? English and true?

I keep thinking about the words for little Luke's tombstone, and there's so little to say, but so much to say. I think the words must be short and simple, because that's what Luke's life was. He only lived for ten months.

SON
little luke
FIFTH SON OF
sir john and
lady helen
de caldicot
BORN AND DIED 1199
BROTHER

How does that look? The more words I think of, the more difficult it is to choose.

the goshawk

My stone was the dark of the moon.

But I didn't want to wrap it up and hide it in the crevice. I needed it. And I think it heard my lonely prayers.

I saw myself, Arthur-in-the-stone, wearing a coat of mail and a helmet as though I were a knight, and my charger was wearing a trapper right down to the ground and a green cloth hood; there were slits for his eyes, and his big ears stuck out of them.

At first I thought the forest was Pike, but then through the trees I saw a castle. And as Arthur-in-the-stone approached the drawbridge, two bells rang. One sounded like our own church bell, grave and kind; the other was like a little bird sounding an alarm.

A goshawk rises out of the castle courtyard, trailing its long leash and wearing its bells. It flies to the top of an elm tree, and its leash catches on a branch. The hawk tries to free itself, it flutters up and down and round and knots itself to the tree.

Now a lady steps out of the gatehouse, and onto the bridge across the moat. She's wearing an orange cloak. It is Lady Alice.

"Sir!" she calls. "Have you seen my goshawk?" And she walks across the bridge.

"Up there!" says Arthur-in-the-stone, pointing to the top of the elm.

"I was feeding her on my fist," Lady Alice says, "and her leash slipped my wrist. She's our only hawk and she's trained to take herons. She sleeps in our chamber." Lady Alice looks at me fearfully. "Whoever you are, I beg you to help me."

"I'll try," says Arthur-in-the-stone, "but I'm not much good at climbing trees."

I dismount and tether my horse to the elm. Then I unfasten my helmet and Lady Alice starts to help me. She unfastens my broad waist belt and my two sword-belts and lays my sword on the ground. She unties my coat of mail at the wrists, and helps me pull it over my head.

"My husband has such a foul temper," Lady Alice says. "If I lose our goshawk, I'll be lost too. My husband will kill me."

She stoops and loosens the thongs of my mail-leggings, and then she grasps the hem of my quilted tunic between her small hands.

"Raise your arms," she says, and she pulls the tunic over my head.

Dressed in nothing but my undershirt and breeches, Arthur-in-the-stone seizes the lowest branch and starts to climb the elm. Up! Quickly up from bole to fork, and fork to branch.

The goshawk stares down on me, and I stare up at the goshawk. Nearer and nearer. Then I reach out and grab her! Now I tug and loosen one of the tree's rotten stumps, and tie the goshawk's leash round it, and throw the stump down from the tree. It falls to the ground, and the goshawk flutters down after it.

At once an old knight reels out of the gatehouse, and he strides across the drawbridge to the foot of the elm. It is my uncle, Sir William, and he is holding a naked sword.

"I've been waiting for you!" he shouts. "Come down and die."

"You can't kill a defenseless boy," says Arthur-in-the-stone.

Sir William gives a dry laugh. "You won't be the first," he says.

"Let me have my sword," I shout. "Hang it on the bottom branch."

"Come down, you coward!" roars Sir William.

I'm standing on a leafless branch. It's dead. Quite dead. First I lower myself onto the branch below me . . . I tug and wrench at the dead branch and suddenly it breaks.

At once I climb down the tree, carrying the dead branch in my left hand.

The rims of Sir William's eyes are red; his eyebrows are white and tangled. But he's seasoned and still very strong. Arthur-in-the-stone grips the dead branch with both hands, shouts, and leaps out of the tree.

Sir William roars. He raises his sword and slashes at me. But I can fend off the blade with the elm branch, and as Sir William rocks back, I use all the strength in my forearms and upper arms to swing the branch after him.

The branch whacks Sir William on the side of his head. It knocks him down, and I launch myself at him and pinion his wrist. I squeeze it and grab his sword as his grasp loosens. Then, as he reaches out and half-rises, I swing the shining sword and cut off Sir William's head.

Lady Alice shrieks. "My husband," she cries. "Why have you killed him?"

"His own treachery killed him," says Arthur-in-the-stone.

"And it has wounded me," says Lady Alice in a low voice.

Two bells ring inside the castle: one safe, one nervous.

I know Sir William's men may come out of the gate-house at any moment. I roll up my hose and pull my quilted tunic over my head. My coat of mail. My helmet. Silently, Lady Alice looks at me, then she lies down beside her husband's body, and her orange cloak covers them both, like the wing of a phoenix. Her goshawk waits beside her, glaring angrily at me.

Arthur-in-the-stone untethers and mounts his horse and, as he rides away, deep into the forest of his life, all the pictures and sounds draw back into my stone again.

Once more, my obsidian was the dark of the moon.

What did it all mean? Why did Sir William want to kill me? And was Lady Alice in danger because of her husband's terrible temper?

Merlin says our questions have their answers inside them. So what is it I need to know?

thin ice

Sian's a wildcat, and sometimes it gets her into trouble.

At dinner, my mother asked her to help make soap, because Dutton slaughtered three sheep yesterday.

"Dutton's mutton," said Sian.

"And then we must scent it with rosemary and lavender," said my mother. "And after that, it's high time Tanwen washed your hair. It hasn't been washed all this month."

Sian just grinned at my mother but, as soon as we were allowed to stand up, she skipped across the hall and swung open the door.

"Come back!" called my father, but Sian ignored him. Serle and I looked at each other; neither he nor I would be able to get away with disobedience like that.

"The little . . ." began my father.

"She hasn't even got her cloak on," my mother said. "Please, Arthur. Go out and get her."

"I'll drag her in," I said.

"And you put on your cloak," said my mother.

"Your mother's right," said my father. "It's freezing again this morning."

Outside, I called for Sian several times, but she didn't reply. She wasn't on the bridge and she wasn't in the Yard, climbing the ladder, so I went to look for her in the stables.

She wasn't there either, but Gatty was. She was helping

Jankin muck out the stables, but when she saw me she lowered her eyes, and drove her twig-broom into the sludge so that it flew up and spattered the stable wall.

"Mind that," said Jankin. "Or Hum'll have me cleaning the walls as well."

Gatty said nothing, and I knew it was because I had upset her. I should have stood up for her when Serle bullied her in the yard. Then I thought how pretty she looked — the wild curls of her fair hair and her pink cheeks spotted with freckles and speckled with manure.

"He can clean it hisself," said Gatty, and she splashed the manure a second time.

"Seen Sian?" I asked.

"No," said Jankin.

"The little wildcat," I said. "I can't find her."

I ran round the back of the house then. Sian wasn't in the sheepfold, and she wasn't in the copse; she wasn't in the herb garden.

This was when I heard a loud crack, and then a scream from the fishpond.

"Sian," I yelled, and I raced round the hedge and over to the pond. Sian had gone through the ice, at least ten steps out. She was in the water up to her shoulders, clutching onto the jagged edge of the ice-sheet with her white fingers.

"Arthur!" she screamed.

"Keep still!" I shouted. "Don't try to move."

"Help!" screamed Sian.

"I'm coming," I called.

At the edge of the pond, I lay down on the ice and began to pull and slide my way across. I looked down, down through the thin ice into the drowning darkness, and saw the darker shapes of gliding carp and trout, and when I looked up again, Gatty was there! She was running round to the other side. Then she, too, bellied onto the ice, and silently began to swim out across it.

Again and again Sian screamed.

Gatty reached her first and grabbed Sian's arm.

"Quiet!" she said fiercely.

When I tried to get hold of Sian's other arm, some of the ice around the hole broke away; then it cracked under me, and I let go of Sian and slid back.

Sian began to scream again.

When I reached out for the second time, I could hear the ice groan and feel it bending.

"Go on!" said Gatty. "Lift, Sian!"

Sian grabbed Gatty's shoulder, and then my hair. She strained, she moaned, and then all at once she slid out onto her stomach, dripping and mucky and wailing, as if she'd somehow given birth to herself. She'd risen from the darkness into the light, and Gatty and I were the mid-wives, pulling her up onto the bending ice.

Then Gatty spread herself out on the ice again, and we began to pull Sian back to the nearest bank.

"How did you know?" I asked Gatty.

"Worked it out, didn't I," Gatty panted.

"She would have drowned," I said.

Then Gatty put her left arm around Sian's shoulders, and I put my right arm round Sian's waist, and together we half-walked, half-hauled her back to the door of the house.

My mother couldn't have heard us, but she knew we were coming, and met us at the door.

"She went through the ice," I said.

"Bring her in!" said my mother.

"Gatty saved her."

"Quickly!" said my mother. "Come in, Gatty."

"'s all right," said Gatty, and she pulled her arm away from Sian's shoulder.

"Sian!" said my mother angrily. "You little wildcat!"

"Gatty saved her," I said again.

Gatty's curls were sprinkled with silver and her lower lip was bleeding; her river eyes were flooded with tears.

ᴅevil's вerries

King Uther said his Saxon enemies call him the "half-dead" king. He beat them in battle, though, and their leaders Octa and Eosa were killed. In my stone, I saw four of the Saxon survivors sitting around a fire in a forest clearing.

One man stands up, and I can see his left arm has been hacked off at the elbow joint. "Good riddance!" he growls.

"Damn them!" says a second man, who has a scar right across his forehead.

"And what if they had won?" a third man demands. "They couldn't stand each other."

"Octa would have slit Eosa's throat."

"Or Eosa would have stuck a knife into Octa."

"*Nil de mortuis* . . ." sneers the scarred man.

"The same to you," says the one-armed man.

"Don't dump on dead men. That's what that means," the scarred man says.

"So what now?" asks the third man. "That's the question."

Beside the fire there's a heap of sacking. Now it begins to shake, and then to growl, and a fourth man sits up. A large gold brooch is pinned to his chest. "Uther won't last," he says. "Not for long."

"How come, Walter?" asks the third man.

"He won the battle, didn't he?" says the scarred man.

"The battle, not the war," says Walter, the fourth man.

"Uther's old and ill. He's weak in body, and weakness sows dragon's teeth."

"What's that?" asks the one-armed man.

"Plant one enemy and one hundred spring up," Walter says. "Uther's had it, one way or the other."

"It's not as if he's got a son," says the third man.

"Only that girl."

"What's her name?"

"Anna."

The scarred man fingers his scar and the one-armed man yawns. A little stick in the fire blossoms — brilliant orange petals. Then it fades again.

"His followers are all at each other's throats," says the second man. "Each of them has his eye on the crown."

"So we'll help them, shall we?" says Walter, grinning.

"What do you mean?" asks the third man.

Walter feels around in the sacking and pulls out a leather bottle, and takes a swig from it. "Ugh!" he says. "Gut rot!" He narrows his eyes at his three companions. "Have seven of our men disguise themselves as beggars . . ."

"That won't take much."

" . . . and follow Uther back to St. Albans, and nose around until they find the king's well."

"Got you!" says the scarred man.

"And crush one hundred devil's berries, and drop them into the water," Walter says.

"Very good, Walter," exclaims the scarred man, and he claps his hands. "That'll help King Uther from this world into the next. And some of his knights with him."

64

ROT AND BAD BLOOD

"Go on, then," barked Johanna, and her whiskers twitched. "Pull down your breeches."

So I turned round and pulled down my breeches.

"Bend over," said Johanna.

I felt Johanna's hot breath on the small of my back as she glared at my tailbone. "It's a mess," she said. "A mess! You understand!"

"Yes," I said meekly.

"You don't," said Johanna. And then the old woman planted her thumbs on either side of my tailbone. "A mess!" she shouted, and suddenly she tore my skin apart as hard as she could.

I yelled, and jerked up, and my eyes filled with tears.

"Devil's part!" exclaimed Johanna. "Cuckoo's beak! What next? There's not even a stump."

"That hurt," I cried.

"Your wound needed breaking," said Johanna. "It's full of rot. It's just a tailbone and it'll never heal until you get out all the bad blood. You understand?"

"Yes," I said, rather shakily.

"Leave the wound open until you wake tomorrow. Then ask Lady Helen to boil horsemint and strong vinegar with honey and barleymeal. Boil them dry, and rub the mixture into your wound."

Johanna's recipes didn't help Luke, and I don't think they'll help me either. All the same, I'm glad I showed her my tailbone because even after what my aunt told me, I still thought it might be growing. For a long time, it has been my second sorrow, the sorrow of my body.

When I got back to the manor, Sian was crouching beside the fire and sobbing, because my father had just beaten her for her disobedience yesterday.

"And the ice has got into her blood," my mother said. "She's sniffing and snuffling like a piglet, and the next thing is she'll catch a fever."

the art of forgetting

"No, Oliver," I protested. "I can't remember."

"Can't," said Oliver. "There's no such word."

"There is," I said, "and I can't. I know you told me what Sheba's father was called . . ."

"I didn't tell you," said Oliver. "The Book of Samuel did."

"All right!" I said. "The Book of Samuel."

"Several times," said Oliver.

"But I can't remember," I said.

Oliver crossed his pudgy arms and sighed. He's quite easy to trick and I think he believed me.

"Anyhow," I added. "What does it matter?"

"I see," said Oliver. "The names of our fathers don't matter."

"Of course they do," I said, raising my voice a little.

"What's wrong with you today?" demanded Oliver. "Can you even remember the name of your own father?"

"You always think I know more than I know," I complained. "I can't remember everything."

"You've never forgotten a name before," said Oliver, frowning.

"My head's full up with names," I said. "I can't fit any more in."

"Shall I tell you what our brains are like?" asked Oliver, and for a while he looked up at the vestry roof. But instead of receiving divine guidance, Oliver was hit on the forehead by a little piece of plaster. I laughed, and Oliver stood up, and rubbed his eyes and dusted his shoulders, and sat down again. Then our lesson continued.

"Our brains," said Oliver, "are like pigs' bladders. The more we fill them, the larger they grow."

"In that case," I said, "some of us would have much bigger heads than others."

"You know what I mean," said Oliver. "Brains are like . . . wombs."

"Or like climbing Tumber Hill," I said. "The higher I climb, the more I can see."

"You could say that," said Oliver. "But why were we talking about brains? Can you remember?"

I pretended not to remember.

"Bichri!" said Oliver triumphantly, waving both hands in the air. "Sheba was the son of Bichri."

hot and important

Up here in my writing-room, I sometimes hear squeaking through the storeroom wall: impatient mice attacking the barrels of wheat and barley. But after Terce this morning I heard something else.

Instead of going straight to my lesson with Oliver, I came up here, and after a while I heard two voices. A man and a woman. They were speaking very quietly so I couldn't hear what they were saying, but I know she kept telling him something, the same thing, and then asking something hot and important. She was begging him.

Then I heard the storeroom door groan. Like thin ice. Quickly I stood up, and when I peered through my broken door panel, I was just in time to see Serle and Tanwen standing in the gallery, and they were in each other's arms.

the Gates of paradise

"This is not the best way to die," says King Uther. He is lying on his bed, in the middle of his hall. His face is blotched, and his hands are joined over his stomach.

"Is there a best way?" the hooded man asks.

"Some ways are worse than others," Uther replies. "To die at a time chosen by your enemies." The king clutches his stomach. Then, feebly, he coughs. "To die in pain," he says. "I am cold and burning."

"Your enemies," says the king's priest, "will be pitched into hell for poisoning you. But you die in peace. You have made your confession; you've received the last rites. The gates of paradise are opening for you."

Ygerna is there; Anna is there. They sit on either side of the king and gently stroke his shoulders and forearms.

And I can see Sir Ector and Kay as well. After a while, King Uther turns his head towards them.

"Where is your second son?" asks the king.

"He's learning," says Sir Ector.

"I need every boy and man in this kingdom," the king says.

"We'll avenge you, sire," says Kay. "We'll drive the Saxons back into the sea."

"What's his name?" asks the king.

"Arthur," says Sir Ector.

"I had a son," King Uther says dreamily.

"He is delirious," the priest says. "A daughter, sire. You have a daughter."

Uther rises to the surface. "I had a son," he says again, and he sounds as if he is talking of another world, or another time, very long ago.

Then Ygerna shudders and begins to sob, and the priest asks the hooded man something, and the hooded man nods, and Sir Ector and Kay stand up and start whispering to the knights and squires nearest to them, and before long the whole hall is a sea of whispers.

King Uther opens his blurred eyes, and the sea slowly subsides, it becomes calm again. "I was dreaming a dream," he says.

"A dream?" asks the hooded man.

King Uther almost smiles. "I will have a son," he says.

"Sire," says the hooded man in his deep voice. "Remember!"

Then King Uther turns to look at Ygerna, and she looks at him, and she is as she was. Her eyes are violet. Her shoulders and arms are rounded and pale and slender, like stripped willow, curving.

"Sire," asks the hooded man, "who will be king when you die?"

"Many men here would be king," says King Uther, "but I have a son who was and will be."

"Do you hear that?" the hooded man calls out, and there is complete silence in the hall.

"You promised me," Uther says to the hooded man.

"I will help him as I have helped you," the hooded man replies, looking into Uther's eyes, "and three kings of Britain before you. I will come for him when his time comes."

Uther tries to sit up. "I give my son God's blessing," he cries out in a loud voice. "I give him my blessing. Let him claim my crown."

"What is his name?" one earl calls out.

"Where is he, then?"

"Who is his mother?"

And then the sea swells again.

King Uther raises both his arms. Wild and unseeing, he looks around the room, and then he reaches out towards Ygerna. He shudders, his teeth chatter. Then he falls back onto his pillow and lies still.

In the silent hall, the priest leans over King Uther's body. With his right forefinger he closes the king's eyes.

+ 68 +
WORDS FOR LUKE

I went to sleep last night wondering whether King Uther's son will claim the crown, and how the hooded man will be able to help him if all the jealous earls and lords are against him.

And this morning I woke up with new words for Luke's tombstone already waiting in my head. All I had to do was arrange them in the right order, and sharpen my quill, and write them down:

> Call him son. Call him brother.
> Fifth son of his loving mother,
> Born with bubbles in his blood.
> Call him bone, and tombstone name.
> But if you read this, call him home.
> Call Little Luke a son in God.

"It's very fine, Arthur," my father said. "Say it again."
So I did.

"This song should be at the bottom of the tombstone," I said, "and at the top, the words should say: LITTLE LUKE, son of Sir John and Lady Helen de Caldicot. Born and died 1199."

"I'll ask Will to carve them," said my father. "He'll need your help."

"Father," I said. "Have you heard of King Uther?"

"No."

"Have you, mother?"

"No."

"Who is he?" my father asked.

"I don't know exactly. I thought you might."

"You didn't make him up?" my mother asked me.

"No," I said. "I don't think so."

"By the way, Arthur," said my father, "your mother tells me that Gatty saved Sian."

"She did. She risked her life."

"What about you?"

"I couldn't have done it without her."

"I see," said my father. "Well, I suppose we should be grateful."

"Really, John!" my mother exclaimed.

despair

Ygerna and the hooded man were waiting for me in my stone; they were standing beneath a lime tree.

"Half his earls and lords want to wear his crown," Ygerna says.

"Of course they do," the hooded man replies. "They're men, aren't they?"

Ygerna shakes her head unhappily.

"So how can a boy of thirteen claim the crown?" asks the hooded man. "That's what you're thinking."

"Yes."

"And how can I help him?"

"Yes."

"You live in this world but you cannot see it clearly," the hooded man says. "You can see no more of it than you see of me. But I can see what you cannot see."

"I don't even know his name," Ygerna wails. "Who are his foster parents? Where does he live?"

"Where England ends and Wales begins," the hooded man replies. "He is your son of the crossing-places."

That's strange. That's what Merlin called me — that day when we met at the mill ford: Arthur of the crossing-places.

"You doubt me, Ygerna," says the hooded man. And then he raises his voice. "When Vortigern wanted to build a castle, it was I who told him to drain the pool under its foundations, and then he saw them with his own eyes: the red dragon and the white dragon, fighting to the death. It was I who spirited the Giants' Ring from Ireland to England, after a whole army of Britons were unable to move it, for all their ropes and hawsers and scaling ladders. It was I who brought Uther to you, and you thought he was your own husband."

"I know!" cried Ygerna. "And maybe it was you who killed Gorlois."

"No," says the hooded man in a cold voice. "I did not do that. I give; I do not take away."

"Giving to one person," Ygerna replies, "sometimes means taking away from another."

"Everything has its own time," says the hooded man. "No sooner does this lime tree drop its leaves than it begins to dream of the spring. Be patient, Ygerna. Your son who was will be."

"My head hears you," Ygerna replies, "but my heart does not. I wish your words comforted me."

"Doubt is like rust which corrodes metal," the hooded man says. "It travels from your brain into your body, and eats you away."

"I haven't seen him since the day he was born," says Ygerna. "He is my son, and I know nothing about him."

"Nothing comes of doubt," says the hooded man, "except inaction and more doubt."

Ygerna grasps the hooded man's right wrist.

"Will you not understand?" she says in a low voice. "I have lost a husband, and I do not have a son."

70

The MANOR COURT

I will never be able to sleep tonight.

I'll sit up here, wrapped in this skin. All night. This candle burning.

I'll write words. They can't change anything but with them I can say my thoughts; I can understand. They're better than fury, aren't they?

But if only words could help Lankin.

Down there in the dark.

If only they could help him, and Jankin and Gatty too. If only Jankin's mother hadn't died in childbirth last winter, and her baby with her . . .

Let me begin again.

Today was the first day of December, the day of the manor court — and it was the worst day of the year. The worst for Jankin's father, and the worst for our manor. How will Jankin and his sister survive the wolf of winter now? And how will Jankin be able to marry Gatty? Hum will never agree to it. How could Hum and Wat Harelip and Howell and Ruth and Slim have sworn those oaths when they knew they were not true? How can there ever be peace in our manor again . . .

Words! Words! My fears keep going round and round. Let me begin again.

Today was the day of the first manor court since my

thirteenth birthday, and everyone living in this manor has to attend as soon as they're thirteen.

Lord Stephen rode in last night because he always presides over the court, and he brought with him his scribe Miles and two servants.

Lord Stephen greeted us all very warmly, and especially Serle. Serle says that he liked serving Lord Stephen as a squire, because Lord Stephen talked to him like a man, and often praised him.

"Other people won't always like what you do," Lord Stephen said. "They don't always like what I do. So we need to be sure of ourselves."

I shouldn't think Lord Stephen likes looking in a mirror, though. I'm taller than he is, and he's a whole head shorter than my father. His eyesight is bad too. He says he can count the leaves on a tree a mile away, but when he's looking at someone or something close to him, he keeps blinking and screwing up his eyes and drawing away. Lord Stephen is quite stout too — in fact, he looks rather like a speckled egg. But he has a very merry smile, and a definite way of speaking that makes people listen to him.

"He's a fox," my father told me once. "He pretends to be less clever than he is."

Very early this morning, the whole household went to church, and then Oliver and Merlin came back to breakfast with us. Hum and Gatty arrived before we'd finished, although Gatty's not allowed to vote because she's only twelve. And by the time the table had been cleared, and Lord Stephen had ensconced himself in the middle, with my father on his right and Hum on his left and his scribe sitting opposite him, there were as many people in the hall as risked the Black Sow and came guising on Hallowe'en.

My father told me then that sixty people live in his manor, but little Luke has died since then. So that's fifty-nine, and of them, fifteen are under age and seven cannot walk.

"Where's Cleg?" my father asked Hum.

"Not here, sir."

"I can see that. Well, where is he?"

"The miller's away, sir."

"And Martha. Where's she?"

"She's away too, sir."

"Where?"

"They must speak for themselves," said Hum.

"They can't if they're not here," my father said.

"A fine of twopence each," said Lord Stephen, "unless they can show good reason."

"Cleg the miller can always show good reason," my father remarked drily, and there was a murmur of agreement in the hall. "He thinks that rules are like his weights and measures: made to be cheated."

"Next!" said Lord Stephen.

Next was the collection of egg-fees from each household that runs hens, and of course all of them do; and then came the collection of a betrothal fee from Ruth's and Howell's fathers.

"When will you marry?" Lord Stephen asked Ruth.

"April, sir," said Ruth.

"No," said Howell in a loud voice. "March!"

That made everyone laugh.

"A good start!" said Lord Stephen, smiling. "Next!"

Once Hum had passed all the fees across the table to Lord Stephen's scribe, the court tried several charges brought by my father against villagers who had broken the king's laws. Brian and Macsen were charged with snaring pheasant and partridge in Pike Forest, and Joan was charged with taking too much deadwood, and Giles was charged with cutting wood from a living tree.

None of them denied the charges, but when she was fined, Joan asked Lord Stephen: "Who are your parents, sir?"

"My parents!" exclaimed Lord Stephen.

"Your first ones," said Joan.

"Joan," said my father, "Lord Stephen asks the questions."

"Let her speak," said Lord Stephen. "Adam and Eve. They were my first parents."

"Yes," said Joan, "and they're mine too."

"So?" asked Lord Stephen.

"I'm poor and you're rich. Why's that, when we got the same parents? Why are you sitting high and mighty over me?"

"Joan!" said my father sternly.

"You and Sir John there and Lady Helen, you got more than enough to eat. I got nothing. I can't even pick up deadwood and I get fined for it."

"Pike Forest belongs to the king, Joan," said Lord Stephen. "His laws may be gentle or they may be harsh, that's not for me to judge. But you and I have no choice: We have to obey them."

"Adam and Eve," screeched Joan.

"One penny," said Lord Stephen. "Next!"

"Who judges the king, then?" Joan asked.

"God judges the king," Lord Stephen replied. "He judges us all."

"You wouldn't live so rich except for us," said Joan.

Lord Stephen sighed. "Stand down!" he ordered Joan.

To begin with, the mood in the hall had been quite good-humored. But Joan's outburst was like the first dark cloud sailing ahead of a storm and, after it, everyone grew quieter, more watchful, and more resentful.

When he tried Macsen, Lord Stephen asked him how to snare a pheasant, and Macsen offered to take him out into Pike there and then and show him how, but even that didn't lift our spirits for long.

"I'm fining you one clipped penny," Lord Stephen said. "I suppose you'll do it again, Macsen."

"I suppose I will, sir," said Macsen.

When Lord Stephen had finished with the offenses against the king's laws, he heard a plea from my father against Joan for letting her cow stray into my father's meadow.

"A second charge, Joan," said Lord Stephen. "This is a bad morning for you."

"Every morning's bad," said Joan.

"Well, what have you to say?"

"Nothing," said Joan, and she glared at my father.

"That's something," said Lord Stephen.

"If I can't feed my cow, she won't milk, and if she don't milk, we can't drink."

"I see," said Lord Stephen, and then he turned and whispered to my father. "Right, Joan," he said crisply. "One day's extra work on Sir John's land before Christmas and another before Easter. Next!"

"Bah!" said Joan, and Lord Stephen's two servants led her back to her place in the hall.

So what would happen if my father ignored Joan's cow eating his hay? Would everyone think they could do the same? Would Dutton let his pig trespass on my father's meadow, and would Cleg the miller try to move some of the land markers, and would Eanbald complain he couldn't afford to pay his tax? I suppose they would. And then law and order in our manor would soon break down.

But Joan's right. My father's quite rich. We're all dressed in linen and there are barrels of corn in our storeroom, and our barn is filled with hay.

So isn't there some way in which my father could help everyone living here, in his care, so that no one will starve this winter? And no one will freeze because there's not enough wood to put on the fire? My father is not unkind.

"Next!" said Lord Stephen.

My father looked at Hum and Hum, slowly, looked up at my father. "Lankin," he mumbled.

"Lankin," repeated Lord Stephen. "Come forward!"

If Lankin stood up straight, he'd be a tall man; but he stoops and shambles along on flat feet. His black hair is short and ragged, as though it has been nibbled by a rat, and he has small dark eyes. When he smiles, his mouth is tight and twisted.

Jankin isn't the same as his father at all. He's always hopeful and laughing, and everyone likes him. But no one likes Lankin much, and a number of people hate him because they say he pilfers their firewood and turf during the night, and steals their bracken to bed his cow, and things like that. They can't prove it, though.

Martha, the miller's daughter, says that Lankin's a peeper. She told me that when he was doing day-work at the mill, Lankin looked through the keyhole into her room, and then came in and tried to fondle her breasts.

But I don't know whether she was telling the truth. And if she was, why didn't she tell her father Cleg, and why didn't he bring a charge against Lankin?

Once, Lankin got into really serious trouble. He swung his right fist, and hit Hum on the side of his jaw. That's something a lot of the villagers would like to do but, all the same, they didn't speak up for Lankin when Hum brought a charge against him. Lord Stephen ordered him to be lashed twenty times with a knotted rope. That was the winter before last, and Lankin nearly died.

Lord Stephen blinked and looked at Lankin. "What is the charge?" he asked.

The charge was brought by Slim. He said Lankin had entered the manor kitchen, and stolen a leg of mutton.

"You hear the charge?" Lord Stephen asked Lankin.

"Never!" said Lankin. "And he knows it." Then he narrowed his eyes at Slim. "I was down at the mill. All day I was, doing my day-work."

"Who will swear oaths?" asked Lord Stephen.

Ruth and Wat Harelip and Howell immediately stood up.

"I was coming out of the church," said Wat, "and he was going down the headland, carrying the leg inside his jerkin. I swear it."

"He's got light fingers," said Howell. "Everyone knows that."

"What do you swear, Howell?" Lord Stephen asked.

"My dog turned the mutton up, didn't he? Down the headland. I swear it."

"And you, Ruth?" asked Lord Stephen.

"Lankin stinks," she said.

"So?"

"The kitchen smelt of him."

"You smelt Lankin?"

"In the kitchen, when I came back," said Ruth.

"You swear that?"

"I swear it."

"Anyhow," said Slim. "I never heard of a sheep with three legs. When me and Ruth went out into the hall, there was four legs, and when we came back there was three."

"You swear that?" asked Lord Stephen.

"I swear it," said Slim.

"I see," said Lord Stephen slowly.

"What about you, Hum?" my father asked.

Hum shrugged.

"Well?"

Hum took in a deep breath and then shook his head.

"Spit it out, man!" said my father. "You're my reeve."

"The truth is," said Hum, "I saw Lankin going into the kitchen . . ."

"That's a lie!" Lankin yelled. "I'll smash your face in."

"Go on, Hum," said Lord Stephen in a level voice.

" . . . and I didn't think twice about it, did I? What with all the coming and going around the manor each day."

"You saw Lankin going into the kitchen?" said Lord Stephen.

Hum pursed his lips and nodded.

"Swear it," said Lord Stephen.

"I did," said Hum. "I was on my way to the hay barn."

"Swear it, then," repeated Lord Stephen.

"Yes, well then!" said Hum. "I do. I swear it."

Everyone in the hall caught their breath, and then there was silence.

"You filthy liar!" said Lankin in a cold, flat voice.

"Five doomsmen in this hall swear against Lankin," Lord Stephen said. "Now who will swear for him?"

No one moved. I looked round the hall and all I could see were pairs of eyes.

"I was down at the mill," said Lankin. "All day I was. Ask Cleg."

"He's not here," said my father.

"He knows I was," said Lankin. "You ask Martha."

"She's not here either," said my father.

Lankin rounded on Hum. "You kept them away," he said, and his voice was rising. "That's what you done."

Hum shook his head.

"I know you. You've set me up."

"No, Lankin," said Hum.

"Where are they, then? You tell me that."

"That's enough, Lankin," said Lord Stephen.

Lankin looked at Hum. "You scum!" he said.

Lord Stephen quietly raised his right hand. "Dooms-men," he began, in that meaningful voice that makes everyone listen to him. "Slim brings the charge but Lankin denies it. As you've heard, five oath-swearers swear against Lankin but no oath-swearers swear for him." Lord Stephen looked around the hall. "Each of you has one vote. Cast it wisely. Cast it before God. Stand up now if you vote that Lankin's guilty."

I didn't dare look, but I looked: More than half the villagers had got to their feet, and while Miles the scribe counted them, they began to whisper.

"Quiet!" called Lord Stephen. "Sit down! All of you. Now then, who votes for Lankin? Stand up if you vote he's innocent."

"What if we're not sure?" I heard myself asking.

"You stand up," said Lord Stephen. "A man is innocent until he's proven guilty."

I stood up. Jankin stood up. Then my mother stood up. Then Dutton slowly got to his feet, and glared at Giles, and Giles stood up as well.

"Is that all?" asked Lord Stephen. He looked at his scribe and raised his eyebrows.

"Seventeen, sir," said the scribe. "Seventeen guilty and five innocent. The others have not voted."

Lord Stephen stared at Lankin, and then he turned and talked very quietly to my father. I couldn't hear what they were saying.

Lord Stephen turned to face Lankin. "Theft," he said in a voice loud enough for everyone to hear, "is a very serious offense. It is punishable by hanging." He blinked and screwed up his eyes. "But Sir John has asked me to reduce your punishment, as he's entitled to do — because he's your lord, and the mutton was his. Lankin, the court finds you guilty of theft, and I therefore sentence you to lose your thieving right hand. Let it be cut off at the wrist."

Lankin said nothing. No one in the hall said a word.

"Take him out," said my father.

Then Lord Stephen's two servants stood up and gripped Lankin under his shoulders and walked him out of the hall. My father followed him, but he didn't look at me.

"This court is suspended," said Lord Stephen, "until the first day of June in the year of our Lord 1200."

At once there was commotion in the hall, and a gang of villagers hurried to the door, all of them eager to witness my father draw his sword.

Then my mother stood up. She slowly walked over to Lord Stephen, and led him and his scribe away into the chamber.

So Gatty and Jankin and I were left in the hall. The three of us huddled together; we put our arms around each other. Jankin was shaking.

Then suddenly Jankin tore himself away. He ran out of the hall, shouting.

Half this night has gone. Slowly it has burned away. Maybe Lankin did steal the mutton; but even if he did, what Slim and Howell and Ruth and Wat Harelip have done, and what Hum has done, is much worse. They've chopped our village into two; they've wrecked Gatty and Jankin's betrothal.

How can they sleep? How can my father sleep? I can still hear Lankin screaming.

butterflies

"You?" exclaims Sir Lamorak, the one with the blue shield with white waves running across it.

"You the judge?" scoffs Sir Owain, the one with the gold shield with a scarlet lion on it. "You think you can judge us?"

"I can," says Arthur-in-the-stone.

"You're no judge," Sir Owain says. "It's for you to learn from us. What's your name?"

"Arthur."

"Arthur! What does that mean?"

"I don't know."

"He doesn't know," says Sir Owain.

"But I'm thirteen," I say, "and on a quest. Like Sir Pellinore."

"Never heard of him," says Sir Owain.

"What quest?" asks Sir Lamorak.

"I don't know. I have to find out."

"You don't know much," says Sir Owain.

"I know the difference between right and wrong," I say.

"Right and wrong are seldom black and white," says Sir Owain.

"Or blue and gold," says Sir Lamorak, and they both start to laugh.

"Each contains the other," says Sir Owain. "What seems right is often also partly wrong."

"And vice versa," adds Sir Lamorak.

"And if you judge us, Arthur," Sir Owain asks, "who will judge you?"

"God," I say. "God judges us all."

"But who will believe us?" asks Sir Owain. "Who do you expect to believe us when we say we were judged by a boy?"

I look at both knights and press my back against the tree. "Close your right hands," I say.

Sir Lamorak and Sir Owain glance at each other, then slowly close their hands.

"Now open them," I say.

The moment they do so, two butterflies fly out — a blue one from Sir Lamorak's hand and a gold one from Sir Owain's hand. Openmouthed, they watch them as they flicker across the glade.

"If anyone doubts you," I say, "or even if you want to see a bright butterfly on a dark day, do as you've just done."

The two knights each get down on one knee in front of me.

"I swear it," says Sir Lamorak.

"I swear it," says Sir Owain.

The picture in my obsidian blurs, it fades. But now I know that Arthur-in-the-stone can do magic. Did he learn it from the hooded man? Or was he born with magical powers?

72

MERLIN AND THE
ARCHBISHOP

Since Lankin's trial the day before yesterday, everyone in
the household has been ill at ease with each other. I still
feel half-angry with my father, and I'm going to ask him
whether he agrees with the things Joan said. I wish I could
talk to Gatty, but Hum is keeping a close watch on her.
Slim and Ruth serve in the hall, of course, but both of
them have avoided my eye.

So unless it's mealtime, or I'm practicing my Yard-
skills or studying with Oliver, I climb up here to my room,
and this is where I'll stay until my teeth chatter. The
words I write comfort me; my stone is my companion.

I wonder whether Merlin knows any magic? He might.
After all, he gave me my seeing stone, and I think he disappeared when we were on top of Tumber Hill, and he
knows about names and numbers and the nine spirits, and
Oliver said some people think his father was an incubus.
The trouble is that Merlin never says yes or no. He closes
his eyes and then he tries to find out the question behind
my question.

Of course I know a boy can't judge two knights, but all
the same Sir Lamorak and Sir Owain were loudmouthed
and mean-minded. They were only interested in themselves. And the last knight I saw in the stone was Sir
William who bawled me down from the tree and tried to

cut off my head. Sir Pellinore, though, was on a quest. "Each of us must have a dream to light our way through this dark world." That's what Sir Pellinore said.

Today, I saw the hooded man in my obsidian. He was sitting in a vestry and talking to a man who was holding a gold staff and wearing a miter shaped like the mouth of a fish. The miter was gold and had a darker gold cross stitched on it, and I think the man was the archbishop of Canterbury.

"We're alone," the archbishop says, "so I'll talk openly. There are too many men in this country with big heads. They all think they can wear the crown."

"King Uther told them about his son," the hooded man replies. "Before he died, he gave his son God's blessing, and said he should claim the crown."

"I've heard about that," the archbishop replies, "but the earls and lords are restless, and not without reason. The Saxons are massing in the north and east again. It won't be long before they attack us."

The hooded man smiles grimly at the archbishop.

"Things can't go on like this," the archbishop says. "Where is he, this son?"

The hooded man gazes at the vestry roof, and shakes his head.

"How old is he?" demands the archbishop.

"Thirteen, Your Grace," says the hooded man.

"Just a boy!" exclaims the archbishop. And he swats the thin air with his right hand. "This kingdom's in jeopardy. Britain needs a leader!"

"This is what you should do," the hooded man says, and his voice is as rich and dark as Slim's pheasant gravy. "Send out messengers to every earl, lord, and knight in the country. Instruct them to come to London by Christmas, without fail, and this is why: to kneel down together and pray to baby Jesus on the night of his birth; to beg the king of mankind to perform a miracle and show us all who should be crowned king of this realm."

The archbishop narrows his eyes. He rolls his golden staff between his two pink palms, first one way, then the other.

"A miracle," he says.

"That's what Christians call it," the hooded man replies.

"And what do you call it?" asked the archbishop.

"Many things seem miraculous until you understand them," the hooded man says, "and some are so marvelous you could call them miracles."

"I will send out my messengers, then," says the archbishop.

the ACORN

My stone again!

I saw my namesake and the hooded man standing under a lych-gate in front of a huge church, and the hooded man was looking at me very strangely, with his left eye open and his right eye closed.

"Why are you looking at me like that?" I ask.

"A fierce wind will blow from the north and the east," the hooded man replies. "It will tear at the trees on the forest. Many branches will bend and break. But in a forest glade an acorn will take root and grow into a sapling. Then all the oaks around it will bow down to it. So will all the beech trees, the ashes, and the elms."

"Is that a prophecy?" I ask.

"It is," the hooded man replies.

"What does it mean?"

"Work it out for yourself," says the hooded man. Then he closes his left eye and opens his right eye, and turns away.

The light went black inside my stone. For a while I scritched and scratched at one of the milky spots on its rough underside, like one of the mice in the storeroom. A fierce wind and a king-tree? I slowly dressed my strange stone in its cloth, and pushed it back into its crevice.

spelling

"How do you spell a word?" Oliver asked me this morning.

"I don't know," I said. "Like it sounds?"

"But two people can say the same word in different ways. Haven't you noticed that?"

"Not really," I said.

I have, of course. Gatty and I often say the same words in different ways. But until I know what my father's plans for me are, I'm going to disappoint Oliver.

"Here in the March we say *us*, but way east from Wenlock people say *uz*. So the same word gets written down in two different ways."

"I see," I said.

"And at court in London, people say *ars*, as if they were talking out of their nostrils, and so they write down that sound. Words are spelled in as many different ways as people speak them."

"I understand," I said.

"Not only that," said Oliver, puffing himself up. "There's more than one way of writing down the same sound."

"Is there?" I asked.

"Look!" said Oliver. He dipped his quill into the inkwell and sounded the words as he began to write them. "*Urth*, and erthe, and now *earth*, they all sound the same, don't they? And what about this? *Woom*, and *woume*, and *woumbe*, and *woombe*, and *womb*: They all sound the same as well."

"Yes, I see," I said.

"Many words are like this," said Oliver. "Words that wear different clothing."

"Language is very difficult," I said.

"It's a beauty and a beast," Oliver replied. "As sharp as the most subtle thoughts we're capable of! As crude as a bludgeon!" Oliver waved his pudgy hand at me. "You'll learn," he said.

"I can only get worse," I replied.

"Whatever do you mean? You can only get better. Now! I've got some news for you."

"News?"

"The guestmaster at Wenlock has sent me a message and he says there'll be room for us at the priory guest house next week. And then you'll be able to see the scriptorium where the monks write and illuminate their manuscripts, and you'll hear them sing the offices. A marvelous sound! I've spoken to your father, and he has agreed to it. What do you think about that?"

What I think is this: I want to visit Wenlock Priory. Of course I do. I am interested in how manuscripts are made, and I want to hear the monks singing. But I don't want my father or Oliver to know this, otherwise they may think that I'm suited to be a monk myself, or a schoolman. I am not. I want to be a squire, and then a knight, and I want to be betrothed to Grace.

the pope's proclamation

It's very strange. In my stone, the archbishop agreed to send his messengers to every earl, lord, and knight in the country to summon them to London; and this afternoon a friar called Fulk rode in and told us he had come with the blessing of the archbishop of Canterbury.

First, he spoke to my father, and then my father asked Hum to summon everyone over the age of twelve to church, and Oliver energetically swung the church bell.

Lankin didn't come. But Cleg the miller did, and so did Martha. Jankin was there: He looked very white, and sat in a pew on his own.

The friar climbed into the pulpit. "I've come all the way from Neuilly in France, and I bring a message from the Holy Father, Pope Innocent himself. Jerusalem is still in the grip of the vile Saracens. Think of Jesus's pain. Think of His sorrow. Now the pope has proclaimed a fourth crusade to exterminate the pagans once and for all. Hundreds of the best men in France have already taken the Cross; they've shown their pity for the land oversea. They've sworn to avenge Him, the king of mankind, and recapture the Holy City."

The friar thumped the pulpit with both his fists. "God wills it!" he shouted. "Drive out and kill the Turks! Recapture Jerusalem! Take pity on the Holy Land."

The friar spoke with such force and feeling that people began to weep. Then I looked at my mother and saw that her eyes too were hot with tears, and I remembered how she reminded my father that Richard Lionheart had "roared and rattled the gates of the Saracens," and brought home a piece of the Holy Cross.

"His Holiness the Pope," the friar called out, "has pronounced an indulgence, and your archbishop commands me to proclaim it. Every single man who takes the Cross, rich and poor, free and bonded, old and young . . . every single man who serves God in the army for one year will be pardoned without penance for whatever sins he has committed during his life, his entire life, so long as he confesses them."

The friar looked round the church. "Without penance," he repeated. "People of God, take the Cross! Sir John, take the Cross! God wills it."

My mother looked at my father, and tears were streaming down her cheeks; my father didn't even blink — he just looked straight ahead.

"I've come here from Lord Stephen at Holt Castle," said the friar, "and before that I preached at Lurkenhope and Knighton. Do you know what one woman did when her husband stood up to take the Cross? She grabbed his belt and stopped him. That night, lying in bed, she heard a great voice saying: 'You've taken my servant away from me, and so, woman, what you love most will be taken away from you.' When she woke next morning, the woman found her own baby dead in the bed beside her. She'd overlaid him and suffocated him."

The friar paused, and then he thumped the pulpit

again. "In the name of Saint Edmund and your own souls," he said earnestly, "stand up and take the Cross!"

There was quite a lot of noise in the church then. Wat Harelip and Howell and Dutton stood up and waved their arms; Brian and Macsen joined in and stamped their feet, and then many people started talking to each other.

But no one in the manor can go on a crusade unless my father chooses to go and takes them with him, or else releases them from their service and permits them to enlist in the foot army. All the women will be against it, because they'll be afraid of going hungry. How would they be able to sow and reap, and make the hay, and look after their animals, without their husbands or their sons?

My father allowed people to talk for a little while. Then he stood up, and raised his right hand, and thanked the friar for preaching the crusade. "Before I can decide, I will need to talk to Lord Stephen," he said, "and the other lords and knights in this middle March. Some of us will say that if we travel east to the land oversea, the Welsh will also travel east, and take over our women and our castles and our manors. I will send word of my decision before the end of the month."

My father doesn't want to take the Cross; I can see that, and I know my mother will be very fearful as well as very proud if he does because she would never be able to figure all the accounts and organize all the day-work. Or would Serle stay here and manage everything? That would be terrible.

Sir William is sixty-four but he told me his crusading years were the best of his life, so he may take the Cross. Poor Grace!

Maybe nothing will come of all this. Today is only the fifth of December, but this has already been the most fearsome and most exciting month of the year. Perhaps the whole of this month will be full of joys and sorrows because the century is ending. I've noticed my mother and Nain and Oliver keep talking about it; they're uncertain and hopeful, and full of prophecies.

In the manor court, people turned against each other, and some of them told lies. But when I looked round our church and saw everyone talking and excited, even Jankin, I thought we were all like one body, one wounded body, longing to be healed and to live in peace and friendship again.

"Some things," said the hooded man, "are so marvelous you could call them miracles."

Today is the feast day of Saint Barbara. She was a beautiful girl who was murdered by her father because she became a Christian. The day after he killed her, he was struck dead by lightning. I think that was a miracle. But when Fulk the friar rode in this morning, and we had to sit down side by side, whether we wanted to or not; all of us children of God; and when we heard his words, helping to heal our village body . . . That was a kind of miracle too.

76

NOThING'S NOT
WORTh hiDING

Arthur-in-the-Stone is standing in the forest clearing with Sir Pellinore, the same glade where we met before, and now the huge tombstone has my words for little Luke carved on it. Through sunlight and shadow the hooded man slowly walks towards us.

"Sir," I say to Sir Pellinore, "will you make me a knight?"

"You're very young," Sir Pellinore replies.

"And then I'll ride through the forest to the fountain, and smack the shield of the Knight of the Black Anvil. Without water from that fountain, little Luke's grave will always be barren. But as soon as I water it, bright flowers will grow on it all the year round."

"The Knight of the Black Anvil is the terror of the Marches," Sir Pellinore says, "and you are very young."

"But the fountain water is the first part of my journey," I reply.

"You need not be a knight to begin," says Sir Pellinore. "How old are you?"

"Thirteen."

"He's too young," says the hooded man. "He's not even a squire, and he can't be a knight before he's a squire. Do you know what will happen if he rides to the fountain? The Knight of the Black Anvil will cut him to pieces."

Sir Pellinore looks me in the eye, and one corner of his mouth keeps twitching.

"Knight me, sir," I say again.

"Well then," says Sir Pellinore. "Kneel down."

"No," says the hooded man.

"The Saxons are massing in the north," Sir Pellinore says. "We need our boys to be men, and each one of them to fight and defend the western kingdom."

"No," says the hooded man more firmly. "If you knight him now, you're sending him to his death."

"I beg you to knight me, sir," I say. "I'm not too young. Give me my sword and spurs . . ."

At this moment there was a gentle tap-tapping at the door. At once I scrambled out of my window seat, scooped up the saffron cloth, and buried my obsidian in it.

"Wait!" I called, quickly winding the cloth around the stone. "Who is it?"

The door creaked, it swung open a little, and Lady Alice put her head around it.

"You!" I exclaimed.

"Me," said Lady Alice, and I remembered she told me that she and Sir William might visit us before Christmas. Lightly Lady Alice stepped into the room. "And what are you hiding from me?"

"Nothing," I said.

"Nothing's not worth hiding," said Lady Alice in her singsong voice, reaching out for the saffron bundle.

"I can't," I said. "I promised Merlin. I mean . . ."

"You mean you don't trust me," said Lady Alice.

"It's not that," I said.

I pushed my obsidian into the crevice between the two

234

blocks of dressed stone, and a beetle scurried out, heading in the opposite direction.

My aunt smiled and took my left hand. "Still warm?" she said. "How's your tailbone?"

"I told Johanna in the village about it. And she broke the wound."

My aunt screwed up her eyes.

"She said it was full of rot."

"She hurt you," said Lady Alice gently.

"Then my mother boiled vinegar and honey and barleymeal and something else — I can't remember — and rubbed the mixture into my wound."

"You poor creature," said my aunt. Her hazel eyes were quick and bright, and she played with a curl of her hair. "I said I might see you again before Christmas," she said.

"Is Grace here?"

"No," said Lady Alice. "Just Sir William. He only came home from France the day before yesterday. But that's his way. The man's sixty-five on Christmas Day, and he can't sit still for a moment."

"But why have you come?" I asked.

"Sir William and Sir John need to talk," replied Lady Alice.

"What about?"

"You're as bad as Tom," Lady Alice said quite sharply.

"Have you ever heard," I asked my aunt, "of the magic fountain in the middle of the forest?"

"Which forest?" asked Lady Alice.

"I don't know. Its water makes bright flowers grow and blossom in each season of the year."

"No," said my aunt. "But I can tell you what to do if you want red roses to bloom at the dead of winter."

"What?"

"In June," said my aunt, "or in July, you pick the buds from a rosebush, and be sure they have long stems. Put them into a little wooden barrel without any water — an ale barrel would do — and then seal the barrel so that it's watertight. Tie a heavy stone to each end of it, and sink it in your stream. *Tu comprends?*"

"I understand," I said.

"And then," said Lady Alice, "in the bleak midwinter you can raise the barrel and take out the rosebuds. Put them in water and they'll soon open."

"I'll try that," I said. "Aunt Alice, since you visited us, Sian fell through the ice into the fishpond, and Oliver got hit by a piece of falling plaster . . ."

Lady Alice shook her head and smiled.

" . . . and then there was the manor court, and it was terrible. Lankin was accused of stealing a leg of mutton from our kitchen, and seventeen people voted that he was guilty, and his thieving hand was cut off at the wrist. And after that the friar Fulk came to preach the new crusade. There's so much to tell you."

"Later," said my aunt. "You must come down to the hall now and greet Sir William." Then she gathered her cloak — not her burnt orange one but a much thicker, darker one, the color of bullace and damsons — and she stepped out into the gallery.

"What's in there?" asked Lady Alice, tapping the storeroom door.

"Corn," I said. "And once, a man and a woman."

Lady Alice looked at me. She raised an eyebrow, and smiled.

foul stroke

You would never guess that my father and Sir William are brothers because they don't look the same and Sir William's so old he could be my father's father. They're about the same height, but my father is quite lean whereas Sir William's body looks like a tree trunk. He has white hair, lots of it, and matted white eyebrows, and his face looks so brown and battered you can tell it has weathered all kinds of storms and adventures. His left eye is stony, so he can't see much out of it, but his right eye is wonderfully knowing and doesn't miss anything.

My mother told me once that big men and women are comfortable with themselves, and that's why they're easy-going and good-humored. But that's not true of my uncle William. He has a ferocious temper, unlike my father. When he loses his temper, Sir William becomes violent, and I know Lady Alice is afraid of him; and because of what I know, I'm afraid for her too.

"So, Arthur!" said Sir William in his loud, deep voice. "Let's have a look at you. You've put on a head of height."

"You haven't seen him for a year," said my mother.

"And now I can only half-see him," said my uncle. "Blast this eye!"

My aunt stepped over to Sir William and slipped her right hand under his left elbow.

"Your aunt keeps talking about you," Sir William barked. "Arthur this . . . Arthur that . . ." He sniffed loudly, and then turned to Lady Alice. "John says he had that friar here too. Yesterday."

Lady Alice glanced at my mother, but my mother kept her eyes lowered.

"Well, Serle!" Sir William demanded. "What about you? Will you go, or do you want the bloody Turks to trample all over Europe?"

"I want to go, sir," said Serle.

"It's high time you were knighted," said Sir William. "You can make your own choices then. How old are you?"

"Seventeen, sir."

"And you've completed your service. Well, John, what about it? Two brothers and one son?"

My father shook his head.

"I'll look after them, Helen," boomed Sir William. "I'll look after them both. Think, John! Remission for all your sins."

"And for yours, William," said my father.

"Not only that," said my uncle. "We'll come back with booty." And then he thumped Lady Alice so hard on her buttocks that she gasped and put her right foot forward. "Am I too old or am I too young?" he boomed.

I looked at my mother but her eyes were still lowered. I know my father beats her sometimes, but he would never be so coarse as to lay a hand on her in front of visitors; and if he did, Nain would probably lay a hand on him.

"What about you, Arthur?" asked Sir William.

"I'll go," I said. "I'll go crusading."

Sir William harrumphed and then spat on the rushes.

"Shrimps don't last long when they get washed out to sea," said Sir William.

"I could go if I were a squire," I said, and I could feel my father staring at me, but I didn't look back at him.

"From what I hear," said Sir William, "no knights from around here will be sailing east anyhow. It will be the counts of Champagne and Normandy, and maybe the Germans. Maybe the lords of the Low Countries."

"Will Lord Stephen go?" I asked.

"Not if Lady Judith has anything to do with it," said Sir William. "Anyhow, he's more at home in a courtroom than a crusade, isn't he?"

"I wouldn't be so sure," said my father.

"There's no appetite here," said Sir William. "No, there'll be no army from England. Just a few adventurers, serving God."

"And serving themselves," said my father. "Lining their own pockets."

"Can you fight?" Sir William asked me.

"I'm learning," I said eagerly.

Sir William rubbed the white nose hairs curling round the bottom of his nostrils.

"Two weeks ago, Tom and Serle and I had a contest, and . . ."

"So I've heard," said Sir William. "And Tom told me he could have won but for Grace, and some damn-fool contest."

"Wordplay," I said.

"Arthur was best," said Sian.

"Knights and squires don't fight with words," said Sir William, "and they don't fight with bows and arrows either. They fight with swords. They fight with lances.

239

Come on, Arthur! Let's see what your swordplay's like. There's time for that before we talk. Isn't there, John?"

And with this, Sir William swung round, and marched off towards the door.

I looked at my father, and he looked at my mother, then sighed. "You'd better go," he said.

"Come on!" called Sir William from outside. "I'm waiting for you."

"I'll be the judge," said Serle, and one side of his mouth curled upwards, and the other didn't. "Go on! I'll get the armor and weapons for you."

As Sir William and I walked down to the Yard, my uncle lengthened his stride so that I could only just keep up with him, and started muttering to himself. "Nothing!" he snapped. "Nothing. Or maybe too much." Suddenly I felt quite nervous of him and wished Serle would hurry and catch up with us.

"Swordplay, then," said Sir William. "Or would you prefer to tilt?"

"No, sir," I said.

"I thought not," said Sir William.

"Tom never hit the shield at all," I said.

"And you were sandbagged," Sir William replied.

As soon as Serle had brought us our jerkins and weapons, Sir William and I crossed swords. Then we jumped back, and began to feint.

"At you!" barked Sir William, and he lunged straight at me. Before I could guard myself with my buckler, he jabbed me fiercely on the bottom of my breastbone.

"One point to Sir William," shouted Serle.

"At you!" I shouted. "At you!" And I drove my sword at

Sir William's heart, but he deflected it with his own sword, and I had to jump out of the way again.

I was much lighter on my feet, but my uncle was the more skillful swordsman, and for a while neither of us was able to land a blow on the other. But my uncle was beginning to breathe very heavily, and so I thought that the longer our fight lasted, the better chance I would have.

"Pax!" said Sir William, dropping his buckler and raising his left hand as he struggled down onto one knee. He was gasping for breath. "I'm getting old," he said.

"Ready?" called Serle. "Are you ready, Sir William?"

At first I didn't notice, but Sir William had taken his sword in his left hand and, as he stood up, he lunged at my right shoulder. There was no time to swing my buckler across my body, or even to step backwards.

"No!" I yelled.

I saw the bright sword driving towards me, and then I heard it: the point, unsharpened as it was, ripping through my leather jerkin.

"Foul stroke!" shouted Serle.

And then I felt it: cold iron burning through my right forearm; the wet warmth of my leaping blood.

Sir William drew back his sword with a jerk, and I cried out at the searing pain, and fell onto my knees.

"Boy!" said Sir William, stumbling forward and catching me. "Have I hurt you?"

I looked up at Sir William's face. My eyeballs felt too big for their sockets, and Sir William began to spin and tumble, like one of Sian's tops.

When I regained consciousness, I was lying beside the

fire in the hall, and my mother and Tanwen were kneeling beside me.

"You've come back," said my mother, and she closed her eyes, and made the sign of the cross on her breast.

"You'll be all right," Tanwen said. "You've lost half your blood, mind!"

"He played foul," I said, and my voice didn't sound like my own.

"With you, of all people," my mother said quietly.

"Where are they?" I asked.

"Gone," said my mother.

"Lady Alice?"

My mother nodded. "It's late now. After Compline." My mother smiled her strange, sad smile. "Sir William says you'll be a good swordsman."

When I heard this, I tried to raise my right hand. I couldn't, though, and my forearm and shoulder blazed with pain.

"Don't do that again," Tanwen said, and she cradled my head between her cool hands.

"Try to sleep now," said my mother. "Sleep and rest."

I slept all night, and in the early morning, Johanna came down to the hall, and looked at my wound, and grumbled, and applied poultices and gave me a potion. After that, I slept again, and now three days have passed and this is the first time I have wanted to climb the staircase to my writing-room.

What did my father and mother and Sir William and Lady Alice need to talk about? Grace and me? Or Serle? Whatever it was, it must have been urgent because Sir William only rode home from France the day before he came here.

Serle might know. I could ask him but he'll only tell me if he knows I won't like the answer.

I wonder whether I was knighted in the stone by Sir Pellinore, and whether I was able to bring back water from the fountain. In any case, I think the hooded man was right after all: A page is too young to fight a fearsome knight.

78

NOT YET

My wound is still oozing blood and water, and so my mother has decided I should not travel to Wenlock Priory until the new year. Oliver is very cross about this, and when he came to sit with me in the hall, he kept tutting that it might be several months before we can arrange another visit, and that to light candles at the shrine of Saint Milburga and hear the monks sing would have illuminated this Advent-tide, and that our visit would have been a stepping-stone in my life.

This is exactly what I fear, and so I hid my own impatience to see the monks writing and illuminating their manuscripts.

I still don't know what my father and mother and Sir William and Lady Alice talked about, and Serle doesn't know either. Sian told me she heard Serle ask my mother, but my mother said it had absolutely nothing to do with him. I hope that is true.

I want to ask my father about my life. I want to ask him about Joan and whether he agrees with what she said at the manor court. And I want to ask him whether Will has carved little Luke's tombstone yet. But this wound has taken away half my energy and half my appetite.

"Sir William fought foul, you know," I told my father.

"Disgraceful!" said my father, and he stared angrily into the gloom on the far side of the hall.

"I was faster than he was."

"I've never heard of such a thing," snapped my father.

"I can't use this arm," I said. "Not for writing or anything."

"I've talked to Oliver about that," my father replied. "When you start your lessons again, for the time being you can write with your left hand."

"You said it's not natural."

"It's necessary," said my father.

A messenger from Lord Stephen rode in this afternoon, but I don't know what he and my father talked about either. Maybe the new crusade. Or the manor court.

Poor Lankin. At least Sir William didn't cut off my right hand.

the archbishop's messenger

Sian and I picked misty sloes in September. As soon as we touched them, their mist disappeared, and they gleamed purple and darkest crimson, like congealed blood.

That's how my seeing stone looked when I unwrapped it this morning. I still can't close my right fist although it's six days since Sir William hurt me, so I just laid the stone on my open palm. After a while it began to grow warm, and then its mist lifted.

It is early, and bright, and very frosty. Arthur-in-the-stone is standing on the first reach of Tumber Hill looking down onto our manor house. The yellowy stone is glowing in the winter sunlight and the thatch is glistening, except that bit which is green and rotten and needs replacing. To my right the churned earth in the pigsty is glinting and, beyond the house, Nine Elms and Great Oak and Pikeside stretch their shining limbs. Everything is very still.

Then I see a messenger ride in from the east, but I can't make out who it is because I'm looking almost straight into the sun. I run down the reach of the hill, past the silent copper beech, past the icy pond, and by the time the messenger rides over the bridge, I am at the door to meet him, panting. The messenger's panting as well, and so is his horse. The three of us are wreathed in mist; we're like ghosts of ourselves.

The messenger is wearing a surcoat with the arch-bishop of Canterbury's gold staff and double silver cross embroidered on it, so I lead him at once into our hall. Sir Ector and Kay are sitting beside the smoky fire.

"God's bones!" says the messenger. "It's cold outside, but even colder inside. You people on the March are made of iron."

"We are," says my father.

"I come at the bidding of the archbishop of Canter-bury."

At once Sir Ector makes the sign of the cross on his forehead.

"Our country needs a king," the messenger says. "Without a king, it's like a boat without a rudder, tossing on the winter sea."

"King Uther has a son," Sir Ector replies. "He said so before he died."

"But his priest denied it," says Kay. "He said Uther was delirious."

"And the king affirmed it," my father insists. "He gave his son God's blessing, and the hooded man told all the earls and lords and knights he would help him."

"The archbishop is aware of all this," the messenger replies

"So what is your message?" my father asks calmly.

"The archbishop is sending messengers to every earl, lord and knight in this country. He bids you come to Lon-don in time for Christmas, without fail."

"So soon!" exclaims Sir Ector.

"To kneel down together in the church of Saint Paul," the messenger says, "and pray to baby Jesus on the night of his birth. Every earl, lord, and knight in this kingdom must beg Jesus to perform a miracle, and show us all who should be crowned king of Britain."

Sir Ector nods and directs the messenger to the kitchen. "Drink as much milk or ale as you wish," he says, "and eat as much bread as you can before you ride on." Then he turns towards the chamber, and signals Kay and Arthur-in-the-stone to follow him.

"It's true," Sir Ector says, "Britain needs its king. I will go to London." He pushes out his lower lip, and then puts his right hand on Kay's shoulder. "Kay," he says, "you came with me before, to kneel to King Uther, and you must come with me now."

Kay inclines his head. "Thank you, sir," he says.

"I haven't forgotten what King Uther said," Sir Ector says. "It's time you were knighted. I will knight you myself in the Church of Saint Paul."

"Sir," says Kay quietly, and he bows his head for a second time.

Now Sir Ector turns to me. He lays his left hand on my shoulder. "And you, Arthur," he says.

"Sir?"

"You're my page. Isn't it right?"

"Yes, sir."

"And you're old enough to be my squire now."

"I am, sir."

Sir Ector smiles. "Well, then! I want you, too, to come with me to London."

No sooner had my father said these wonderful words than my obsidian began to sparkle. It became cold in my right hand, and looked as though it had been touched by the hand of Jack Frost, like the manor and the frozen fields inside it.

Arthur-in-the-stone is not me. We look and talk like each other. But he can do magic, and I cannot. He has killed Sir William, but I have not. It was my uncle who nearly killed me!

Sir Ector and Kay are not exactly the same as my father and Serle either. They may live here at Caldicot, but they have also been to the court of old King Uther, who no one's ever heard of, and who may never have existed.

And now, all three of us are going to ride to London at the bidding of the archbishop of Canterbury; but actually, I've been wounded and can't even ride as far as Wenlock.

the knight in the yellow dress

Early this morning my stone made me laugh. It made me want to punch the air with both fists, but I can't do that because my right forearm is extremely sore.

The court is packed out with knights and ladies. Some are waiting for an audience with Queen Ygerna, some are sitting at long tables and drinking, some are playing chess, and there's one squire walking up and down and around on his own. It's Kay!

Now there's quite a rumpus at the hall door, and then a fully armed knight rides into the court, holding up a woman's dress. It's dusty yellow, the color of ripe green-gages, and I see it's decorated across the breast and at the sleeves with hundreds of tiny pearls.

Now this knight dismounts and, still holding the dress, stalks up to the queen. "There's a knight in this court called Laurin," the knight says in a low voice. "Laurin fought with me, and threw me, so he has sent me here to you to do with me as you wish."

"What about that dress?" Queen Ygerna asks. "What are you carrying it around for? Who does it belong to?"

"Me," replies the knight.

"You?" says the queen.

"It's mine," says the knight.

"You wear women's clothes then?" the queen asks.

"I do," the knight replies.

At this, some of the knights and ladies in the court shake their heads, and some laugh.

"What's so strange about that?" the knight asks. "It would be stranger if I didn't."

"Are you a knight?" asks Ygerna.

"When I wear this dress," the knight replies, "I am a woman. But when I'm dressed in this armor, anyone who comes up against me will find I'm a knight."

Hearing this, everyone in court begins to laugh again.

Now Kay pushes his way through the crowd, and puts his nose in the knight's face. "So Laurin threw you, did he?" he says rudely, and he looks the young knight up and down. "A good night's work!"

"Kay," says the queen. "That's most unworthy of you."

"Laurin flattened you, did he?" Kay goes on. "Well! That can't have been too difficult."

Now the court grows restless and uncomfortable with Kay's rudeness. Some of the knights start to call out, and the ladies groan.

"Kay," says the queen, "why can't you hold your tongue?"

"Because it tells the truth."

"It's far too sharp. You have no grounds at all for insulting this woman."

"Thank you, ma'am," the knight says to the queen, and then she rounds on Kay. "I'll stop your mouth," she says.

"What with?" says Kay. "Kisses?"

"I'll drop you in the river. I'll make you drink so much water you're awash inside."

251

"Just you try," says Kay. "If anyone's going to get wet, it's you, my lady. Wet from head to toe with your own stinking sweat before you lay a single finger on me."

"On your own head be it," the knight replies.

"You're your own worst enemy, Kay," says Queen Ygerna. "There's a devil inside you." And then she turns to the young woman. "Kay has insulted you," she says, "and I give you permission to joust with him."

The knight bows to the queen, and then she clanks across the court, and mounts her horse.

"Are you well mounted, lady?" Kay jeers. "Are you sitting comfortably?" Then he strides past her and outside the court, he pulls on his fustian tunic and his coat of mail, his helmet and gauntlets, and mounts his horse.

When they ride the first end, neither Kay nor the young woman are able to balance their lances; they both miss, and gallop down to the opposite ends of the tilting yard. But when they gallop against each other again, separated only by a wooden railing, Kay hits the young woman right on the base of her breastbone — exactly where Sir William hit me, before he wounded me. But the young woman's as tough as a stone pillar. She sits upright in her saddle, and trots down to the far end of the yard.

As they gallop towards each other for the third time, Kay bawls at the young woman. But that doesn't stop her! She drives her lance right into Kay's shield and he's unable to keep his balance. His mount pulls up, and he topples over sideways, and clatters to the ground.

Quickly the young woman dismounts and pounces on Kay. Then she picks him up, and the knights and ladies cheer and shout.

Kay tries to jab the young woman with his metal elbows and scratch her with his gauntlets. He thrashes with his feet. But the lady won't let go of him.

"Kay!" she says. "I've swept you off your feet!"

The young woman carries Kay across the tilting yard and down to the river, and all the knights and ladies surge after them. Kay yells, but it makes no difference. The young woman swings Kay and throws him in headfirst. She stops his loud mouth, and the swift currents at once sweep him out and downstream.

Kay has a difficult time of it wading back to the riverbank. But when he reaches it, there are plenty of strong arms outstretched to welcome him.

Kay coughs and spits the river out of his throat and lungs, while the young woman looks at him and smiles an inward smile. Her eyes are bright, and I see one of them is fierce, and the other very tender.

"That's for your insolence, Kay," she says in her low, husky voice.

If only Serle could be taught a lesson like this, it might stop him from strutting round Caldicot, and throwing his weight about. It might stop the insults in his mouth.

81

TANWEN'S SECRET

Gatty and I have found out something. It's a secret that can't be hidden for much longer, because it's growing, and when my father and mother find out about it, they will be very angry, and there will be a great deal of trouble.

This year the winter has shown its white fist so early that our cattle and sheep are already going hungry.

"I'm hungry myself half the time," Gatty told me. "It gnaws at my insides, and cramps me up. Hunger's like a toothache — you keep thinking about it."

After he had talked with Hum this morning, my father told me we have more hay in our barn than for several years and that he's allowing each family to take as much hay as one person can carry.

"One load each," my father said. "It won't harm us, and it will help them. You remember what Joan said in court? If she can't feed her cow, the cow won't milk, and if the cow doesn't milk, she won't have anything to drink." My father shook his head. "The last thing I want is to lose any villagers," he said. "We're shorthanded enough as it is."

"And hunger hurts," I said with some feeling.

"In this manor, Arthur," my father replied, "children do not give their opinions unless they're asked for them. How's your arm?"

"Getting better," I said.

"Good. You've been cooped up here for too long. Why don't you go out to the barn and help Hum?"

"Fieldwork," said Serle.

"No, Serle," said my father. "Not fieldwork. Hum's in charge, and Arthur will assist him. You know that."

"Reeve-work then," said Serle.

The barn was packed with people and the air was thick with dust and chaff; it was sweet with the scents of summer.

Gatty was tying hay into small, tight bundles; Brian stood up on the top of a hill of hay, throwing forkfuls down to Macsen; Will was bundling and Giles was stacking and Dutton kept trying to lift an enormous load onto his head and shoulders — his face was as red as a coxcomb; Johanna was choking; and I saw Howell trip up Martha so that she fell headfirst into a bed of hay, and then he fell on top of her, laughing; Ruth kept sniffing and spitting; and Slim was sneezing. Everyone was! Then Wat Harelip headed for the door, dragging an enormous bundle of hay behind him, but Hum at once ran after him.

"Carry!" he bawled. "As much as you can carry, not as much as you can haul."

Wat grinned sheepishly.

"Cabbage ears!" shouted Hum.

"Hum!" I called out. "I can help you."

Hum glared at me. "You know what your father said."

"He's given me permission," I said.

"Are you making that up?"

"No!" I said indignantly. "Ask him if you like."

"Right!" said Hum. "You can oversee them. One load for each person, and no more than that."

"All right," I said.

"And me and Gatty will carry our loads," Hum said.

"Not two loads."

"Says who?" demanded Hum, and he thrust his face too close to mine.

"I'm sure my father didn't mean that," I said uncomfortably.

"I'm the reeve, aren't I?" demanded Hum. "I'll do as I want. Anyhow, there's enough hay in here."

"I know," I said unhappily.

"You're as bad as the rest," Hum said angrily. "You don't care nothing except for yourself."

"That's not true," I said, raising my voice.

Now Joan joined in. "You seen my Matty?" she said.

"Who's Matty?" I asked.

"My sheep! She's down on her knees, begging for food. Hasn't got the strength left to stand up."

"That's terrible," I said.

"He's good with words, that one," said Hum, "but he's as bad as the rest."

"Let him be," shouted Gatty.

"Why's that, then?" said Joan. "You soft on him?"

"Not!" said Gatty indignantly, swiping wisps of hay out of her hair. "Arthur's all right."

"That's enough of that," said Hum. "Come on, Gatty! I'll load you up."

By the time Hum had bundled and carted off his own load of hay, the barn had grown quite quiet again. It shook its old, creaking shoulders, and breathed deeply, and I knew that, before nightfall, all the mice and rats would be out and about, eating their fill and gossiping.

Only Tanwen and I were left in the barn, and then Gatty walked back in again.

"Come on," I said. "Let's try and get some milk from the kitchen."

"I haven't done my load yet," Tanwen said.

"Do it after," said Gatty.

Slim was back in the kitchen beating batter, and he wanted to get rid of us, so he let us take a whole pan of creamy milk, and some collops too.

"I know where we can go," I said, and I led Tanwen and Gatty out of the kitchen and into the little stone building just behind it.

"I've never been in here," said Gatty.

The armory is quiet and still. The two windows are barred so that if the Welsh raiders do come again, they won't be able to steal our armor.

In the space between the windows, my father's armor hangs on the shouldered stand Will made for it, with his new flat-topped helmet perched above it. Doublets and coifs hang from nails hammered along one wall, and so does my father's old coat of mail. It's quite rusty now. His new one only comes down to his knees, split to the waist, so that he can ride in it.

"Look at it all!" marveled Gatty, and she rippled her fingers over the chain mail and slid them across the plate metal. Then she picked up a pair of fustian breeches from the wooden shelf and disturbed a whole family of wood lice. Some rolled into balls, and some headed for the pile of woolen pads, and some scurried along the shelf and disappeared down a cobwebby crack.

"What's this made of, then?" asked Gatty, rubbing the breeches between her right thumb and forefinger.

"I don't know," I said, "but it's very tough. The crusaders brought it home from El-Fustat in Egypt. That's why it's called fustian."

"What's Egypt?" asked Gatty.

Before I could reply, Gatty swung shut the heavy oak door and saw all the weapons behind it: my father's sword in its scabbard, and his lance which is ten feet long, and his shield, and all the weapons Serle and I use when we practice in the Yard.

"Look at this!" gasped Gatty.

It was my father's skull-splitter.

"That's for if his sword snaps," I said.

"It's that thick in here I can't breathe," Tanwen said.

"Do you want to try some armor on?" I asked Gatty.

"Yes," said Gatty eagerly.

I looked at Tanwen and narrowed my eyes.

"Who do you think I am?" she said.

So then I shook out a fustian tunic for Gatty, and she pulled it over her head, and put her arms through the holes.

"Really," I said, "you should begin at the bottom and work up. Otherwise, you get top-heavy and fall over sideways."

"Come on!" said Tanwen. "It's hot in here."

"This next," I said, and I unhooked the old coat of mail from the wall.

"I can't wear that," laughed Gatty.

"And I can't carry it," I said. "Not with this arm."

So Tanwen held up the coat of mail and Gatty reached back with her left arm, then her right arm, and slipped it on.

"God's bones!" she shouted in excitement.

"Sshh!" I said.

"It's not as heavy as I thought," said Gatty. "Not in one place, I mean. It's heavy all around."

"It's much too long for you," I said. "It's dragging on the ground."

"It's so thick in here," said Tanwen. "I'm feeling . . ."

And then Tanwen collapsed. Her eyes were closed, and her face was very white.

"Tanwen!" I exclaimed. "Are you all right?"

But she didn't answer.

"She's out," said Gatty. "Reckon I know what that is."

"What?"

"She's pregnant," said Gatty.

"Pregnant?"

"She was sick as a cat last week."

Tanwen's eyelids began to flutter. Then she opened her eyes, and stared at us.

"What happened?" she asked.

"You fainted," I replied.

Tanwen sat up. "First time I done that," she said, and then she shivered. "It's cold in here."

"You're pregnant," Gatty said.

"No," said Tanwen.

"You are and all."

Tanwen said nothing.

"How many months?" said Gatty.

Tanwen put her head between her knees.

"Four, I reckon," said Gatty knowledgeably. "Can't go much further than that without it showing."

Gatty sometimes surprises me with how much she knows. I don't think Grace would know anything like that.

Tanwen got to her feet, rather unsteadily. "Take that off!" she told Gatty. "We shouldn't be in here. I can't stand this place, anyhow."

Gatty slipped off the coat of mail. It clinked and chinked and fell in a soft heap at her feet.

"Come on, then," Gatty said to Tanwen, and she took her arm.

"Let me be," said Tanwen. "I'm not, anyhow."

"You are and all," said Gatty.

"Nothing to do with you," Tanwen said very fiercely. She glared at us both. Then she picked up one of my father's gauntlets, flung it down on the floor, and stormed out through the armory door.

"Who's the father, then?" Gatty asked me. "You tell me that."

"I don't know," I said.

But I do know, and I wish I didn't.

82

KING JOHN'S
CHRISTMAS PRESENT

There are only sixteen more days this century, and scarcely a day goes by without something happening. Yesterday in the armory, Gatty and I discovered Tanwen's secret, and today another king's messenger rode in, but he wasn't the same man who came before — the one who cursed all the time and souped up our latrine.

This messenger told us that all over the country, King John's earls, lords, and knights are allowing their tenants to commit offenses against forest animals, and against the trees and undergrowth. The king's new laws instruct my father to prevent anyone on his manor from axing living oak trees or ashes, or even cutting their branches. Not only that, the laws say each villager must pay his wood-penny to my father twice each year if he wants to pick up deadwood, and that in any case he can only bring home five loads — one for spring, summer, and autumn, and two for the winter.

Five loads! How will people in the village be able to cook pottage and stay warm? Does King John want his people to freeze? And where can Will get true wood now to make our tables and stools and shelves?

"Our new king seems very eager to be liked," said my father sarcastically. "These new restrictions are not just."

"They're just according to the king's forest laws," the messenger replied.

"Exactly," said my father. "The king does just as he pleases, and now it pleases him to call unjust rules laws."

Then the messenger told my father that King John intends to appoint a warden for each of his forests.

"But I am the warden of Pike Forest," said my father angrily.

"You will be answerable to him," the messenger said. "From now on, you will pay him all the king's dues you've collected, and he will inspect Pike Forest each month. He and the chief forester will hear cases concerning offenses against the king's animals and trees."

My father is angry not only because the king's new laws reduce his authority, but also because they will cause suffering and everyone will think that he made them. My father may be firm but he's also fair.

The messenger raised his document with the king's red wax disk depending from it. "This is King John's word," he announced. "His loyal earls, lords, and knights are the strength and health of his kingdom, and the king requires them to enforce his laws."

My father nodded but he didn't even offer the messenger rye bread and cheese and ale. He simply walked away into the chamber.

My mother looked at the man. "You're welcome to eat and drink before you ride on," she said.

"I could eat a horse," the messenger said.

"The way things are going," said my mother, "our people here will have to eat grass. They'll have to eat the hens that lay for them. These new laws are very harsh."

"I didn't draw them up," the messenger said.

"I know," said my mother.

"I'm only their voice," the messenger said.

At supper, my father was still angry. "I said the worst was to come," he complained. "A warden for Pike Forest! And dues no one can pay." My father drank a draft of ale. "Well," he said, "I'm not going to stop anyone. They can all collect as much deadwood as they can find."

"But what about the warden?" asked my mother.

"Hang the warden!" said my father coldly. "And hang King John's Christmas present to all his English people."

83

NINE GIFTS

I have been thinking about Tanwen and her baby, and what will happen to her and Serle. And I've been thinking about King John and his new laws, and how all the freezing fieldstones hunch their shoulders and grit their teeth and say nothing. I've been thinking about how the night stars are sometimes so clear they seem to be trilling.

And then this morning Oliver and I talked about how Mary's cousin, Elizabeth, became pregnant, even though she was more than fifty years old, and about the meaning of the gifts that the three wise men of the East brought to baby Jesus.

So I have decided to bring gifts to Jesus as well, nine of them because my number is nine, and this is what I've written:

I bring you my body, darling dear:
My ripening song, my jubilant ear.
That's what Mary sings.

Alleluia!

Well! I bring surprise — this sweet fragrance
Made with love and hope in patience.
That's what Elizabeth says.

Wonder!

I come with a trill and a blue light
And followers stumbling through the night.
That's what the star sings.

Rrrrr!

Well, my lamb, I've got you this fleece
So your old mother can get some peace.
That's what Tom the shepherd says.

Yan! Tan!

I bring not a word, the sound that's silent,
And I'm the broken tooth of a giant.
That's what the stone seems to say.

(   )

I bring you guffaws and loops of mist,
A band of brown hair for your right wrist.
That's what the donkey says.

Eeyore!

I bring you my crown and an uneasy dream
Of new laws and honor, duty and scheme.
That's what King John says.

Heigh-ho!

Open your hand for this glove:
The name of the song in my throat is love.
That's what the ringdove says.

Coo-oo!

But what can I bring you? I bring me,
Whatever I am and all I will be.
That's what each child sings.

Little Jesus!

the sword
in the stone

I have seen brightnesses, but never a brightness like this.

The sun silvering the backs of the shaking alder leaves, and our orchard mounds of newly picked apples, and the man at Ludlow Fair with a yellow and red and green hat and jingling golden bells: All these things are dancing bright, but they are not deep and lasting, and neither was our fallowfield this summer, thick with poppies and cornflowers and trembling fritillaries. This brightness was different.

Each knight wears an oatmeal linen coat over his tunic and breeches, and on the front and back of each coat there has been stitched the shape of a large shield. One shield is flying with five crimson eagles and one is roaring with a purple lion and one is barking with three greyhounds and one is swimming with a swarm of tiddlers — and they're all silver and rose. One shield is midnight blue, with seven stars shining out of it, and one is quartered gold and white, with a black anvil in the middle, so it may be the shield of the Knight of the Black Anvil. Burnt orange stripes and damson squares, pewter circles and triangles yellow as oak leaves are yellow before they turn green; thundercloud ravens and summer-sky-blue keys, bright blood-red crosses and a saffron griffin and a foxy red-brown . . . I've never seen such a panoply of colors and designs as illuminate these shields.

Oliver says that this is what some of the manuscripts at Wenlock Priory are like: borders and whole pages decorated with forever colors, as rich as the colors in early evening sunlight before dusk fades them.

The knights are all standing at the eastern end of a churchyard, staring at something: and behind them there's an enormous pigeon-grey church. I know what it is: the church of Saint Paul.

Now I can see what the knights are staring at. A sword! A naked sword stuck into an anvil, which is sitting on a huge block of dressed stone. The stone is marble, and there's gold lettering cut into it:

HE WHO PULLS THIS SWORD
OUT OF THIS STONE AND ANVIL
IS THE TRUEBORN KING OF ALL BRITAIN

The archbishop of Canterbury, dove-white and scarlet and gold, walks slowly out of the church, and at once some of the knights hurry towards him, and lead him up to the sword in the stone.

"It was not here and it is here," the archbishop says. "Let it be the same with our king. Let him who was, come to be."

Many knights press round the great slab of marble, eager to be the first to try to draw the sword from the stone.

The archbishop raises his golden staff, and then the chill north wind claps its hands, and slaps everyone in the churchyard. The archbishop's vestments tug and ripple, and all the linen surcoats of the knights jump and dance.

The churchyard's in uproar! Oyster and garnet, gold and beech-green and flames. Waves of color! A wind-walloped sea!

"I command you all," the archbishop says, raising his voice above the rising wind. "Come into this church. No man here is to touch this sword until we have all got down on our kneebones. We must pray to baby Jesus to perform a miracle, and beg Him to show us all the trueborn king."

splatting and
sword-pulling

"Yes," said my father. "Woodcocks and larks and a swan."

"Swan," I cried. "We haven't eaten swan since last Christmas."

"And boar's head," said my father. "You haven't forgotten that."

I cried out in excitement and started to sing, and my voice reverberated around the chamber:

> "Welcome to you gathered here!
> You will have good talk, good cheer
> And you'll eat the best of fare
> And sing before you go.
>
> Bring on the first dish of meat!
> A boar's head. That's what you'll eat
> With spicy mustard, subtle, wet,
> And sing before you go."

"Very good," said my father, smiling. "But this isn't a singing lesson."

"I know, sir. I do know some of the right words for carving."

"How do you carve a partridge?" my father asked.

"You wing it," I said.

"You do wing it. That's right. And how do you carve a pigeon?"

"You thigh it, sir."

"That's right, Arthur. And a hen?"

"You spoil it."

"Very good. What about a capon?"

"You . . . you unbrace it."

"No, you don't. That's a duck. You unbrace a duck but you sauce a capon. A rabbit?"

"I don't know, sir."

"No, well, you unlace it. Because it's got so many tendons and sinews inside it. Birds and four-legged beasts and fish: We carve each of them with a different word."

"I love words," I said. But then I wished I hadn't. "But Oliver says I'm slow at reading and even slower at writing," I added.

"How do you carve a pike, then?" my father asked.

At this moment, my mother threw open the door. "John!" she cried. "Please come out here!" And she walked quickly over to us.

"You splat it," said my father, and he closed his eyes and took a deep breath. "What is it, Helen?" he asked.

"Arthur," said my mother, "you go into the hall. I need to talk to your father."

"Splat!" said my father.

I stood up and bowed. "Thank you, father," I said.

There was no one in the hall except for Sian, who had taken a piece of charcoal out of the fire and was busy blackening her fingernails with it.

"Then I'll be like the witch," she said.

"Black Annis, you mean?"

"Yes, and I'll eat you."

"Where is everyone?" I asked.

"When I came in from out," said Sian, "Tanwen was lying down by the fire and sobbing. When I asked her what was wrong, she ran out."

"Where's Serle?"

"He and mother were arguing — up in the gallery."

"What about?"

"Serle shouted at her! Then he came leaping down the staircase, and mother was calling after him."

"What about Nain?" I asked.

"I don't know. Arthur, do witches have black toenails too?"

For a while I waited in the hall, but my father and mother stayed behind their silent chamber door. So after Sian had blackened her toenails, and gobbled me up, I put on my heavy cloak and rabbitskin cap and came up here to my writing-room.

I wanted to see which knights tried to pull the sword out of the stone, and as soon as my obsidian had grown warm, it showed me.

There's a green gloom in the churchyard, and the ivy covering the gravestones is wet and shining.

"All right!" booms one knight with a face as flat as a spade and a surcoat with two scarlet stripes on it. "I've got the strength of two men. I'll give it a try."

He steps up onto the plinth and grabs the sword and three times he tries to wrench it out of the stone.

"I can't move the damned thing," he snorts.

"Go on, then," says a knight with a copper face and copper hair, and a surcoat shield with three castles on it. And he steps up onto the plinth.

"Get out of the way!" shouts the Knight of the Black Anvil. "I'm the man to be king."

The archbishop watches as twelve earls, lords, and knights try to pull the sword from the stone. But none of them succeeds.

"None of you is the trueborn king," says the archbishop. "The one we're looking for is not here."

"Where did this stone come from, anyhow?" asks the spade-faced knight.

"It was not here and it is here," the archbishop replies. "It is a marvel; and when the sword is pulled from the stone, it will be a miracle. Baby Jesus will show us our new king in his own time."

"I doubt it," says a knight whose surcoat shield is white with pink spots all over it, and looks as if it has caught some disease.

"You men are the first to reach London, but hundreds more are on their way," says the archbishop. "Ten of you must stand guard here by night and day. Let everyone know about the sword in the stone, and let anyone who wishes try to pull it out. This is my advice."

"Amen," the knights reply.

"And let no man here return home," says the archbishop. "Let us hold a joust and tournament on New Year's Day. By then, I believe we'll know our trueborn king."

Then the archbishop and the knights faded into my dark stone as sharp-edged stars fade into lightening sky.

For a while I sat in my window seat and hugged my poor right arm and shoulder. I think it must have been the hooded man who spirited the block of marble and the sword and the anvil into Saint Paul's churchyard, because it was he who advised the archbishop to summon all the earls and lords and knights in the country to London. But where has he gone? He wasn't in the churchyard.

I know the hooded man promised to help King Uther's son and come for him when his time came; but even if he rides to London, he won't be allowed to try to pull the sword from the stone, will he? He's not old enough to be a knight. He may not even be a squire.

When I came down to the hall again, Nain was there alone, and she told me why my mother interrupted my carving lessons with my father. "Tanwen fainted in front of us," she said. "And when she opened her eyes again, she began to sob. And in the end, she told us she was having a baby, and four months gone."

I didn't tell Nain about what happened in the armory. Sometimes it's better not to let on how much you already know.

Nain sniffed and hawked and spat on the rushes. "Ugh!" she said. "My mouth keeps filling up. Remember when Serle sat up against Tanwen on the beach? 'Tanwen's white fire,' that's what I told him, 'and it's dangerous to play with white fire.' I knew what was going on."

"What will happen?" I asked Nain.

"What weapon?" said Nain.

"Not weapon, Nain," I said "Happen! What will happen?"

"Speak properly, boy," said Nain. "Tanwen will leave your mother's service. The slut!"

"She's not," I protested.

"And Helen says she'll ask Ruth to serve her in the chamber."

"But it's not just her fault. My father will have to help her."

Nain grunted.

"What about Serle?" I asked.

Nain sucked in her cheeks. "He'll do penance."

"And that's all?"

Nain sighed. "How can your father knight him?" she said. "He can't now. Not yet. And he was going to knight him on Christmas Day."

"I didn't know that," I cried.

"The fool!" said Nain. "Still, he's not the first. And you," she said sharply, "you make sure you're not the next. Where was I?"

"Serle's punishment."

"Your father will take away his hawk . . . I don't know what. I told Helen she's never been strict enough. Your father should have beaten Serle much more often."

"Poor Serle," I said.

Nain sniffed. "No good will come of this," she said. "When I'm dead and buried and food for the worms, there'll still be trouble in this manor because of this. You'll see."

Serle did laugh a lot on Hallowe'en, and he was quite gentle when little Luke died; but during the last few weeks he has seemed to be angry with everyone, and sometimes he has been unkind to me — he told Tom and Grace I'm only a fair-weather friend, and he called me a cuckoo and said my father doesn't want me to be a squire.

He said he hated me then.

But now I think I understand why. Since Serle found out Tanwen was having his baby, he must have felt very worried and upset. He could have talked to me.

86

RIDING TO
LONDON

Arthur-in-the-stone is riding Pip and Sir Ector's riding Anguish and Kay's riding Gwinam. Merlin's traveling with us too. He's riding Sorry.

"I can't promise to keep you company all the way," Merlin says. "But I'll ride as far as Oxford."

I've never seen Kay so happy. "These are the last miles of my life as a squire," he tells me. "Our father says that, in London, he'll knight me."

"What's London like?" I ask.

"It's not like anything," my father says. "You'll see."

"What do you want it to be like?" asks Merlin. "That's the first question."

There are one hundred and sixty long miles between Ludlow and London Bridge, and I have never seen any of them before. This mile is flat, and it looks as though the next one will be too. Some way down the track, three elms are signaling, but there are no other trees here, only bushes and scrub.

Behind Sir Ector and Kay and Merlin and me, a large dark cloud pours upwards. It's like a grey tower, with turrets and a pinnacle; a charcoal tunnel, slowly revolving in the air.

We travelers ride on, but the cloud gallops faster. Soon it overtakes us.

Enormous drops like blisters burst on the track, and kick up little puffs of dust.

Sir Ector and Kay and I pull down our caps and wind our cloaks around us. And Merlin pulls up his floppy hood.

christmas

I am living in two worlds.

In my seeing stone, I'm riding east. Hundreds of knights are on their way to London. Kay is going to be knighted. And in Saint Paul's churchyard, ten knights are standing guard by night and day over the sword in the stone.

But here at Caldicot, it is Christmastide!

I can't write down everything, sweet and sour, that has happened during the last three days or Oliver will complain I'm wasting too much parchment; and anyhow, it's colder than ever up here in my writing-room. Even my left hand feels cold and stiff.

After Mass on Christmas morning, Hum strutted into the hall, blowing the pipe and banging the tabor. Slim followed him, holding up the boar's head on a silver dish, and everyone stood up and sang:

"Bring on the first dish of meat!
A boar's head. That's what you'll eat . . ."

Well, not everyone sang! There were forty-nine of us, and some bawled, some warbled, and the very little ones just went on crying.

On Christmas Eve, my mother and Ruth and Sian and I cut as much holly and yew and ivy and mistletoe as we could carry, and decorated the hall with it. All the rusty old hanging nails were still waiting up on the walls, jammed into the mortar, and I hadn't noticed one of them since last Christmas. Then each tenant hauled a huge Yule log up to the hall to keep our fire burning for twelve days and twelve nights. Brian and Macsen stacked them all outside the hall door, and my father helped them.

Oliver told us at Mass that our hearts are like waiting cradles, and that Jesus must be born in each of us this Christmastide. I've heard him say that before and I like it. Then he reminded us about the new crusade, and he began to denounce the Saracens, and kept driving his right fist into the socket of his left palm.

I could feel my father growing impatient, and then I saw him look at my mother and roll his eyes. Sian saw him too, and she rolled her eyes at me, and I know I shouldn't have done but I turned round and rolled my eyes at Gatty, and when I turned round for a second time, just about everyone in church was rolling their eyes and laughing.

Yes, everyone in the family, even Nain, had a warm bath in the chamber before Christmas — for three days, Ruth and Martha were busy carrying water into the kitchen, and heating it over the fire. Yes, my father gave a white loaf to each man who sat at our feast. And yes, at the end of the feast, my father and Giles and Joan exchanged riddles, new and old, as they always do.

"What's most like a stallion?" my father asked.

"A mare," said Joan. "What grows with its root upward and its head downward?"

"An icicle," said my father. "What do I keep in my pocket but you throw away?"

"Snot!" said Giles. "Your snot in your kerchief. Who goes round and round this hall and leaves his gloves on the ledges?"

"Snow does," said Joan. "What about this? Which beast has its tail between its eyes?"

My father and Giles frowned and looked at each other.

"Its tail between its eyes . . ." repeated my father. "Does anyone know?"

"Spitfire!" said Sian unexpectedly. "Spitfire did! I saw her like that when she licked herself."

"Sian!" exclaimed my mother.

Then everyone laughed, and Dutton went lolloping along the benches, walloping everyone with poor Stupid's bladder which he'd half filled with rattling peas.

"One more," said Giles. "How many calves' tails do you need to climb from earth to heaven?"

"One," shouted Joan. "One if it's long enough."

"And this is the last one," my father said. "What was the most precious burden ever borne, and who carried it?"

But before Joan or Giles or anyone else could answer my father, the door burst open, and a wodwo stumbled into the hall. He had a garland of rosemary around his neck, and clumps of black hair flapped against his chest and back. It grew in tufts on the back of his hands and forearms and below his knees. He was wearing a sheep skin — I wondered whether it was poor Matty's — and as he lumbered across the hall, pointing at my mother, he shouted out strange words and half words: "I, I, glim, glim-gleam, you, breast bitty-breast, you, unna, tinna, I, you, Henna, Helen, dara, dick!"

My mother pretended not to know the wildman was

Wat Harelip. She screamed as he clambered right over the table towards her, reaching out with his hairy hands. Then my father put his arms right round her, and Dutton smacked Wat with his bladder until he fell over backwards, right into Johanna's lap, and everyone cheered.

Yes, we prayed all the prayers and ate the sweetmeats and told the jokes and played the games and sang all the songs that link Christmases like a chain of winter flowers — golden stars and stinking hellebore, paradise plants and rosemary: So that here, in our hall on the Welsh Marches, we were all part of the story that began when Jesus was born and will not end until Domesday.

"I know that answer," Oliver suddenly bellowed.

"But what is the question?" Merlin asked. "Do you know what the question is, Oliver?"

"I know the precious burden," said Oliver. "The answer should be baby Jesus and his mother Mary when they fled to Egypt. Baby Jesus and Mary and the ass who carried them. That's what the answer should be."

"It is the answer," said my father, smiling.

"Ah!" said Oliver, and he beamed.

"What about the god, then?" demanded Nain.

"What was that, Nain?" my father asked.

"Carried away by boat from this middle-world."

"God?" said Oliver.

Nain sniffed and shook her head. "Knowing little is worse than knowing nothing," she said.

Now that I'm thirteen, I realize that although Christmas was the same as it has always been, it was not the same. And I want to write down the three things that have made this Christmas different.

Saint Stephen's Day was fine and quite mild, so almost

everyone in the manor came to the Yard for the games, but I wasn't allowed to compete because my right arm is still rather sore.

There were three cockfights, and Will's cock was the winner. Cleg the miller won the wrestling contest as he did last year, and I'm not surprised because he's a whole head taller than anyone else, and his chest's as broad as a cart-horse's.

Then it was the leaping contest. My father stretched out a length of rope and everyone had to jump from behind it, and Gatty and I pushed little sticks into the hard ground to mark the jumps. Johanna was first, and she leaped rather less than one of my father's strides, and everyone started to laugh. Sian leaped five feet and Serle leaped thirteen feet, and for a while Hum was the leader with sixteen feet, and Oliver lifted his frock and ran up to leap, but then he stopped because his knees hurt.

"Well then, Merlin," my father called out.

"No," said Merlin.

"Yes," shouted Sian.

"A leap of faith!" said Oliver.

"Come on, Merlin!" said my mother, smiling and clapping her hands.

"All right," said Merlin. And everyone laughed and called out encouragement and insults.

It happened so quickly. As if it were over before it began. Merlin stepped ten paces back from the rope and then, on his light feet, he bounded up to the rope and sprang into the air.

Forty-seven feet! Merlin leaped forty-seven feet. Some people hid their eyes; and some began to yell and cheer.

"Again!"

"Do it again, Merlin!"

"Impossible!"

"Magic!"

"Again!"

"Once is quite enough," said Merlin quietly. "One sip from the chalice of feats."

"Feats?" I said.

"Juggling nine apples, and the spurt of speed, and the snapping mouth, and the stepping on a flying lance, the stunning-shot, and this — this salmon-leap."

Oliver rubbed his red mouth with the back of his hand, and said nothing.

"You can do these things?" my father asked. "These feats?"

"Oh yes!" said Merlin, quite modestly.

"But I've never heard of them," I said.

"No," said Merlin. He thought for a moment. "Well! Just as you're learning swordplay and tilting and archery here, I learned these feats. Once upon a time."

"But that leap!" I said. "It's magic."

"Is it?" asked Merlin.

In the autumn, Oliver asked Merlin whether he denied Christ, and Merlin said he did not, not for a moment, but that we'd all do well to call on the nine spirits, each with a bottomless chalice.

"Cow dung!" That's what Oliver replied. "There's no room in the house of Christ for nine spirits."

But what if there is? What if it's possible to believe in the nine spirits as well as in Christ? Merlin does. Or is he a heretic? Is it true that he'd be burned if my father didn't protect him?

I know it's Christmastide, and Jesus must be born

again in my waiting heart, but I think Merlin understands more than anyone else in this manor, and part of what he knows is very old, and as magic as my seeing stone. Or at least it seems miraculous. The hooded man told the archbishop that "Many things seem miraculous until you understand them — and some are so marvelous you could call them miracles."

So the first thing that made this Christmas different was Merlin's salmon-leap. And the second was the red roses.

Yesterday, we had three visitors. Two musicians first, a man with a five-string fiddle and his daughter. She was my age. Her face was very white, and she had dark shadows under her eyes, but her voice was clear and piercing.

> "Love without heartache, love without fear
> Is fire without flame and flame without heat.
> *Dulcis amor!*
>
> Love without heartache, love without fear
> Is day without sunlight, hive without honey.
> *Dulcis amor!*
>
> Love without heartache, love without fear
> Is summer without flower, winter without frost.
> *Dulcis amor!*"

That's what this girl sang, and while she was still singing, our third visitor arrived. It was Thomas, Sir William and Lady Alice's messenger, with gifts for us.

For my mother, an ivory comb with thirty-five white teeth, one for each year of her life; for my father, a linen kerchief with a scarlet *J* stitched by Grace in one corner; for Serle a studded belt; and for Sian a little silver ring with a blue stone set into it. And for me, six long-stemmed red roses, just opening.

"Lady Alice says they need water — water from the fountain in the middle of the forest," said Thomas.

"Which forest?" demanded my father. "What does she mean?"

"It's because I told her about a magic fountain," I said.

"All your fancies!" said my father rather testily.

Christmas is like an enclosing wall. A fold. We're inside it, eating and drinking and keeping warm and singing, but we know all the year's hungers and terrors and lessons and anxieties and opportunities and sorrows are still there on the outside. We know they're all waiting for us, just as the Knight of the Black Anvil lies in wait for anyone who rides to the forest fountain, and we haven't forgotten them.

I've never thought about this before, the way in which Christmastide is the one and only stopping-place in the long dance of the year. So this is the third thing which has made this Christmas different.

The Christmas fold: Most of us are inside it, but not all of us. Not Tanwen. Poor Tanwen. She didn't come to our feast; she didn't come to the Yard. I haven't even seen her since she ran out of the hall. No mother; no father. Who will look after her? Has Serle gone to see her? Has he taken meat and a white loaf and ale for her and her baby?

Not Lankin. He's not inside the fold. Since the trial, he has stayed inside his hut, and only Jankin and Johanna have seen him.

Will Jankin and Gatty still be betrothed? Will Hum

and Lankin ever agree to it? And will Lankin's wound fester, and will he die?

For that matter, what will become of Serle? He prayed at Mass and sat at the feast and competed in the Yard, but he was very quiet and everyone is talking behind his back.

Poor Serle. This Christmastide, he has been inside and outside the fold.

As we sat near the fire, sipping ale, I grasped his right elbow. "Serle," I said, very quietly.

"What?" said Serle in a dull, flat voice.

Slowly he turned and looked at me, and I looked straight back at him, and smiled.

Serle lowered his eyes.

Kay has traveled the last miles of his life as a squire. He's standing in front of the high altar in the church of Saint Paul, and Arthur-in-the-stone is standing beside him. Sir Ector and the archbishop of Canterbury are facing us, and all around us, in the gloom, I can see a company of knights — the Knight of the Black Anvil and the copper-colored knight and the spade-faced knight, the ten knights who have guarded the sword in the stone, the hundreds of knights who have ridden to London.

I can't see Merlin anywhere. Well! He said he'd only ride with us as far as Oxford, but I thought he might change his mind.

Kay keeps rubbing the top of his head. It must be sore because it has been shaved, and he has a bald spot as big and round as an egg yolk.

Kay's wearing a white robe and, over that, a scarlet cloak with a white belt, because he's ready to shed blood fighting for the Church, and will always try to be pure in mind and body.

"Kay," says the archbishop. His voice is loud and deep, and it echoes around the church. "Why do you wish to become a knight?"

Kay doesn't reply.

"To amass treasure?" demands the archbishop. "To lay your hands on booty?"

"To amass . . ." the echo answers. "To lay your hands . . ."

"Or so that other people have to bow down before you?" continues the archbishop.

"No," says Kay in a firm voice. "I wish to become a knight so I may serve Christ the Lord, pure in mind and pure in body. So I may live for Christ as He died for me."

"Whom will you protect?" asks the archbishop.

"All those who need my protection," Kay replies. "In this kingdom, too many people suffer injustice. The rich rob the poor; the strong trample the weak. Widows and orphans are defenseless. I will oppose evil wherever I find it."

"It is said, and well said," says the archbishop.

"Said . . ." booms the great church. "Said . . . well said . . ."

Now Kay gets down onto his left knee, and Sir Ector picks up Kay's sword from the high altar. He raises it and it hovers over Kay's right shoulder, its tip glinting like the wing of a dragonfly.

Three times and lightly my father taps Kay on the shoulder.

"In the name of God and Saint Edmund," he says, "I dub you knight. Sir Kay, be gallant. Be courteous. Be loyal."

At once all the knights in the church begin to call out "Sir Kay! Sir Kay!" And now they break rank, and crowd round us; they slap Kay's back, and shake him by the right hand. And Kay, Sir Kay, turns towards me . . .

All at once, my seeing stone went dark. Dark as a raven's wing. An old nail-head. Dark as the fresh earth on little Luke's grave.

fourth son

Slim served cold carp with a hot, spicy sauce for dinner this morning and, as soon as we'd finished, Will came wading into the hall.

"I'm sorry and all," he said. "I know it's Christmastide and all, but I finished it, and it's proper to put it up before the end of the year."

Will laid the stone on the end of the long table, and my father and mother inspected it.

"Very handsome," my father said. "Come and have a look, Arthur! Will has cut your letters so deep they'll last one hundred years."

One hundred years! 1299. Will this manor still be here then? And will Caldicots still be the lords of it? Five generations?

"Call him son! Call him brother!" my father said. "Very good, Arthur! You must say your poem when we put up the stone. We'll do it this afternoon, and then I want you and Sian to help me make an icehouse."

"And Gatty?" I asked.

"Good idea," my father said. "In case Sian needs to be rescued."

Then I looked at little Luke's tombstone.

"Father," I cried. "It's wrong."

"Wrong?"

"Look! It says fourth son. Luke wasn't your fourth son."

My father bent over the tombstone, and sighed gently.

"Yes," he said. "So it does." Then he looked up at me. "Well! I wrote it down for Will. It doesn't matter."

"Doesn't matter?" I cried. "Serle, me, Matthew, Mark, Luke . . ." I began to shiver and I couldn't stop.

How can my father have mislaid one of his sons? Or did he mean to write "fourth"? That could only mean that one of his sons is not his son. It's not me, is it? Am I not my father's son? How can I find out?

Perhaps I can ask my mother, or Nain. It's no good asking my father, he doesn't tell me anything.

Tanwen loved little Luke and, when he was so ill, she often sat up all night nursing him. So my mother sent Ruth down to Tanwen's cottage, and asked her to meet us at the lych-gate, and help put up Luke's tombstone.

Tanwen wouldn't come, though, so my mother went down to her cottage herself, and brought her to the graveyard. She had an arm round Tanwen's waist.

But perhaps it would have been better if Tanwen hadn't come. Serle nodded curtly to her, but then he stood as far away from her as he could, on the opposite side of the grave, with his heels on Mark's grave, and he kept biting his lower lip. Nain turned her back on Tanwen, and when I spoke my poem, Tanwen began to shake and then to weep without making a sound, and I knew she was thinking about her own baby, and what will happen to it.

"A mother whose baby is taken away from her must not weep," said Oliver. "Our Lord God shows great kindness when he takes a child away from this foul world. Babies and children, they're alive. They are angels."

When Oliver said this, I remembered how Merlin told me that Oliver was wrong and a heretic. I looked at Merlin, but he had put one arm around Tanwen, and did not look at me.

Will dug a little trench right next to Luke's head, and lowered the bottom of the gravestone into it. Then we packed black earth around it, and I said my poem, and each of us touched the stone. My mother and father were first — but is it true? Have they only had four sons?

Nain followed them and as she touched the stone, she said, "May the birds of Rhiannon sing over you." Serle was next, then me and Sian. Oliver followed us. Then Merlin and Tanwen. And if our tears and longings count for anything, Luke's gravestone will stand upright forever.

There are just two more days in this century — today and tomorrow — and I think time gives authority to words. "Little Luke. Fourth son of Sir John and Lady Helen de Caldicot." In one hundred years, people will believe what this tombstone says, whether or not it is true. But I am alive now, and I need to find out.

the turning of
the century

"It's time you and I talked."

That's what my father said to me, up on the top of Tumber Hill.

The huge bonfire blazed. Its heart was brighter and darker than anything I've ever seen, and it spat golden and orange fireflies at the stars. All around us, white faces and black faces gamboled and gallumphed and gallivanted and shouted and sang.

I saw Gatty and Jankin in the shadows, their eyes shining, and Sian spitfiring around the flames, clapping and jumping; I saw Merlin striding along the hilltop with his dark cloak behind him.

Away north, I could see fires burning at Wart Hill and Woolston and Black Knoll and Prior's Holt. To the south I saw fires at Brandhill and Downton-on-the-Rock, Leintwardine Manor and far Stormer; and away to the southwest, there was a ninth fire, so far off that it kept blinking, white and cold and uncertain of itself, like a fallen star. My father said he thought this fire was at Stanage, or else Stow Hill.

Nine fires and our own fire, roaring and crackling. But away west in front of us, there was nothing but a mask of darkness — Pike Forest and the wilderness of Wales.

My father and I stood shoulder to shoulder, looking

out, looking ahead; and far below, Oliver began to toll the church bell.

Each toll was like a deep breath, followed by long silence. The old year was dying.

Then the bell stopped tolling and, high on the hill, we all stood silent. Humans and animals and birds and trees: We held our breath.

All at once, Oliver began to peal the bell as fast as he could. He rang it and rang it, and we all cheered and hugged each other. The new century had begun!

Nothing was different, but everything seemed so. The gift of the new century to each of us is hope and intention and energy, and these things can cause great changes.

"It's time you and I talked," my father said.

"Your plans for me, you mean?" I asked falteringly.

"Yes," said my father. "After all, you can't see in the dark, can you?"

Then he took my sore right arm and, holding a flaming brand, gently and firmly guided me down Tumber Hill.

"In the morning, then," said my father. "The first morning of the new century. Can you wait until then?"

lightly and fiercely

My stone was glowing through its filthy saffron cloth. I swear it was.

I knew I wouldn't be able to sleep. Not after my father's promise to talk to me. So as soon as everyone was breathing deeply, I lit two candles and came up here to my writing-room.

At once I pulled my obsidian out of its crevice, and unwrapped it. It was alive. It was seeing and speaking again, and now it has shown me something quite wonderful. A New Year miracle.

Sir Ector and Sir Kay and Arthur-in-the-stone are cantering along London wall, and I'm carrying my father's banner. There are knights and squires riding beside us, in front of us, behind us; all the knights are wearing shining armor, and the squires are carrying their lords' banners.

"Today we'll tourney," my father says to Kay. "Tomorrow we'll joust."

"Agreed," shouts Kay.

We're all in high spirits, and so is the west wind. It guffaws and tugs at all our banners; it whistles through the bars of the knights' visors.

Now I can see the tournament field: a throng of ladies and knights and squires and horses, pavilions, little striped tents. I can hear such a hubbub: talk and laughter and singing and braying trumpets.

"No!" yells Kay. Then he pulls up so sharply that

Gwinam throws back his head and whinnies, and kicks up his front hooves.

"What is it?" asks my father.

"My sword!"

"Sir Kay!" my father exclaims.

"Arthur! You dressed me. Surely you noticed."

"No, Kay," says Sir Ector. "Blame yourself."

"Please," says Kay. "Please, Arthur, will you go back and get it from our lodging?"

"We'll wait for you beside the judges' tent," my father says.

I wheel Pip round. I turn my back on all the rainbow colors and the trumpets, and gallop as fast as I can into grey London.

I know Arthur-in-the-stone didn't want to let Kay down. He had only just been knighted, and this was his first fighting tournament. But if Serle left something behind, I wouldn't go to get it. He has so often been unkind to me during this past year. No! Arthur-in-the-stone and I are the same and not the same.

I clatter down the highway past the church of Saint Paul, and then I thread my way through the narrow streets, right and left and left and right, until I reach our lodgings.

Without dismounting, I lean out of my saddle and knock at the door. I bang the door a second time. I hammer it a third time. But there's no one at home. The door's locked and the windows are barred. Maybe everyone has gone to watch the tournament.

"What can I do?" I say. "Kay must have a sword today."

Arthur-in-the-stone pulls at the roots of his hair in the

way I always do when I'm thinking, and then shouts, "I know! I know what!"

My voice bounces from wall to wall all the way down the string-thin street. "Sir Kay needs a sword and he'll have a sword. I'll go back to the churchyard."

I gallop back to the lych-gate, dismount, and tie Pip to it.

"Wait here!" I say, and Pip looks at me with the mournful look of a horse well used to waiting.

I have ridden so hard from tournament to lodgings, lodgings to lych-gate, but now I'm behaving as if there's all the time in the world.

Somehow I know that unless I am quite calm, I will never do anything really well. I must not rush or snatch. I must always unhurry.

Look! I walk in under the shadow of the great church, and round to the eastern end.

I walk up to the huge block of dressed stone, decorated with gold lettering, with the sword and anvil sitting on it.

Slowly I step up onto the plinth of stone.

There is no one else in the churchyard. Just Arthur-in-the-stone, and a dozen London pigeons, pink-eyed, purple breasted.

I stare at the sword, and I think I look almost angry, yet very calm. I stare until there's nothing else in the world except for the sword and me.

I open my left palm, and grasp the winter-cold hilt. I close my eyes and open my eyes. Lightly and fiercely I pull the sword, and it slides out of the stone.

the whole armor

At dawn it was so cold in my writing-room, and so cold outside. But I was burning.

Oliver was already up. I saw him on his way over to the church and called out to him. We exchanged New Year's greetings, and then I told him how we could all hear the Watch Night bell, all of us up on top of Tumber Hill.

Oliver produced his Bible from inside his cloak. "Choose a page," he said. "And now close your eyes . . ."

I made a circle in the air with my right forefinger, and then dabbed the page.

"The Letter of Saint Paul to the Ephesians," Oliver announced. "'Take the helmet of salvation and the sword of the Spirit, which is the word of God.' There, Arthur, what does that tell you?"

"The truth!" I shouted. "I have taken the sword. I have! I took it out of the stone!"

"What are you talking about?" said Oliver.

"I've seen a miracle," I cried. "A light in the dark before dawn."

"New Year madness," said Oliver, snapping his Bible shut. "You're not the first either. Last night I met Joan and Brian when they came down from the hill, and they clutched at me and begged me to bless them."

"Why?"

"They were afraid. They said they saw Merlin flying down from Tumber Hill."

"Tumber Hill," I exclaimed. "He did disappear once, and he can leap like a salmon, but I don't think he can fly."

"Merlin hasn't got wings, has he?" said Oliver. "Of course he can't fly. Now Arthur, you chose those words and they chose you."

"Yes, Oliver."

"Put on the belt of truth and the breastplate of righteousness. That's what Saint Paul tells us. Hold up your shield of faith. Brandish the sword of the Spirit, which is the word of the Lord. That's the way of life you've chosen for yourself, Arthur. Put on the whole armor of God."

93

KING OF BRITAIN

How can everyone sleep this long? They're like squirrels. Like dormice.

Nain and Serle and Sian and Ruth and Slim and Martha were all still asleep when I ran back into the hall, and my father and mother were still in their chamber, so I kept running. Up the stairs and along the balcony and into my writing-room!

In my stone and in my life, the old century has ended, the new century begun, and everything is quickening.

Or is it flying? Brian's and Joan's eyes must have been playing tricks on them. Had they drunk too much ale?

First my stone fizzes like sharp stars dancing on a freezing night. Then it grows quiet, it darkens and deepens. It invites me into it.

I can see my ears sticking out. My mouth opening like a fish. My wide nostrils. I grin; then I scowl, and bare my teeth at my stone . . .

Now I can see him. He's riding towards me, waving his sword.

Arthur! Arthur-in-my-stone! Take me with you!

My namesake trots onto the tournament field, past seven knights all dressed in orange and gold. Each knight is captive to a lady who holds a long orange cord attached to the bridle of his horse.

Raising the sword, I canter down the lists and past the long pavilion, until I reach the judges' tent. I see Kay waiting there, and sit straight up in my saddle. I brandish the sword. A slice of blinding sunlight!

Kay looks at the sword. He knows at once it isn't his, and he knows where it comes from. He bites his lower lip as Serle always does when he's nervous.

Politely I reverse the sword and offer the hilt to Kay.

"Thank you, Arthur," he says. "Thank you very much."

"I've never been to a tournament," I say. "I want to see everything!"

"Ride around then," Kay replies. "I'll find my father and meet you back here."

Then I ride away, but my stone can still see Kay. He trots along the ground and finds Sir Ector at the far side of the pavilion, outside the second judges' tent.

Sir Ector stares at the sword.

"I got tired of waiting for Arthur," Kay says, "so I went back into the city myself."

"But that's not your sword."

"No! I rode past the church and . . . I am the king, father."

"You?"

"I am the king, I must be."

At this moment, I ride back into the stone again.

I meet Sir Ector and Kay at the tent which looks like a castle, with knights waving banners and guarding it, and little turrets as green as beech leaves.

My father looks at me, and then at Kay.

"Follow me!" he commands us, and at once he spurs Anguish, and gallops straight out of the tournament field towards the church of Saint Paul.

"Father!" I call out. "Wait! I want to see the tournament. Please!"

It's no use, though. My words are no more than mouthfuls of air.

Inside the church, my father tells Kay, "Put your right hand on the Bible. . . . Now! How did you come by this sword, Kay?"

Kay bites his lip again. "Arthur brought it to me," he says.

"Then give it back to him," my father says. "Arthur, how did you come by this sword?"

"I rode back to our lodging, but there was nobody there. Not one servant. The door was locked and all the windows were barred."

"And then?" Sir Ector asks me.

"I didn't know what to do. Then I thought of the sword in the churchyard, and so I rode here as fast as I could. I pulled it out of the stone."

"Was anyone guarding it?" Sir Ector says.

"No one, sir."

"Kay," snaps Sir Ector. "Stop biting your lip! You'll tear it to pieces."

And now my father gazes at me; he looks right into me with his unblinking, silver-grey eyes.

"Then I believe you are the king of this country," he says.

"I can't be," I say.

"No one could draw this sword unless he's the trueborn king."

"But I'm not."

"Show me!" says Sir Ector, leading the way out of the church. "Can you fit the sword back into the stone and then pull it out again?"

"I think I can," I say.

Now I slide the sword back into the stone, almost up to the hilt. Sir Ector steps up onto the plinth and tries to pull it out. He bends his back to it, but the sword remains fast in the stone.

"You try, Kay," my father says, and Kay tries to snatch the sword out of the stone.

"Now you!" my father says, and I step up to the stone. I stare at the sword until there's nothing else in the world except for the sword and me. Then I grasp the hilt. All around us, a storm of sparrows rush to and fro across the churchyard. The biting steel and rough stone whisper; they softly sigh, as a grass blade sighs when it is drawn from its green scabbard, and I slide the sword out of the stone for a second time.

At once Sir Ector gets down onto his right knee, the one that sometimes hurts him, and Kay gets down beside him.

"Father!" I say, starting forward.

"No," he says. "I am not your father."

"What do you mean?" I cry.

"You are not my son, born of my blood."

"Father!" I cry.

"Listen, Arthur," Sir Ector says. "Before you were born, when Uther was still a king, a stranger rode in to Caldicot. A hooded man. This hooded man asked me and your mother to be foster parents.

"'To foster a boy unborn.' That's what the hooded man said.

"'Who are the parents?' we asked.

"But the hooded man could not say, or else he would not tell us.

"All the same, your mother and I were glad to agree.

301

Your mother had been ill and was unable to have any more children, and we were glad of a sibling for Kay.

"'I will bring him to you when he is two days old,' the hooded man told us, 'and you must raise him as your own son. Have him christened Arthur but, for as long as this century lasts, do not tell him he's your foster son. I will watch over him. I will come for him when his time comes.'"

"Father!" I cry.

"Now I know who you are," Sir Ector says. "You are the son King Uther spoke of when I knelt to him. You are the son of King Uther and Queen Ygerna."

I reach out for Sir Ector and Sir Kay, and raise them both to their feet. Should I be happy? I feel so sad.

"But you are my father," I say. "You are the man I will always owe most to."

Sir Ector and Sir Kay stand apart from me. There is a distance between us now, for all that we wish there was not.

"You've cared as much for me as for Kay," I say, "and if ever I become king, as you say I will, you can ask me for whatever you want. I will not fail you. God forbid that I should fail you."

"Sire," my father says to me. "Only this. Kay is your foster brother. When you become king, honor him."

BLOOD-TRUTHS

My heart began to quicken as I followed my father into the chamber. He gestured to me to sit on one side of the Great Bed, and then he sat down in his dressing chair.

"Why now?" he began. "Why not yesterday or tomorrow? I know you've been impatient, haven't you?"

"Yes, father."

My father stood up again. "I was the same when I was thirteen," he said. "Well, firstly I've had to make decisions and arrangements, and they take time. Secondly, I gave a solemn undertaking . . ."

"To my mother, you mean?"

"Be patient! You'll understand why and to whom in good time. Now! Some of the things I have to tell you will make you glad. But some will not. You must be brave, Arthur, and bravery means facing and accepting the truth."

"Yes, father," I said in a low voice.

"I've tried to act in your best interests," my father said. "I always have and I always will. So, then. Do you remember I said you'd make a good schoolman?"

My heart began to bang in my chest.

"Well?"

"Yes, father," I said in a low voice.

"And so you would. You're that clever. That's what Oliver says, and Merlin as well. Yes, and I think you'd make a good priest, too," my father said. "But what I be-lieve is that you'd make an even better squire."

"Father!" I cried, and I stood up.

"Sit down!" said my father. "A squire and then a knight. That's what you want, isn't it?"

"Oh yes!" I cried.

"You're good enough at your Yard-skills," said my fa-ther. "Just about! Though you need to sharpen up your swordplay, don't you?"

"I will," I cried.

"Anyhow," said my father, "there's more to knighthood than fighting skills. A good deal more, though not all knights seem to think so. But first things first! Three years' service as a squire."

"With you, sir?" I asked.

"You want to serve with me?" my father replied. "I thought you wanted to go away into service. The same as Serle."

"It doesn't matter," I said.

"Well, why have I gone to all this trouble, then?" said my father, smiling.

"You mean . . ."

"I mean," said my father.

"With Sir William?"

"Certainly not!" my father replied very firmly. "I've arranged for you to go into service with Lord Stephen."

"Lord Stephen!" I exclaimed. "But you said one de Caldicot would be quite enough for him."

"I did, Arthur. But do you remember the manor court? Lord Stephen liked the way you stood up for Lankin. 'That young son of yours,' he said to me, 'he's his own man.'"

"He said that?"

"He asked for you as his squire."

"Asked for me!"

"So that's all right?"

I leaped up again and this time my father didn't stop me. I bowed to him, and then I embraced him.

"When will I go?" I asked.

"At Eastertide," my father replied. "Your arm has almost healed, hasn't it?"

"Yes, father."

"Well, now you must practice."

"I will," I cried. "Each morning."

"Now!" said my father. "Sit down again."

He dragged his dressing chair across the chamber to the side of the bed.

"This isn't so easy," he said. Then he reached out and took my right hand. "Arthur," he said, "you are not my blood-son. You are my foster son. And Lady Helen, she's your foster mother."

First I stared at my father and prayed he wasn't telling me the truth. Then I lowered my eyes.

"I almost knew," I said. My voice sounded very strange: as if it came from somewhere outside my body. "Fourth son. That's what it said on Luke's tombstone. Who is he, then? Who is my first father?"

My father cleared his throat. "Sir William," he said.

"Sir William!" I yelped, and I pulled my hand away from my father's warm hand.

My father nodded. "My brother," he said.

"But that means . . . that means Grace is my sister."

"Your half-sister," said my father.

"Who is my mother, then?" I demanded.

"Be calm," said my father, laying his firm hand over

305

mine again. "Sir William's your blood-father. I can't tell you who your mother is, because I don't know. A woman living on his manor."

"At Gortanore?"

"So I believe."

"You mean it's like Serle and Tanwen."

"In a way, yes," said my father. "But the fact is Sir William was already married. To Lady Tilda. So she and Sir William agreed it would be better if the baby — if you, Arthur — were taken away."

"Better?" I said.

"Yes."

"Who for?"

"Everyone," said my father.

"Not for my mother," I said bleakly.

"So Sir William asked Lady Helen and me whether we'd foster you. And that's what happened, Arthur. We were glad to have a brother for Serle because Lady Helen had been very ill, and we supposed she'd never have another child. And anyhow, I wanted to help my brother."

"But Grace," I said.

"I know," said my father. "This does mean, of course, that you can't be betrothed to her, and I know that's what you hoped."

"We both did," I said sadly.

"But you're not losing her," my father said. "She's your own half-sister. We'll find you another wife."

"Does Sir William know you're telling me?" I asked.

"That's why he and Lady Alice came over before Christmas," my father replied. "To discuss everything."

"And to wound me," I said.

"Yes, well . . ." said my father grimly.

"I thought you were talking about our betrothal and my going into service."

"Sir William and I had this understanding," said my father. "We were free to bring you up as we chose on condition I didn't tell you anything until now."

"Why now?" I asked.

"Because now you're old enough to understand. Last night was a crossing-place. Today is a starting-place."

"Who knows I'm Sir William's son," I asked, "except for you and my mother?"

"Nain," my father replied. "Nain and Merlin. That's all."

"Not Serle?"

"No. He was only three when Sir William brought you over. And we led everyone on the manor to believe you were Lady Helen's own baby."

"Lady Alice," I said. "She knows."

"Well, she does now," said my father slowly, and he pursed his lips. "I think I'd better tell you the whole story, Arthur. Your aunt Tilda died in giving birth to Grace. Very soon after that, Sir William married again, he married Lady Alice and didn't think it was a good idea to tell her everything . . ."

"About me, you mean?"

"About you, yes . . . and everything."

"What, father?"

My father frowned, and then sniffed. "Your blood-mother, Arthur, well, she was married. But you know how forceful Sir William is."

"Yes, father."

"Well, one Sunday morning, your mother's young husband stood up in church and accused Sir William, and threatened him. In church! In front of all his tenants! Can you imagine?"

"What did Sir William do?" I asked.

"Not long after that," said my father, "this young man disappeared. He just disappeared." Slowly, very slowly, my father drew in his breath: It sounded like water beginning to seethe in a pan. "I don't know," he said. "I don't! But there were more ugly accusations. I do know there were rumors that he was murdered."

"That Sir William murdered him," I said.

"But no one could prove it," said my father. "Still, you can see why Sir William didn't want Lady Alice to know. Her own parents were dead but her guardian uncle would never have agreed to their marriage. So he kept quiet. But of course Alice hadn't been married long before she heard about the sending away of a baby and a young man's disappearance. But I don't think Lady Alice ever knew there was a connection between them and Sir William."

"I think she may have done," I said.

"You do, do you," said my father, and he looked at me thoughtfully.

"Father," I said, "how do you know all this — about the husband's threats in church, and the rumors?"

"Thomas!" said my father abruptly. "He's my brother's messenger, but he's loyal to me."

"I don't like Sir William," I said. "I don't care whether he's my father or not."

"I understand," said my father quite calmly. "But this is a time for facts, not feelings. Lady Helen and I have brought you up, but Sir William's responsible for your inheritance. You are listening?"

"Yes, father."

"You know Sir William owns three manors — the one at Gortanore, and one at Catmole, and one over the sea in Champagne? He has set aside the estate at Catmole for you, Arthur. And without that . . ."

"Serle told me you didn't want me to be a squire," I said. "He said that if I became a knight, you'd have to give me a parcel of Caldicot land, and that would weaken the manor. He said I'd never be able to make a good marriage. He said . . ."

"What?" asked my father gently.

"He said I was . . ." My throat tightened. "He said I was . . . I was a cuckoo." And with that, I burst into tears.

My father sat quietly beside me, his right hand over mine once more. He waited while I sniffed and snuffled like a dismal mole.

"Serle's jealous," said my father. "He's been afraid you'll take away the ground he stands on."

"Have you told him?" I asked. "What you've told me?"

My father shook his head. "No," he said.

"Can I tell him?"

"I will talk to him first," my father replied. "You go and find Lady Helen and comfort her. I do believe she thinks she's losing a son."

"Lady Helen's my mother," I cried, "and she's the woman I'll always owe most to. You are my father."

"And you're no cuckoo," my father said. He stood up and stretched. "You're your own young man."

I reached out, and my father pulled me to my feet.

"I'm proud of you," he said. "Who we are isn't only a matter of blood; it's what we make of ourselves. And you, Arthur, are fit to be a king!"

The Christmas fold! It has been breached.

For four days everything my father has told me has buzzed inside my head and my heart. It has followed me everywhere — the hall, my writing-room, the stables, the church, up and down the stream. The only way I can escape is into my other world: my obsidian.

But what kind of escape is that? Arthur-in-the-stone is no more Sir Ector's son than I am Sir John's son. But I never knew that until I pulled the sword from the stone, and Sir Ector told me King Uther was my father and Ygerna my mother. When I saw myself in the stone, begging Sir Pellinore to knight me, and dreaming butterflies into the fists of Sir Lamorak and Sir Owain, and riding to London, I never realized I was also the baby the hooded man delivered to Sir Ector and his wife. So now at last I understand why the stone showed me King Uther and Ygerna. They're the beginning of my own stone-story.

In the stone, Sir William tried to kill me when he ambushed me up in the tree. But I killed him. And then, when he came here before Christmas, he wounded me. Sometimes what happens in my life echoes what happens in the stone, sometimes it's the other way round. But my stone also shows me people and places I've never seen before — the fortress of Tintagel, King Uther, Ygerna, the hooded man.

The archbishop is standing beside the sword in the

stone. Around him stand all the great men of Britain, and around them, packing the whole churchyard and the highway beyond it, jostle the people of London.

One by one the earls and lords and knights step up onto the plinth. They grunt and strain and yell and spit on their palms, they growl and crack their bones and curse: but not one of them can shift the sword in the stone.

"Sir Ector tells us his squire Arthur can do it," the archbishop says.

"I swear it," says my father.

"Prove it!" shout one hundred knights, and they're none too friendly.

"Show us, Arthur," the archbishop says to me.

So I step up onto the plinth for the third time. I know what I have to do. I gaze at the sword until the stamping earls and the hooting lords and the whistling knights and all the people of London seem to fall away from me, and there is a great space around me. I stare until there's nothing else in the world except for the sword and me. . . .

First they gasp, the earls and lords and knights, like a hundred swords cutting the cold air; then for a moment they're silent, and then they all begin to shout. They're angry, they argue.

But look! The hooded man is stepping out of the crowd of townspeople. I didn't even know he was here.

He works his way through the throng and steps up onto the plinth beside the archbishop and me.

"A boy!" he calls out, and his grand, dark voice rings around the crowd. "A boy who can pull this sword from the stone, when all you grown men, you great men cannot. This seems like a miracle!" The hooded man paused. "And that's what Christians call it. A miracle!"

The tide of voices rises; it swells and rolls around the churchyard; then it ebbs again.

The hooded man raises his right hand. "I have helped four kings of Britain," he calls out. "Listen carefully!

"As soon as King Uther saw Ygerna, he burned with passion for her, and he followed her and Duke Gorlois into Cornwall. On the same night Gorlois was killed, I changed Uther's appearance, so that he looked exactly like Ygerna's husband. In every part of his body. Then Uther went to Ygerna in her chamber — in the fortress at Tintagel. And that night Ygerna conceived a child."

"Impossible!" one knight shouts.

"Rubbish!"

"Prove it!"

"Do you disbelieve your own king?" the hooded man asks. "Many men here heard Uther's dying words. 'I have a son who was and will be.' That's what your king told you. 'I give my son God's blessing. Let him claim my crown.'"

The hooded man glares at all the earls, lords, and knights. "You're blinded by your own ambition," he shouts. "Your jealousy! Listen to me! Ygerna gave birth to a son and, as he promised, King Uther entrusted that boy to me. He gave him to me, wrapped in gold cloth, on the day he was born.

"I know what you do not and see what you cannot," the hooded man calls out. "Nothing in the world is impossible, but there's always a price. I gave King Uther his heart's desire, but he never saw his son again. Ygerna has never seen her son again. I found him foster parents, a knight and his wife who were loyal to the king, strict, and kind. They had a young son of their own who was almost three, and his mother weaned him and fed Ygerna's baby with her own

312

milk. But I never told them whose child they were fostering.

"This foster father, this good knight, stands here before you," the hooded man calls out. "So does his firstborn son. Sir Ector! Sir Kay!"

Now the hooded man turns toward me, and inclines his head. He opens the palm of his right hand. "King Uther's son! Ygerna's son!" he declares, and his voice is as powerful as thunder. "Arthur! The trueborn king of all Britain."

Many of the townsfolk begin to clap and cheer, but most of the knights are shaking their heads.

"What if he is?" one man yells.

"A boy king?"

"Never!"

"Against the Saxons?"

The hooded man's voice rises again over the restless crowd. "I told King Uther I would come for his son. And I tell you all, you men of Britain, I tell you all: Arthur's time has come!"

+ 96 +

BLOOD ON THE SNOW

Last night was twelfth night.

First we hoisted the last of the Yuletide logs onto the fire, and pulled down all the holly and ivy, the rosemary and bay, and laid them on it. Then we asked Nain to tell us the story she always tells on Twelfth Night, about another fire and another time.

When my mother and her brothers were children, they set fire to the hay barn, and their father, the dragon, had to rescue them.

"Right inside the barn Helen was," said Nain, "and close to the flames. She was poppy-cheeked, her eyeballs were hot, and she was down on her knees, crying out the words and sounds."

"What sounds?" I asked.

"The old ones," my grandmother said, "for fire to swallow fire."

"Helen thought she could put out the fire with words?" exclaimed my father.

"She did."

"She was wrong," my father said.

"She was right," said Nain, "and maybe she would have done if the flames had been less hungry. But it was too late. They roared and ate up all the hay."

After Nain's story, Hum played the pipe and banged the tabor and we all danced, we drank and sang. Then my father announced that Lord Stephen had asked me to be his new squire, and everyone cheered.

Not Gatty, though. When I grinned at her, she lowered her eyes.

Most people drank so much ale they could scarcely stagger out of the hall. Will and Dutton were the last to leave, on all fours, snorting and mooing and baaing.

"It smells like snow," my father said, and he bolted the door. Christmastide had come to an end.

Serle and Sian and I shook hands with our parents and Nain. We asked God to keep us safe while we slept. Then we curled up by the fire.

"I wish . . ." said Sian, and she yawned.

"What do you wish?" I whispered after a while.

Sian didn't reply. All evening she'd spitfired around the hall. But the moment she stopped and lay down, my little sister fell asleep.

I was wide awake, though. While Nain and Serle came to the crossing-place between waking and sleep, my head and heart were still busy with all that has been, and what is to come.

Tanwen! She wasn't with us in the hall, singing and dancing. Surely my father will let her stay here at Caldicot, and her baby with her. I must ask Serle about this. I can understand why Sir William wanted me to be taken away from Gortanore, but Serle's not married and Tanwen's not married . . .

Grace will be sad as well when Sir William tells her . . . When we sat up in the tree, we talked and talked, and Grace took my arm, and she said she'd never marry Serle and it would be all right if we were betrothed. She asked me to try and find out my parents' plans, and now I have . . .

I don't like Sir William, and I never will. He's a bully. He slaps Lady Alice and makes her manage the day-work and do all the accounts . . .

She's right to be afraid of him. She knows he murdered my mother's husband . . .

Poor Lady Alice! She only found out after she married Sir William. Whom could she talk to? Her own mother and father were dead and she was an only child. She couldn't talk to Tom or Grace: Sir William was their own father.

So she told me. Up on Tumber Hill, where the wolf-wind could tear at her words as soon as it heard them, and rip them into pieces.

"Sir William murdered a young man," she said. "He buried him in the forest."

There! I have written it down. My third sorrow! Sir William is a murderer! My own father is a man-slaughterer.

I haven't told anyone and I never will, because of my promise to Lady Alice. I nearly told my father, though.

My father says I must go to Gortanore before Easter. He says it's time Sir William and I talked to each other as father and son. But I'm my mother's son as well. No matter what, I will find out who she is before I go to Lord Stephen.

"Dear God," I said under my breath, "in the wilderness of the night and the night of my fears, in my fears of the unknown, be my companion!"

Beside the fire, Tempest and Storm stirred, and then they began to growl. And then I heard the sheep in the fold: They were baaing and squealing.

I leaped up and the hounds leaped up.

"Serle!" I said. "The sheep!"

Serle began to gabble. He was drowned in sleep.

"The sheep!" I said more loudly, and I shook my brother's shoulder. Then I stepped into my boots and unbolted the hall door.

It was snowing! Large, soft flakes. A skyful of feathers, swaying and settling under the wide eye of the moon.

All December was iron-hard; ice covered the pond and Jac. Frost stalked through the manor almost every night. But this was the first snowfall of the winter and I ran out into it, joyful and fearful.

Gatty was already there, standing beside the fold. And all the sheep were jammed against each other, mewling and wailing.

Gatty pointed.

At her feet, there was blood on the snow. A mouthful of wool. A track where something heavy had just been dragged away.

"They got what they came for," Gatty said.

"A whole sheep!" I exclaimed.

"Wolves help themselves," said Gatty. "We can't do nothing."

That's not what Tempest and Storm thought, though. They ran away through the snow towards the forest, barking.

"Stands to reason," said Gatty. "If we're hungry, them wolves are hungry."

"Where is everyone?" I cried. "I couldn't wake Serle."

"Ale-sleep!" said Gatty, and she looked at me in the moonlight. "Arthur," she said. "Will you remember?"

"What?"

"Harold and Brice," said Gatty.

"Of course."

"And Sian on that ice."

"I know," I said. "And you wearing the armor. It's always us."

"You're going," said Gatty.

"Yes," I said quietly.

"Can you walk there?" Gatty asked.

"Of course!" I said. "It's not oversea. Not like Jerusalem."

"You said we'd go to Ludlow Fair."

"Oh Gatty!"

Hundreds of snow pearls were shining in Gatty's curls. And they kept settling on her long eyelashes.

"You promised," she said.

"We'll go before Easter," I said. "I promise you. All the stalls there! The criers and the crowds. And the freak show! That's worth being beaten for, any time."

"What about the stream then?" Gatty said.

"That too. We'll walk upstream towards Wistanstow."

Gatty lowered her head. "It's all there is," she said in a dead voice.

I looked at the blood. The falling snow. I listened to the terrified sheep.

"I'll tell my father you drove the wolves off," I said. "You and me."

"It doesn't make no difference," Gatty mumbled.

I took both her hands. "What about Jankin, then?" I asked.

Gatty shrugged.

"He still wants to be betrothed, doesn't he?"

Gatty nodded. "It's Lankin," she said sadly.

"Oh Gatty!" I said.

And under the moon and her green halo, we reached out and embraced.

unhooded

"He's green," says the spade-faced knight.

"Then he needs your support," the hooded man replies.

"He's never spilled blood, has he?" asked the Knight of the Black Anvil.

"Nothing but milk," replies the copper-colored knight.

"That's not true," says Arthur-in-the-stone. "I killed a man."

"You?" jeers the copper knight. "What with? A bunch of feathers?"

"First with an elm branch and then with his own sword."

"Nonsense!" says the spade-faced knight.

"He's just a child," scoffs the Knight of the Black Anvil.

"And you are the same men King Uther trusted?" the hooded man demands. "Three times Arthur has pulled the sword from the stone, and still you deny him. This boy is King Uther's trueborn son."

Now the huge crowd of townspeople surrounding the earls and lords and knights begins to cheer. They wave. They brandish cudgels and sharpened sticks. They stamp on the ground.

"The king!" they shout. "Arthur the king!"

"This is God's will," the archbishop proclaims, and he raises his crucifix.

Hearing this, the townspeople cheer more loudly.

"Arthur!" they shout. "Crown Arthur!" And they begin to shuffle towards the knights, shaking their cudgels and holding up their sticks.

"All you knights are armed with swords and shields," the hooded man calls out. "Are you going to use them against your own people?"

"Have faith!" declares the archbishop. "This is a matter of faith!"

"Is that what you're going to do?" the hooded man demands.

"Arthur!" the crowd insists. "Arthur the king!"

"I warn you," the hooded man says. "For each man you kill, a dozen will spring up. They will overwhelm you."

Now the earls and lords and knights turn to one another. They begin to talk, and argue . . .

Quietly, I slipped out of my window seat. In the stone cell of my writing-room, I got down onto my right knee and closed my eyes. I folded into myself, quiet and compact as a nut, still cradling my warm obsidian between my hands. For a long time I waited.

"Arthur my king!"

"I swear my allegiance."

"I will be your liege man."

"Here and always."

When I opened my eyes again, all the great men of Britain, earls and lords and knights, were kneeling in front of me: brave men and bullies, shrewd men, blunt men and the woolly-headed, loyal men, honest men, the unjust and grasping, and the men who stop at nothing — liars, manslaughterers.

Five crimson eagles fly for me and the purple lion roars for me, three greyhounds bark for me, and a swarm of tiddlers, silver and rose, swims for me. Seven bright stars shine for me.

"You have all sworn oaths," I say in a clear voice, "and I swear to you before Christ the Lord I will be loyal to you. I will be just to rich and poor alike. I will root out evil wherever I see it. I will lead you by serving you and serve you by leading you as long as I live."

Then I turn to the archbishop. "Your Grace," I say, "I have not seen my own mother since the day I was born. Will you send for Queen Ygerna and bring her here for my coronation?"

The archbishop inclines his head. "As Christ the Lord loved his own mother," he proclaims, "it shall be so. And Christ the Lord will guide you."

"Your own blood will lead you," the hooded man calls out. "The nine spirits will nourish you."

Then he raises his right hand, and sweeps back his floppy hood. It is Merlin! Merlin is the hooded man!

But of course! The same slateshine eyes; the same powerful, deep voice. How can I not have recognized him? Merlin! You gave me my wonderful obsidian, my seeing stone, and you've been there in my stone all the time, waiting for me to find you. It was you who counseled King Vortigern to drain the pool and you who changed King Uther's appearance; on the day I was born, you delivered me to Sir Ector and his wife. And it was you who promised King Uther, my blood-father, that you would watch over me and come for me.

"Merlin!" I cry, and I reach out towards him.

Merlin smiles and unsmiles. "Arthur!" he says. "The king! But what kind of king? No, I haven't finished with you yet. I've only just begun!"

98

AT ONCE

"Where have you been?" my father demanded as soon as I opened the hall door.

"With Lankin."

"Lankin! Why?"

"Gatty says he won't let Jankin marry her. Never! I thought I could persuade him to change his mind."

"You should have been in the Yard," my father said.

"I know, but . . ."

"No!" said my father. "Sons obey their fathers. Squires obey their lords."

"I'm sorry, father."

My father held out his hands to the fire, and then he rubbed them together. "It was brave of you, certainly," he said. "How is Lankin?"

"Very stubborn," I said. "And very bitter. He says Hum will go to hell."

"What about his wrist?" my father asked.

"I think it's rotting. His whole hut stinks."

"Well," said my father, "a messenger rode in for you."

"For me?"

"From Lord Stephen. We looked for you everywhere."

My heart began to patter. "He hasn't changed his mind, has he?"

"Well . . . yes, Arthur," my father replied. "In a way, he has."

"No!" I cried.

"But not in the way you fear," my father said calmly. "No! Lord Stephen wants you to go into service with him at once."

"At once?"

"You remember that friar, Fulk, who came here and preached the crusade?"

"Of course," I said.

"Well, Arthur, Lord Stephen has decided to take the Cross."

"Father!" I cried.

"Yes, and he has asked my permission to take you with him."

My father put his right hand through my arm, and for a while we paced round and round the hall.

"He wants you to ride over in three days' time," he said. "It will cost us a great deal, of course. You'll need a whole suit of armor to be made for you, but I think Sir William will pay for that. And then you'll need a new mount."

"What's wrong with Pip?"

"Nothing," said my father. "But he's no warhorse. He couldn't carry you to the gates of Jerusalem. But first things first! You must talk to your mother about your clothing. Will's making a chest for you, and Ruth will help you to pack it."

"My longbow?" I cried.

"I want Will to cut you a new set of arrows," my father said, "and they can be sent after you. Lord Stephen will have plenty of practice-swords and lances and shields."

"But I wanted to see Lady Alice," I said, "and Grace, and you said I should talk to Sir William."

"There's no time for that now," said my father.

Then I thought of my lost mother. . . . Does she want to know about me?

"And I wanted . . ." I began.

"It can't be helped," said my father. "Anyhow, I wouldn't be surprised if you met Sir William on crusade. Adventure and the land oversea burn in his blood. Do you remember how he challenged Serle and me to go with him?"

"I remember what the friar said."

"Yes," said my father. "The pope's indulgence. No matter how terrible a man's crime, he will be pardoned without penance if he dies in combat during the crusade, or serves in God's army for one year."

My father said no more, and I said nothing, but we each knew what the other was thinking.

"Three days!" I cried. "But I promised Gatty."

"What?" asked my father.

At that moment, my mother came half running in from the kitchen, followed by Sian. "Arthur!" she cried. "My crusader son!" The she opened her arms and pulled me to her, and hugged me tightly.

"I can't breathe," I said.

"No!" said Sian loudly.

"What, Sian?" said my father.

"I say Arthur can't go," she announced. "Serle can!"

"Now!" said my father. "There's a great deal to do. Clothes . . . your longbow . . . the arrows . . . I'll arrange for an armorer to ride over to Holt and measure you up, and I'll talk to Lord Stephen about the horse."

"Merlin," I said. "I need to talk to him."

"Slim's waiting for you," my mother said, "and you can choose whatever you like for dinner tomorrow."

"A meat tile," I cried. "Chicken and crayfish and millet."

"And I'll ask Oliver to say prayers for you," my father said, "with everyone in church. Then you can say your good-byes."

"Serle!" I cried. "I was going to ask him everything. About Lord Stephen: what he's like and what he'll expect of me. And I wanted to explain . . . Have you told him?"

"I have," said my father, "and there'll be time for you to talk to him. Some things you can do, some you can't. But first, Arthur, before you do anything . . . Are you listening?"

"Yes, father."

"Step into yourself. Make sense of everything. Take the hounds, now, while it's still light, and climb Tumber Hill. Stand right on the top, and stare out in every direction. Then, when you come down again, you'll be ready."

"Thank you, father," I said. And I bowed to him and my mother.

99

WHAT MATTERS

"Gatty," I said. "You know I promised we'd go before Easter?"

"The fair?" said Gatty.

"Yes."

"And the stream," said Gatty.

"I know," I said. "But I can't. Lord Stephen has sent a messenger, and I'm to ride over to Holt in three days' time."

Gatty slowly pushed out her lower lip.

"I wanted us to go," I said.

"Tomorrow, then?" said Gatty.

"I can't!" I cried. "There's so much to do. But one day we will go, Gatty. I promise you."

Gatty brushed the curls off her forehead.

"You remember that friar who preached the crusade? Lord Stephen and I are joining the crusade."

Gatty looked at me under her eyelashes, and they were trembling. "Jerusalem," she said in a desolate, faraway voice, as if she were naming something that had been lost to her forever.

"Oh, Gatty!" I cried.

"Don't matter," said Gatty quietly, and she took a step back from me. "Jankin says you went down and talked to Lankin."

"Yes."

"What about?"

"You. You and Jankin."

"You went down for me?"

"Yes, Gatty."

"Here comes Serle," Gatty said. "I'll be going, anyhow."

Then Gatty tossed her head and her curls danced. I watched her as she walked away.

"I'll see you before I go," I called out.

"Saying your good-byes?" said Serle, and he raised his eyebrows.

"Serle! Our father's told you."

"Yes."

"And you know Lord Stephen's taking the Cross?"

"So everything's all right for you."

"Not for me," I cried. "For you, Serle. You said I was a cuckoo and that I was trying to push you out. But it's not like that. You'll inherit Caldicot. All of it."

"Sir William's a wealthy man," Serle said in his sharp voice, "much richer than his younger brother. Tom will inherit Gortanore, but you'll take the second manor at Catmole and that's larger than this one."

"But there's enough for both of us," I said, "and for Tom as well. Isn't that a good thing?"

Serle said nothing.

"What about Tanwen?" I asked. "If you had told me, I would have helped if I could."

Again Serle said nothing.

"Can't she stay here? I asked. "It's your baby too."

Serle shook his head. "My father wants her to go away," he said.

"But what do you want?" I asked.

"It doesn't matter what I want," Serle said in a flat voice. "I don't know, anyway."

"Serle," I said. "We're not blood-brothers. We're cousins. There's nothing for us to argue about. Can't we make peace before I go?"

"It's all right for you," Serle said again, and very bitterly.

"How is it all right for me?" I replied in a loud voice. "How would you like Sir William for a father? How would you like not to know who your mother is, or where she is? All you think about is yourself."

Then I turned away from Serle. I took long strides, with Tempest and Storm leaping beside me. I ran. I raced past the fishpond and the orchard, the copper beech. Then the hill slope began to tug at my calves and thighs and I had to slow down. I was panting, and the snow was almost as deep as my forefinger. There is no quick way to reach the top of Tumber Hill.

He was already there, sitting on a large rock.

"Merlin!" I cried. "I need to talk to you."

"I suppose you do," said Merlin.

"You're in the stone," I panted.

"Ah," said Merlin. "So you've found me."

I flopped down beside him.

"Sit on this rock," said Merlin, and he shuffled along it to make room for me.

"You're the hooded man," I said. "Aren't you?"

"But who are you?" asked Merlin. "And who are you to be? That's what matters."

For a while we sat on the high hill, and the bright sky around us breathed and shimmered and flowered.

"I am Arthur the king!" I said. "And I'm squire-in-waiting to Lord Stephen. I'm the foster son of Sir John and Lady Helen de Caldicot. I have two fathers, two mothers . . . My life here! My life in the stone! What does it all mean?"

"What do you think it means?" asked Merlin.

"My stone's smoky, or it fizzes, but then its eye opens. It shows me part of what's going to happen, or has already happened, and it takes me on amazing journeys. I don't know why."

I remembered then what my father had told me, and looked north and south, even farther than the New Year bonfires. I looked west into dark and shining Wales.

"Merlin," I said, "my stone has shown me dragons fighting and burning passion and magic and argument, wise words and foul plots, great kindness, cruelty. It's showing me what's best and worst, and right and wrong, and I'm part of it."

"And that's not enough?" asked Merlin.

"Well, I think it's showing me I'm on a quest, but I don't know exactly where."

"And by the time you find out," Merlin said, "you'll have grown into your name."

"That's what Sir Pellinore told me," I cried. "In the forest."

"He did, yes," Merlin replied. "And I said that anyone without a quest is lost to himself."

"I see," I said.

"You're beginning to," said Merlin, smiling and unsmiling. "So, then. You'll take your stone with you."

100

SONG OF THE NORTH STAR

Of course I'll take it with me!

My wolf-skull. Moon-bruise. Heart of Caldicot. It is my life, part of it. My seeing stone.

When will I sit in this window seat again? With my knees up, my ink-perch beside me. A cream page on my lap. With this quill.

Downstairs, everyone is asleep. The hall's furry with warmth and thick breathing. But this writing-room, it is corpse-cold. I think I can hear the music of the North Star.

Listen! Its voice is the clean, sharp voice of the white-faced girl who sang for us at Christmas. Ice and fire! That's what the star is singing. The song of my king-self, and of a squire setting out for Jerusalem.

WORD LIST

BEADLE a petty official; a messenger of a law court

BOGGART a goblin, perhaps half the size of a human, and twice as hairy

BOWYER a person who makes (or sells) bows

BUCKLER a small round shield

BULLACE a small purple plum

CAPON a rooster fattened for eating

CHANGELING a fairy child secretly exchanged (by the fairies) for a human one

CLIPPED PENNY a silver penny cut in half or into quarters

COEUR-DE-LION (FRENCH) Lionheart. A nickname given to Richard I (1189–99)

COLLOPS small slices of meat

DESTRIER a charger or warhorse

DINNER the main meal of the day, taken between 9 A.M. and 11 A.M.

DOOMSMEN tenants, both men and women, who served as jurors at the manor court (literally, "judgment men")

DOVECOTE a little house for doves or pigeons to roost and breed in, usually raised above the ground

FALLOWFIELD land left uncultivated for one or more growing seasons, so as to make the soil richer

FLETCHER a person who makes arrows

FLEUR DE SOUVENANCE (FRENCH) a flower, sometimes real, sometimes made of jewels, to serve as a reminder or keepsake

331

FLIGHT   the feathering at the notched end of an arrow

FLYTING   a dispute; an insult contest

FORD   a shallow place in a river or stream where people and animals can wade across

FRITILLARY   a species of butterfly

GLEBE   land belonging to the church

GOGONIANT!   (WELSH) Glory be!

GONFANON   a battle standard

GOSHAWK   a large short-winged hawk

GREENGAGE   a variety of plum, colored green

GUISERS   people who disguised themselves at Hallowe'en as a protection against evil spirits

HART   a male deer (especially a red deer)

HAWSER   a very thick rope

INDULGENCE   a pardon for one's sins, granted by the church

JACK   a short, close-fitting leather jacket

JERKIN   a short, close-fitting, often sleeveless jacket

JOUST   a war game in which two mounted opponents try to unseat each other, using lances

JUMPER   a robber (who "jumps" through windows)

THE LAND OVERSEA   the name for the territory, including Palestine and the Nile Delta, over which Christians and Muslims fought during the Crusades

LIEGE MAN   a loyal follower

LYCH-GATE   a roofed gate at the entrance to a churchyard

THE MARCHES   the borderland between England and Wales

NASAL   a strip of metal bolted to a helmet, covering a knight's nose

OBSIDIAN   volcanic glass, usually black, believed by some cultures to have magical powers

PANTER   head of the pantry, where food and tableware were kept; sometimes called a pantler

PARRY to ward off or deflect the thrust of a sword

PORTCULLIS a heavy iron grating lowered to bar the gateway to a castle

PRIME, TERCE, VESPERS, COMPLINE sets of prayers said at daybreak, midmorning, late afternoon, and the end of the evening. In all, the church assigned seven periods of the day to prayer and worship: matins/lauds, prime, terce, sext, none, vespers, and compline

PUMICED scoured, smoothed, or erased with a pumice stone

QUINTAIN a post, or the object attached to it, used for practice at jousting with a lance

REEVE the overseer (or steward) of a manor

ROE a small species of deer

ROUNSEY a strong horse without special breeding used mainly by knights and travelers

SCYTHE an implement with a handle and a long, thin, curved blade used for cutting grass and grain

STEW a fishpond

TABOR a small drum

TITHE one tenth of one's income, or the produce of one's land, paid as a tax to support the church and its clergy

TOURNAMENT a magnificent sporting and social occasion at which knights engaged in a series of contests

TOURNEY to take part in a tournament

WATTLE a weaving of sticks and twigs used in the building of walls and roofs as well as for making fences

WIMPLE a cloth covering for the woman's head arranged so that only her face is exposed

WODWO a wildman, covered in hair or leaves; sometimes called a woodwose

ABOUT THE AUTHOR

KEVIN CROSSLEY-HOLLAND fell in love with the Middle Ages and Anglo-Saxon poetry while he was an undergraduate at Oxford University. He wrote his first work for children, a retelling of a medieval romance, in a London park, during lunch breaks from his job as a children's book editor. In 1985, he received the Carnegie Medal for his novel *Storm*. A longtime resident of the United States, where he taught at the University of St. Thomas in Minnesota, Kevin now lives with his wife, Linda, on the coast of the North Sea in Norfolk, England. The second book in the Arthur trilogy, *At the Crossing-Places*, is being published this fall.

Arthur's journey continues in the marvelous
second book of the Arthur trilogy

AT THE CROSSING-PLACES
by Kevin Crossley-Holland

ice and flames

The first day of my new life began with ice and ended with
flames.

As soon as I woke, I was wide-eyed awake. Under my
badgerskin it was warm, and for a little while I lay still as a
huntsman in a covert. I stared around me at the high hall
where I have slept and woken almost every day of my life. I
tried to wake my brother and sister by making faces at
them. I listened for a moment to my grandmother Nain
snuffling and one of the hounds groaning and grinding
his teeth. Then I leaped up. The whole world was waiting
for me.

When I unbolted the hall door and tugged it open, the
ice in the jambs clattered down. Then I saw Gatty. She was
standing beside the mounting block with my horse, Pip. I
had to look twice because she was dressed in dirty sacking,
sparkling with frost, and all I could see were her large, river
eyes and one fair curl.

"Gatty!" I exclaimed.

"Jankin said I could."

"How long have you been here?"

Gatty ignored my question. "The biggest saddlebags we got," she said.

I kicked at the shards and thorns of pearly ice and, barefoot, I walked out and slapped Pip on the rump.

"You look as if you've been here half the night," I said.

Gatty lowered her eyes and shook her head dumbly.

"Oh Gatty! When I reach Jerusalem, I will send you a message. I'll try to."

Gatty stared at the ground. "Don't matter," she mumbled.

"It does matter," I said. "We're friends."

"Can't be," Gatty replied. "Not with the likes of you."

"But we are. We rescued Sian when she went through the ice, and we separated the bulls and drove off the wolves together. Didn't we?"

Gatty sniffed. "You could load up," she said.

"Nobody's awake yet."

"I can help, can't I?"

"You're frozen."

"When are you coming back?" Gatty demanded.

"Three years," I said. "Two, maybe."

Gatty shuddered and hunched her shoulders.

"Go on, Gatty," I urged. "Get out of this cold. I'll see you before I leave."

Gatty looked at me. She gazed at me as gravely as the painting of Mary on the church wall, and her long eyelashes flickered. Then she turned away.

Nain and my brother and sister and Ruth, our chamber-servant, were still asleep, so I hurried back across the hall. Missing out the fourth and fifth steps, and the ninth and tenth, the ones that always creak, I ran up the staircase and along the gallery to my freezing writing-room.

That's where I've hidden my seeing stone since Merlin gave it to me last summer. We were up on top of Tumber Hill when he unwound this saffron bundle. Inside it was a flat black stone, my obsidian, just a little larger than the palm of my hand, deep as an eye of dark water, and it flashed in the sunlight.

"Until the day you die you will never own anything as precious as this," Merlin told me. "But no one must know you own it, or see it, or learn anything about it."

Merlin is right. My seeing stone is my other world. My guide. My echo. I can't leave that behind!

I pulled the stone out of the gap in the wall and ran back downstairs. I went straight out to Pip and jammed the saffron bundle into the very bottom of one of the saddlebags.

All morning I was very busy. I cut reed scabbards for my quills and shaved acorn stoppers for my ink bottles, and I wrapped my valuable parchment pages in shaggy towels. I stuffed my saddlebags with writing materials and clothing and in my wooden chest, which is going to be sent after me, I laid more clothing, my new flight of arrows, my ivory chesspieces, and my mail-coat. Then I went round the village and found Merlin, and Oliver the priest, and Jankin, who was mucking out the stables, and took my leave of them; but Gatty and her father Hum weren't in their cottage. After that, I set up the board for the Saxon and Viking game and showed Sian how to play one more time. Then I had a rough-and-tumble with Tempest and Storm, our running-hounds, and Storm tore my right sleeve, so Ruth had to mend it. And then I decided to take my own practice sword with me, and my brother Serle said in that case I ought to clean it properly, otherwise Lord Stephen would be sure to notice and it would reflect poorly on him and my father, but he didn't offer to help.

We were still eating dinner when Lord Stephen's rider, Simon, arrived to escort me to the castle at Holt and my new life as Lord Stephen's squire.

I've met Simon before. He's very thin and his cheekbones are so sharp they look as if they might shear through his skin. He usually looks rather melancholy, but I like him because he has a very long upper lip, like a horse, and makes quiet jokes, mainly against himself.

"Simon!" exclaimed my father — my foster father, that is. "You look like a snowman. Come and eat with us."

"Thank you, Sir John."

"I hope your ride has given you an appetite," my foster father said. "You look as if you could eat a horse."

"I am a horse," said Simon in a hollow, dark voice, and his upper lip looked even longer than before.

Although I've wanted to be a squire so much, and for so long, it still felt painful to be leaving Caldicot. I think Sir John knew that, and as soon as he had said grace after dinner, he walked across the hall and picked up my traveling cloak and whirled it around my shoulders.

Then I embraced everyone — Sir John and Lady Helen, who held me to her so tightly I thought I would burst, then Serle, and Sian, and Nain on her two sticks.

They all came out of the hall to wave us good-bye.

Sir John looked up at me in the saddle. "Do you remember what I told you on New Year's morning?" he asked me quietly.

"I think so."

"I told you I'm proud of you. I told you that who we are isn't only a matter of blood; it's what we make of ourselves."

"I do remember," I replied.

"And I said that you, Arthur, are fit to be a king."

With that, Sir John slapped my left thigh, and Pip started forward. I heard Tempest and Storm barking. I heard my family calling out, wishing me a safe journey, wishing me joy, wishing me peace, wishing me Godspeed.

So Simon and I crunched away into the snow, which wasn't falling so much as circling us and blowing upward. When I turned round in the saddle, everyone was still standing outside, silent and waving. When I turned round for a second time, they had gone. Gone as if they had never been. Snowflakes on my eyelids, my cheeks; the huge blurred hulk of the manor house, patient and grey; nothing else.

I looked around me for Gatty: I kept looking for her. Day after day of fieldwork, barnwork, stablework, and half the time she's hungry. I'm sure she had been waiting for hours in the dark. I hope she was somewhere warm.

As we rode away from the manor, we passed Joan and Will and Dutton dragging back deadwood from the forest. I pulled up and greeted them, and they wished me good health.

"You tell Lord Stephen what I said," Joan instructed me.

"What was that?"

"At the manor court. I can't even pick up deadwood and I get fined. He's so high and mighty, but he wouldn't live that rich except for us."

For a while, Simon and I rode side by side down the track that leads west through Pike Forest. But before long, the forest closed in around us, and I felt like a hare caught in a trap, snagged and dragged back by everything I was leaving behind. I kept thinking about all the things that have happened during the first few days of this new century.

On New Year's Day, Sir John told me I could be a squire. He said he'd arranged for me to go into service with Lord Stephen at Easter. When I heard that, I leaped up and embraced him. But no sooner had he told me this than he shocked me by saying that he and Lady Helen are not my true parents, my blood-parents. They're my foster parents. But I've lived with them since I was only a few days old, and I'll always think of them as my mother and father.

Then Sir John told me my blood-father is his own brother, Sir William de Gortanore. He's vile and violent. Worse than that, he's a murderer, and I don't want to see him again.

And my blood-mother . . . who is she? I don't even know who she is, or whether she's still alive. I don't know where she is, but I'm going to find her.

And then, after all this, Lord Stephen sent word to say that he wanted me to come not at Easter but in three days' time. He has decided to take the Cross. We're going to join the crusade that Fulk, the friar, preached about when he came to Caldicot last autumn. So that may mean there won't be time to meet my blood-father. . . .

I must have been thinking about these things for a long time because when I looked around me, we were already passing the forest hamlet of Clunbury.

We reined in, and I drank a few mouthfuls of milk from Simon's gourd.

"Slow going in this weather," Simon said. "We must push on or the dark will overtake us."

This tenth day of January, it has been one of those days when it gets dark before it gets dark, and by the time we neared Clun there was very little light left.

"Lord Stephen told me to get back ahead of you," Simon said. "Follow this track. Just before you come to an open field, there's a track up to the castle on your right."

With that, Simon cantered off, while Pip and I continued to pick our way along the snowy track, stepping over branches that had fallen across it, wading through hidden pools of mud and mush.

Holt Castle is on top of a small, steep hill, and as I was riding up to it, a rider came dashing out of the courtyard and across the drawbridge. Down the hill toward me pelted the horse and rider, and the horse was whinnying and neighing. Down the hill they came, sliding, slithering, forelegs splaying, the rider yelling, desperate and yelling, and the horse almost wailing, and then I saw the rider was a girl and the hem of her cloak was on fire.

Orange flames! Blue flames! The girl's cloak was alight, and her horse's belly and flanks were scorched and smoking.

As they careered toward me, the girl helpless, her horse wild, I swung Pip round to meet them sideways and braced myself.

We were hurled to the ground. Pip snorted, he trumpeted and, but for the blanket of snow, I would have broken every bone in my body. At once I scrambled up and staggered through the snow. I dragged the girl out of her saddle. I pulled her down into the snow, and heaped it over her feet and legs, right up to her hips.

The girl's horse, meanwhile, just dived into a drift; it writhed and wriggled and neighed pitifully.

I looked at the girl, and she looked at me. She had a blaze of red-gold hair, tied back at the neck, and tawny eyes the color of horse chestnuts.

I gave her a hand and pulled her up, and she blew out her pink cheeks and smiled.

"He bolted!" she exclaimed.

"You were on fire. Your horse's mane was burning."

"Poor Dancer," said the girl.

"Are you all right?"

"I think so," said the girl, brushing away the snow from her legs and feet and inspecting herself. "My cloak's ruined. And your nose is bleeding."

"What happened?"

"I don't know. Before I left the hall, I was sitting beside the fire with my uncle."

"Who's that?"

"My uncle? Lord Stephen, of course! The fire was spitting and cracking, and one of the cinders must have caught inside my hem. Who are you, anyhow?"

"Arthur," I said. "Arthur de Caldicot."

"Arthur!" cried the girl. "The new squire." She got to her feet and shook herself. "And I'm Winifred. Winifred de Verdon. You may call me Winnie."

Together we walked our poor horses up the steep path and across the drawbridge, and then we tied them to the mounting block in the courtyard. Winnie led me through the storeroom and up the circular stone staircase to the hall. She threw open the hall door, and there I saw Lord Stephen de Holt and Lady Judith and his whole household waiting to greet me.

Lord Stephen took one look at us, the snow and filth and soot smeared all over us, Winnie's scorched cloak, my bleeding nose and then, seeing neither of us was seriously hurt, he burst out laughing.

Not Lady Judith, though. She is a whole head taller than Lord Stephen, and she bore down on Winnie and buried her in her arms.

"Arthur . . ." announced Winnie, wrestling herself free, "Arthur saved me. Me and Dancer. Otherwise, Dancer would be ten miles away, and I'd be smoke and ashes."

When Winnie had explained, Lord Stephen gave me a curious, lopsided smile. "Well, Arthur," he said, "what use is chivalry if it doesn't begin at home?"

Lady Judith looked down the beak of her nose and then she smoothed Winnie's blaze of red-gold hair. "I warned you not to leave so late," she said. "Now you'll have to stay here tonight." And with that, Lady Judith put an arm round Winnie's shoulders and ushered her out of the hall and up the second flight of stairs.

I am writing this by poor candlelight, crouched in one corner of the hall. Instead of my grandmother Nain and Serle and Sian and Ruth and Tempest and Storm, my sleeping companions tonight are Simon, and Miles the scribe, whom I met at our manor court, and Rahere the musician, and Rowena and Izzie, who are both chamber-servants, and they're all asleep.

There's so much more to write, about Lord Stephen and Lady Judith, and about Winnie — she's a year younger than I am, and Lord Stephen says she comes to Holt quite often. I want to write about this castle, and everyone here, but I can't stop yawning.

Today I have crossed from ice to flames.